Poor Ghost!

Gabriel Flynn was born in 1991 and grew up in Manchester. His writing has appeared in *Five Dials, Best British Short Stories* and the *White Review*, whose short story prize he was shortlisted for in 2020. He lives in Berlin.

Poor Ghost!

Gabriel Flynn

Sceptre

First published in Great Britain in 2025 by Sceptre
An imprint of Hodder & Stoughton Limited
An Hachette UK company

The authorised representative in the EEA is Hachette Ireland, 8 Castlecourt Centre,
Dublin 15, D15 XTP3, Ireland (email: info@hbgi.ie)

1

A CIP catalogue record for this title is available from the British Library

Hardback ISBN 9781399740739
Trade Paperback ISBN 9781399740746
ebook ISBN 9781399740753

Typeset in Sabon MT by
Palimpsest Book Production Ltd, Falkirk, Stirlingshire

Printed and bound in Great Britain by Clays Ltd, Elcograf S.p.A.

Hodder & Stoughton policy is to use papers that are natural, renewable
and recyclable products and made from wood grown in sustainable
forests. The logging and manufacturing processes are expected to
conform to the environmental regulations of the country of origin.

Hodder & Stoughton Limited
Carmelite House
50 Victoria Embankment
London EC4Y 0DZ

www.sceptrebooks.co.uk

For Nicolas Flynn

'Tis sweet and commendable in your nature, Hamlet,
To give these mourning duties to your father.
But you must know your father lost a father,
That father lost, lost his, and the survivor bound
In filial obligation for some term
To do obsequious sorrow. But to persever
In obstinate condolement is a course
Of impious stubbornness. 'Tis unmanly grief.
It shows a will most incorrect to heaven,
A heart unfortified, a mind impatient,
An understanding simple and unschool'd.

Claudius in *Hamlet*, Shakespeare

The plane descended from the low clouds and the outskirts of Manchester appeared below: roads and sports fields, rings and crescents of little red terraces, the silver roofs of factories and warehouses. After we had landed, the crowd jostled and groaned for twenty minutes before the carousel began to move and I caught sight of the large suitcase, which I recognised by the strip of gaffer tape that sealed a gash on its front pocket. I dragged it over the out-of-service travellators from the terminal to the station, where I bought a ticket from the machine, presented it to the guard blocking the platform entrance, and sprinted to make a train heading into the city. Beyond the windows, darkness fell over the semi-detached suburban houses and the skyline on the horizon: skyscrapers with red lights flashing at their highest points surrounded by phosphorescent murk. I got off at Piccadilly station and made my way along the platform, across the brightly lit concourse. The digital clock opposite the Burger King read 20:57, but the station was so empty that it could have been the dead of night – a few late commuters climbed the approach to the station, earbuds in, heads bowed; a few drunks were arguing outside the Spar while a wary-looking woman stood waiting under the bus shelter. On Piccadilly Gardens, a flock of pigeons were eating chips and doner meat from a tray near the fountain and three men in black raincoats with smooth, pale heads and rough, red faces huddled by the door of the Wetherspoon's, smoking. They were the kind of men one saw everywhere here and it shocked me to see them now after two years in Cambridge, Massachusetts, where besides the few addicts who hung around in Central Square, raving and begging for money under the constant surveillance of the police, one rarely saw a face whose scowl had set into wrinkles or any other such signs that life was a struggle above all else.

I stopped at the junction of Portland and Oxford Street because I had forgotten where I was going and which was the best way to get there. 'Any change, pal?' said a man who sat cross-legged in the doorway of the betting shop next to the McDonald's, his dog sleeping on a blanket beside him. I reached into my jeans pocket, pulled out a five-dollar bill, and said that it was all I had and he could have it if he wanted. He shrugged. 'Go on then. Better than nowt, isn't it?' I dropped it in his cup. 'Have a good night, mate. God bless.' I walked along Chepstow Street, dead except for the lights glowing in the windows of the Peveril of the Peak, until I rounded the corner and the new skyscrapers came into view and I could use them to guide me towards Tom's flat.

Soon, I could see Tom's building poking above the rooftops, the windows of its upper floors lit up against the dark sky. It was a 60s block of council flats named Calico Court that stood on Deansgate Interchange, a large roundabout on the ring road. Since I'd last been home, Tom had bought a one-bed flat on the eighth floor. I hadn't visited yet but I knew where it was because, as a teenager, I had an older friend named Rob who had a flat on the twelfth floor of the adjacent building. We used to go back there after gigs and parties to keep drinking beer and taking speed until the sun rose. Then we'd switch to ketamine and drink Southern Comfort and lemonade until the evening, when I would walk the three miles back to my mum's house to sleep. Whenever I thought of this part of the city, I always pictured the view from Rob's window on one of those dreary Sundays: tower blocks and red-brick houses with dark slate rooftops sprawling for miles towards the moors over Salford. Tom had bought the flat while I was in America, far away from those sad years and immersed in academic life. He gave me a tour via FaceTime and, though I feigned enthusiasm, he could see that the thought of living in a Hulme council flat depressed me. For him, it was simply practical. It wasn't that he didn't see how the whole of Manchester was dark and wet, choked with cars, littered with rubbish, neglected and brooding with violent resentment, but that he could protect himself from the world outside. As a result, he'd been able to save some money and build a good life despite never moving away. In contrast, I had always defined success only by how far away I'd managed to get from home, a trait I must have inherited from my parents, both of whom travelled lightly through their lives, inclined as they were to pack up and leave if ever they reached a dead end.

Whenever I returned to Manchester, which I had done rarely since moving away and not for five years, I always behaved haughtily, softened my vowels and pronounced my *t*s, because I was afraid that if I didn't, the distance between me and the city would disappear and I would be part of it again, as it had never ceased to be a part of me. It was true that the longer I remained in America, the more ideal-ised my idea of my home city had become, and the more

I bought into its grand self-mythology. Sometimes, I walked along Massachusetts Avenue, listening to The Fall in my headphones and singing along, believing that Manchester was the best city in the world, that it was somehow special. When I made an off-colour joke in the presence of my grad school peers and it met with faces of incomprehension, even concern, I missed the quick wit of Mancunians, for whom no joke was too dark. When I felt alienated by the well-paved streets and tidy lawns of Cambridge, I was susceptible to conjuring nostalgic tableaux: rain falling on the Ship Canal, a waterlogged football pitch at Turn Moss on a foggy Sunday morning in November, the owner of Marhaba Café spinning a naan by his tandoor oven. Sometimes I took these for images of home. But if I missed the city, I missed it hopelessly, as a thing that had disappeared, leaving only an atmosphere and a few impressions, never as a place to which I might seriously return. Now that I was here again, it was the US that seemed imaginary: the clapboard house near Inman Square where I rented a room on the first floor, Harvard Yard on a winter evening when the steps of Widener Library are lit up from below, and Mia's house in Orono, Maine, where we had spent a week with just each other for company before I finally decided I had to pack up and leave. Even as I took my seat on the early Greyhound back to Boston and watched the miles of fields and woodlands beside the I-95, the romance of being heartbroken in America was not lost on me. Even now, pressing the buzzer at the gate of Calico Court, it still wasn't.

Since I'd been away, Tom had fallen in love with a woman called Mel. We had been introduced via FaceTime and Tom had told me about her and their relationship, but we had yet to meet in person. She was there now – Tom had texted to say she was making dinner – and I was apprehensive about meeting her because I felt wild and dishevelled. A hand-written sign was taped to the mirror in the lift. It read, 'Stop pissing in the lift. We know who you are.' I was smiling at these words when the lift opened onto the small hallway and I saw Tom, standing at his door wearing boxer shorts and a T-shirt and smiling back at me. 'Is it you that's been pissing in the lift?' He opened his arms for an embrace. I almost could have cried when I put my face in his shoulder and recognised the familiar laundry smell of his T-shirt. 'Eh? Well, is it?' I shook my head on his shoulder as he patted my back. 'Come inside.' The flat looked different to the way it had when he gave me a tour with the camera on his phone. It had appeared almost derelict then, with plaster hanging off the walls and exposed lightbulbs dangling from the ceilings. Now, it had been renovated, fitted with laminate flooring and track lighting, and the walls had been freshly painted. I followed him into the living room, where Mel was sitting on the sofa, her legs folded beneath her, looking like a person who had found a place where she felt content and comfortable. 'This is Luca,' Tom said. She smiled and said, 'Hiya, love,' as she rose to her feet to hug me. When she sat down, Tom took his place beside her, placing an arm around her shoulder. 'What do you want to do, buddy? Do you want to have a shower and then we can have some dinner?' I said I wanted to sit and talk with them, to meet Mel properly, but I wasn't in the best state. From the way they made gentle motions of dismissal and looked at me sympathetically, I could tell that Tom had already guessed what had happened, more or less accurately, and had briefed Mel in advance of my arrival. Tom returned his attention to the book of Sudoku puzzles in his lap and said, 'Go and have a shower,' while Mel looked at me again, focused and curious, as though she were busy trying to match the person standing in front of her to the one from Tom's stories, as though she were a tiny bit amused.

And it was amusing, a person's best-laid plans falling apart. A man who puts on airs and gets shown up for who he really is, a man who turns his nose up at the people he thinks he's left behind, only to find himself once again among them: that's funny. Especially in the North of England, where the humble are revered and the full of themselves castigated. I didn't think that could be me because I never felt that I belonged in that Northern world to begin with, having been born in America and raised by my single mother as a foreigner, though a white foreigner who easily passed for a local. I never thought I was better than the North, just different to it. When I left, I was only trying to find a proper place for myself. But I knew it didn't look that way to others. To them, every move I made only confirmed more emphatically that the problem had been me, not the city, and I looked ever more deluded for holding on to the belief that a better fate lay just around the corner, if only I could find it.

I put on some fresh clothes and dried off my hair. Now the hall smelled of curry and I felt my stomach open up. I realised I'd hardly eaten all day. 'Have you got anything to drink?' I asked Tom.

'Now?' he said. 'It's ten p.m. on a weeknight. Have a cigarette instead.' He directed me to the pouch of tobacco on the living-room table and we stepped together onto the small balcony. 'Look at them.' He pointed across the roundabout to the new skyscrapers that now dominated the skyline, surrounded by cranes, the concrete skeletons of their upper floors visible where the final glass panels had not yet been installed. 'The whole city was sold to investors and that's what we get in return.'

'They're ugly.'

'They're a disgrace.'

We stood shivering in silence while I smoked half the cigarette until Tom took a drag and flicked it over the balcony. 'Come on. Let's eat.'

We ate Mel's curry and rice at the table in the living room and tried to make conversation, but it was difficult to talk without getting into my situation, which none of us wanted to go near. I especially wanted to avoid the topic of Mia and my abortive visit to Maine and feared that Tom might ask at any moment what had happened there. Instead, Mel asked about how Tom and I knew each other and we told stories from when we were school friends at Oakwood in Chorlton. Our perspectives on this time were inconsistent, but we kept that disguised until Mel asked whether it was a good school; then I said it was horrible and had damaged me irreparably while Tom said that it had been fine, and probably far better than what many people had to live with. After we'd eaten, we all sat on the sofa and watched 24 Hours in Police Custody on Tom's laptop. The episode dealt with a man who had been killed by a punch to the head outside a nightclub in Leeds. Tom focused on the show while Mel and I asked each other questions between the exciting moments, keeping our eyes fixed on the screen to help maintain the pretence that I hadn't arrived there in a state of crisis. I asked her about her work as an immigration lawyer and her family in Nottingham. She asked me tentatively what it was like to be a graduate student in America and I said it was a harrowing experience which, if it didn't eat you from the inside out, would transform you into a demon and make you insufferable to everyone except your own kind. 'Every noble value with which you arrive,' I began, and then I stopped myself because I saw in Mel's eyes that I was already more animated than was dignified.

'Do you want to go to bed?' Tom asked. 'We can leave you alone.'

'I think it's time,' I said, though it was only half past six in my head.

Tom unfolded the sofa and Mel brought me a pillow and a small duvet. 'You might want this,' she said as she handed me an eye mask. We said goodnight and I heard them shuffling around in the bedroom next door. Then I turned the light off and lay down on the hard sofa bed to try and sleep.

But I couldn't sleep. When Tom and Mel's muffled voices died away, I heard only the low buzz of an adaptor plug and, when I took it out at the wall, the traffic on the ring road, the odd siren. The city's murky light filtered in through the venetian blinds. I put on the eye mask Mel had given me but it was too tight for my big head and worse, not being able to see only drew my attention further towards my agitated mental state. I wanted to turn my phone on to see if Mia had texted but I resisted the urge because I knew that if she hadn't, I would only feel worse. So, I got up, took a bottle of beer from the fridge, rolled another cigarette and crept out onto the balcony. The smoke tasted bad and hurt my throat, but the cigarette did its job and connected me to past moments where I had smoked in the hope that it would make my dissatisfaction profound. I was thinking about Mia and realising what I already knew: that our relationship was over and the reason was simply that she had finally seen who I really was and hadn't liked it, just as I had always feared she would. I flicked the cigarette over the balcony, watched the glowing tip spiral towards the car park, and went inside wishing that I could rinse its foul taste out of my mouth. I turned my phone on to see if I had a message from Mia. I didn't, and I looked at our chat on WhatsApp. I waited to see if the word 'online' would appear beneath her name. I clicked on her profile picture and then I turned off the phone again.

I was in the first semester of my second year when I met Mia, behind schedule and preparing with dread for the oral exams that all graduate students had to take before they were permitted to move on to the later stages of their PhD. It was autumn, when Bostonians put on their baseball caps, shiny sunglasses, and goose-down gilets and drive out to New Hampshire and Vermont to look at the turning leaves and eat beef jerky and trail mix from sandwich bags. I was invited on several such expeditions by some of the well-meaning peers with whom I sometimes ate lunch but I declined them all because I was always behind with work and because I felt ashamed of myself when I spent time with these people, whose lives were so much more orderly than mine, who belonged where they were. Perhaps in a few weeks, I said. But the leaves turned quickly. They were amber and gold and then they fell, dried up, turned to mulch. Then the trees were bare, the temperature dropped below freezing, and the foggy nights came closing in. I was just as behind as I had always been while the tenth of April, the date of my general exam, drew closer every day.

I had a desk in a dark corner of the fifth-floor stacks, where I sat, paralysed by worry, while in the reading rooms below, amid such a general hush as I had never heard before, the great scholars of the future were assembled in their hundreds, reading the great scholars of the past and present, furrowing their brows at articles, journals, charts, and monographs, newspapers, patents, codices, and bestiaries, microfilm and microfiche, ledgers, manuscripts, transcripts, typescripts, affidavits, samizdat, and facsimiles. They were working on the relationship between church and state in modern Egypt, the economics of respiratory illnesses in nineteenth-century France, and the Judaic foundations of Spinoza's philosophy of substance. They were working on the Anglo-Indian tea trade, the poetry of Early Modern Central Asia, the death penalty in Singapore, the role of eunuchs in medieval West Africa, agriculture under Khrushchev, the ritual uses of Incantation Bowls in Upper Mesopotamia and Syria, the ecology of fracking, the memorialisation of the Holocaust in Lithuania, the politics of sleep, the future of anthropology, bondage and sado-masochism, Sardinian separatism. I knew because I had asked them, just as they had asked me. 'What do you work on?' It was the question that everyone loved to ask and which I hated because, unlike those hundreds of others, I had no satisfactory answer. In my application, I had lied about my interests – I borrowed them all from the super-visor whom I had let steer my path because it was easier than asking myself what I cared about – but now I wanted to do work that mattered; I was lost, and when my peers asked what I worked on, I said only 'literature' or, if I was feeling confident, 'modern literature' or 'the novel'.

These encounters could be managed if my interlocutor was a student of government or economics, because many of them had not read a book in years. But they were torturous if they took place with the graduate students in the English department, who saw in my evasiveness a weak adversary whom they could prey on. They spoke like lawyers and had the deadly eyes of seagulls and CEOs.

'Where did you study?' they asked me when we spoke in the red-carpeted halls. 'Oxford or Cambridge?' When I told them the name of the modern university where I had studied, they looked offended, as though I had made the place up. These were not readers as I had known them. They were not rebellious sorts whose searches for some-place authentic had washed them up on the shores of literature. They were not harmless, diligent misfits who fitted in better on the pages of a medieval poem than they ever did at school. They were businesspeople. They knew who had been hired at which universities and on what length of contract, what grade of pay. They knew their fields like paranoid farmers, watching them at night with shotguns on their laps. They did not confide their doubts, fears and weaknesses, and they did not make jokes. Most were several years younger than me and possessed a preter-natural youthfulness; this presented itself not only in the radiance of their skin and the whiteness of their teeth but in their deference to authority and evident trust that the world was in its proper order. If anything had begun to intrude on that illusion, it was only the ever-shrinking job market, which threatened to deny them the careers they believed were their birthright, turning the better among them into trade unionists and the rest into aspiring management consultants.

First I tried to write them off by telling myself that I had something they didn't: life experience. I knew a bit about ordinary suffering and the same could not be said of them. Yes, they had a lot of *book learning*, but had they ever tried rubbing speed into their arseholes? Had they ever been arrested for stealing a tub of hummus from Tesco? Had they ever woken up crying on the floor of a stranger's flat in Bradford? No. Only it turned out that these experiences had a limited applicability to the practice of literary scholarship, whereas their summer schools and library internships turned out to be quite useful. I came to understand that these people had been raised in stable homes on the bourgeois values of aspiration and constant self-improvement, and it was only through getting to know them that I realised I hadn't. Their composure threw my early life into relief. The centrepiece of my after-school routine had been the episode of *The Simpsons* that aired daily at 6 p.m., while they had kept busy schedules packed with sporting activities and lessons in music and Latin. While I was skipping school to get stoned and play *The Legend of Zelda*, they had been diligent pupils at fine preparatory schools where learning was taken seriously by teachers and students alike. For them, history was the teleological progress of spirit towards self-consciousness and freedom; it was Napoleon traversing Europe on horseback with not just the Grand Armée but late modernity in tow. For me, it was a wall display about Queen Victoria whose upper right corner had detached from the Blu Tack and drooped inward to conceal the monarch's left eye; it was Mr Wheelan lugging the old TV to our classroom, one hand gripping the frame of its rolling stand and the other clutching his VHS of *Britain at War*. I had been to a provincial university, built to educate the post-war masses. They had studied at Princeton and Yale, read the greater part of the Western Canon, and talked about Virgil and Dante as naturally as my friends and I talked about Zadie Smith and David Foster Wallace. To catch up with them would have taken another lifetime and every day I felt my workload was double theirs: there was everything I had to do – reading for classes, weekly assignments, reading through the list for my general exams – and everything I had failed to do when I was younger. I could not read a single text without thinking that I was probably the only student in my cohort who hadn't already read it and lamenting the wasted years of my youth when I should have, if only circumstances had been otherwise: if only my dad hadn't died, if only my parents had been able to secure themselves a comfortable living, if only I had known of an antidote to despondency that would let me exploit the opportunities that fell my way instead of using them as weapons with which to torture myself.

Nobody smoked. At first, I thought that I could step out and smoke a cigarette on the street as one could in Manchester or London, but passers-by held their throats and gasped for air; children eyed me fearfully. One white-haired man walked by as I puffed on a morning Marlboro during orientation week and shook his head. 'What's your problem?' called the angry Mancunian who lived inside of me. The man turned and shook his head again. 'In my day,' I understood him to be saying, 'a Harvard man took care of himself, respected science, and led a dignified life.'

I might have taken his advice and tried to assimilate. That would have been wise. Instead, I doubled down. Giving up smoking would have been an admission that I had been raised poorly, that my parents had taught me all the wrong lessons, that I did not know how to live. Nobody drank either, at least not the way I did, a pint after the library that was always two or three, in deep gulps, interspersed with cigarette breaks, seeing off the hours as though there was nothing better to do.

If I could only have buckled down and read – read and read and read – I might have got where I needed to go, but something was missing. I had frazzled my young brain with computer games and drugs. I had not had the proper schooling at the proper time and I lacked discipline and a vision of a better life. I fidgeted and fucked about. Whether these were injuries of my class, symptoms of the age, or merely personal defects, I couldn't decide. I had leveraged my relative disadvantage when applying for the scholarship that paid my way, playing up my leaving school without qualifications before seeing the error of my ways and discovering the redemptive power of literary education. It was a story that flattered the right people and so afforded me a novel kind of mobility. But it held no currency here. To have lived an errant, wasteful, self-annihilatory life was no cause for pride. And that story had ceased to console me anyway. The real appeal of literature had been that it connected one to something bigger than oneself. I had grown up in the time after history, without religion, not even knowing my grandparents. To take seriously novels and poems written by people who had died hundreds of years ago and to write your thoughts in pencil between theirs was to join a succession of generations originating in the past and stretching into the future and so illuminate your dingy world with the cumulative power of your predecessors' ideas and the belief that they could help you change it. To look at the buses crawling up and down Oxford Road on a rainy morning in November and see a scene no less human, no less ripe with the potential for transformation, no less deserving of its own mode of representation than Homer's Greece or Joyce's Dublin – the promise, in other words, that one's own world could be filled with historical meaning – was enough to make me stop messing around and work. But all of that had now been subsumed by the narrow parameters of personal success: the goal was no longer to understand and remake the world, but to publish articles and get a job.

It was past midnight now, dinner time in Maine. The thought of Mia eating a small bowl of pasta alone at the table by the french windows overlooking the garden did not make me wish we were still together. I was glad I had left. It hurt me to think that she had gone off me, but the days that we had just spent together, after I had left Cambridge in a fit of resolve and gone to stay with her, had surely confirmed what I always suspected: that we were not suited to one another, that our strong attraction derived from our more self-mutilating compulsions. I was standing in the middle of the living room now. What else was there to do? I could not have felt further away from sleep. I went back to the kitchen and took another bottle of beer from the fridge, turned my phone back on again and opened our chat. The last message she had sent me was five days earlier and read 'Can you get toilet paper?' I scrolled through a few weeks until I got to the one picture she had sent me of herself, sitting on the bus back to Maine with the blue sky above the freeway behind her. She was looking into the camera, her gaze level and steady, so that I felt when I looked at the photo that she was looking at me and not the other way around. It always took me a moment to see how beautiful she was and to remember how much I wanted that private, serious look to be fixed on me again. I turned off my phone and buried my face in my hands. The alcohol had gone to my head and I wanted to keep going but it was too depressing to think about getting drunk on my own in silence while Tom and Mel slept in the next room.

So I lay down on the sofa bed and remembered a moment I was happy with Mia. We had been in New York for the weekend and were on the train to Boston, drinking cans of beer that we had bought in Penn Station – her idea. Across the aisle, a woman our age was on a business phone call that seemed to have been going on for an hour. Her voice was pinched and nasal and only the uppermost portion of her little head was visible above the headrest.

'If that woman were a nut, she'd be a peanut,' I said.

Behind their calm surface, Mia's eyes lit up with amusement. 'What would I be?'

I turned towards her and looked her up and down with a kind of mock dispassion. She kept her stern composure and her blue-grey eyes fixed on mine, but I could see the muscles in her face twitching: a smile breaking out because she liked to be looked at that way and I could seldom manage it. 'You're a pistachio.'

She looked pleased with herself as she turned away, jutting her chin out, to take a sip from her can of beer. 'The intellectual nut. Difficult but rewarding.'

'And what would I be?'

Mia smiled as though she already knew the answer and didn't want to say it.

'Come on. I can take it.'

'You'd be a Brazil. Or a walnut.'

'That's not so bad. I thought you were going to say a hazelnut.'

'Hard and sour?'

'Cheap and abundant.'

She rested her head on my shoulder. 'You're a walnut.'

I kissed the hair on her scalp, though she wasn't as affectionate as I and didn't like to exchange these kinds of small kisses, especially not in public, or at least not with me. She shifted, looking for a comfortable position. 'The intellectual nut,' I tutted. 'Are you pleased with yourself now?'

'Shhh,' she said.

Then the train passed beneath a bridge and I saw our figures reflected in the dark window: Mia's head resting on my shoulder, her eyes closed. For the first time, I believed that it would work with us, that we could become a couple and go about our lives together, and I remained still, the way I do when a cat licks my hand, wanting the moment to last as long as possible and knowing that it was beyond my control.

Things might have turned out better with us had we been able to visit each other more easily. She was only a few hundred miles away from Cambridge, on a year-long residency at the University of Maine, where she was writing about the poet Elizabeth Bishop's late years on the island of North Haven. If either of us had been able to drive, we might have seen each other most weekends, but we couldn't. 'Poets don't drive,' she told me matter-of-factly. There was the option of a train from Boston to Brunswick, but Maine is a bigger state than one imagines and Brunswick was nowhere close. The only viable option was the seven-hour ride by Greyhound. Mia had made this trip on the day we first met, when she gave a reading on a dark November night at Harvard. It was, I later understood, mostly on account of the long journey that she looked weary that night, but at the time, I mistook her tiredness for the existential sort and thought it was our first affinity.

She was in her early thirties and already a lecturer with two well-received collections of poems to her name, as well as several scholarly articles. I was younger and still swelling with nervous ambition, terrified that I would achieve nothing, while she had accomplished many of her life's goals ahead of schedule and was more worried that she was growing bored. My head was full of the names of professors and universities, books and articles, scholarships and salaries, all the stuff that was, if not behind her, so normal a feature of her life's scenery that my excitement must have made me look like a child. I didn't know all of this the night we met but I knew some because I had googled her name when I recognised it among the list of upcoming speakers on a poster in the English department's corridor. I remembered her name from my happy undergraduate years on the south coast of England, when I had often taken the train up to London to browse the bookshops and galleries and go along with friends to launch parties and readings. I had even read a poem of hers in a journal I'd bought at one of those readings. It was called 'Saint Burning in a Parked Car' and I could still recall its eerie atmosphere. I could almost remember a few lines to do with rain falling on the windshield of a car and wanting to be snow. The poster in the English department read: 'Tuesday, November 13, Mia Knight (University College London) in conversation with Jocasta Pulaski, Harvard Carnegie Professor of Poetry. Dr Knight will read from her latest collection of poems and discuss her work-in-progress on Elizabeth Bishop.' I took my phone out of the ridiculous satchel I had purchased in a bid to fit in better among my peers and typed her name into the browser. The search returned a few pages of results and a row of photos: these were from the websites of her publisher, her agent, the university that employed her, as well as from newspapers and magazines that had reviewed her work or interviewed her. I clicked through the photographs until I landed on one that held my attention. Her expression was serious, but undercut by a look of sympathy that emanated from her eyes. She had a fine, Oxbridge sort of face with small, delicate features, but her demeanour was punkish in a way that did not speak of boarding schools and family homes in Berkshire. There was a roughness about her that led me to think we might get along.

I had spent the afternoon in my carrel, reading a few pages of a novel and allowing a thought to divert my attention and gather pace until I was once again cursing my inability to integrate and develop. Then shortly after six, I packed my books away, took the elevator to the ground floor, and exited via the large double doors in the grand entrance hall, making small talk with the security guard while he checked my bag for books as though I had more in common with him than with my peers, as though he saw it that way too. Harvard Yard was quiet. Across the lawn, spotlights illuminated the white-painted steeple of the memorial church. The air was cold in that north-eastern way, dry and biting. I crossed Quincy Street towards the Barker Center and stopped to check the time. I was early. If I went inside now, I would have to make conversation with the other attendees. So I concealed myself in one of the many secret corners that I knew, a stone bench surrounded by bushes in the corner of the courtyard, and lit a cigarette. That was when Mia emerged from the double doors of the Barker Center. She stepped out wearing only a black turtleneck and jeans, shuddered at the cold, and resisted a furtive glance either side of her – a sign that she was conscious of the possibility of being watched. She raised her nose to the cold air and looked about searchingly, a look whose meaning I understood well. Placing my cigarette in my mouth and drawing on it slowly so that the circular ember of its tip would be sure to catch her eye in the darkness, I stepped forth at a pace meant to suggest peripatetic contemplation. Our eyes met across the courtyard. I smiled. She took a tentative step forward. I took the pack of Marlboro Lights from my inside pocket and extended them towards her. She came forward, drew one, and placed a hand on her chest, indicating gratitude. She took the lighter from my hand, lit her cigarette, and took a thirsty drag. 'Thank you,' she said.

'Not a problem. You're lucky to find a cigarette around here.'

'You're English,' she said. 'Northern.'

'What about you?'

'London. But I'm in Maine this year.'

'What's in Maine?'

'Fir and birch trees. Little harbours with lighthouses and clapboard churches.'

'Sounds nice.'

'Moose.'

'Have you seen a moose?'

'No,' she said. 'They're rarer than you'd think, and bigger.'

'How big?'

Two professors entered the courtyard. One was Dana Cushing, the Victorianist. The other was Gladys de Rijke. I had taken her 'Comparative Romanticisms' seminar in my first year and she had given me a B+. At Harvard, that was tantamount to an invitation to leave the university. Through their large spectacles, they regarded us with mild disapproval.

'I'd better go inside.' Mia was holding her cigarette by her side to conceal it from the professors. 'I'm reading tonight.'

'Are you?' I said, though I knew full well who she was. 'Then I'm on my way to your reading.'

'Where do you put these?' She held up the cigarette.

'They don't provide a place for them. They don't want to encourage it. Here.' I flicked mine into the hard earth of a flower bed and she did the same.

'Nice to meet you,' she said, meeting my eyes directly.

'You too. I'll see you in there.'

'Thank you for the cigarette.' She entered the Barker Center via the double doors while I stood in the cold for a few minutes longer before following her inside. I entered the large, wood-panelled reading room at the optimal time, once most people had arrived but before the reading had begun. Just as I took a seat at the back of the room, beside a row of undergraduates, a silence fell and Professor Pulaski stepped up to the lectern. She began by introducing Mia, listing her publications and achievements, before describing her work, while Mia stood, head bowed, beside her. When her turn came to take to the lectern, she did so gracefully but with a stylish lack of deference. She seemed to take up little space, to hold her hands close to her sides, and yet she commanded attention with her poise and her intensity. Her speech, which began with an expression of gratitude for the generous introduction, was measured and precise. She made no jokes or other attempts to set the crowd at ease and instead treated the whole occasion with utmost seriousness, a seriousness I might earlier have thought excessively high-minded, but which now struck me as precisely what my life was missing. I sat up straighter in my seat, though I was sitting too far away for her to see me as clearly as I could see her.

Her poems were tightly wound. They made an impression of clarity, even simplicity, so that your instinct was to nod in agreement rather than to strain in confusion, but although their syntax made a kind of sense, it was not easy to say exactly what the poems were about. They alluded to men and women, lovers, fathers and mothers, though all of these figures had an archetypal quality in the poems. There were often places of lying down – beds, baths, graves – and elemental, almost religious objects like blood and water, skin and paper. As she read, her intonation seemed to alternate between passion and dispassion, so that she sometimes seemed to be pleading with us, insisting we understand what she was saying, while at other times she might have been reading the list of ingredients on a cereal box. Despite the conventions I had learned from academic literary criticism, my favourite interpretive game was to guess from an author's work what they were like as a person. Mia Knight, I guessed, must have had a very tender centre to require such a spiky exterior.

The reading was followed by a round of applause and a volley of eloquent responses from the hosting professor. Then the conversation turned to Mia's current project on the later life and work of Elizabeth Bishop. She spoke clearly, with received pronunciation that sounded learned rather than bred from an early age. She spoke of bays and basins, cod fish, fisheries, and schooners, pronouncing the words in a way that drew one's attention to their individual syllables. She spoke of the prosaic quality of Bishop's metre and, to illustrate what she meant, recited several lines from memory. Next, there came questions from the audience. A young associate professor in a tight suit asked a long question about Robert Lowell and John Berryman, which seemed to offend Mia, who dismissed it with tactful but firm conviction while the man wrote rapidly in the notebook on his lap. Next, an elderly emeritus asked an even longer question about Marianne Moore and the Presbyterian Church, which Mia did not appear eager to answer and whose grammatical structure, anyway, did not readily invite a response. She looked relieved when the poet-in-residence asked a question, which moved the discussion onto the subject of 'lyric affect'. A volt of excitement was palpable among the graduate students. A row of undergraduates slipped out quietly as the conversation went on. The emeritus tipped his head back towards the high ceiling. Closer to the front, there was much raising of hands, crossing and re-crossing of suit-trousered legs. The clock was about to strike half past seven when Professor Pulaski interrupted the discussion to say that we had run out of time and to thank Dr Knight for making the journey from Maine to be with us. These remarks were met with applause, which gave way to an excited murmur of conversation around the room.

Unlike in Britain, where events of this kind were followed by a visit to the pub, at Harvard they were followed by a dinner. Professors sometimes invited promising graduate students, whom they felt might benefit from meeting the invited speaker, but I was nobody's promising student. Since the only advisor with whom I'd had a good relationship in my first year had left for a job at NYU, I had become ever more isolated and estranged from my superiors. Mia was still at the front of the room, being schmoozed by a cluster of professors. There was no chance that she would speak to me in such circumstances. To the professors, that would have been as surprising as her speaking to the catering staff, who were beginning to clear the seminar room of the complimentary soup, bread rolls and fruit that were laid out on a long table at the back – so rigid were the lines between the classes: undergraduates and graduate students, the tenured and untenured. I stood alone beneath the bronze bust of John Harvard and ate a few slices of melon from a paper plate. Half the attendees had left by the time Mia was escorted from the room by Professor Pulaski in her bright red blazer and Eric Weld, Professor of Critical Theory, with his spiky hair and long black coat. Professor Weld held the oak door open demurely as Mia passed through, before adjusting his tie and ushering through an associate professor, the poet-in-residence, and two fourth-year graduate students: Samantha Liu and Chase Fagan. Samantha's invitation made sense, I thought, watching from afar and sucking the flesh from a melon rind. She was one of Pulaski's star students and had just published her first collection of poems. But there was no reason that Chase Fagan should have been invited. His work had nothing to do with poetry. He was simply the most obsequious student in the department. Chase walked at the back of the entourage as they passed the tall windows of the reading room, exaggerating his laughter to make clear that he could hear whatever was being said at the front of the group, which I knew from experience was unlikely to be funny. Maybe he would end up sitting opposite Mia at the dinner. Maybe she would fall for him, that little shit Chase Fagan.

A few of my peers were going for drinks at Daedalus and I joined them because I didn't want to go home. After a couple of rounds of eight-dollar IPAs and a long conversation about whether it was strictly necessary to have published a well-received monograph to secure a tenure-track job, or whether in certain rare circumstances, a few articles in prestigious journals would suffice, I was just about to excuse myself when I looked across the bar and saw Chase appear through the door. My heart sped up as Samantha followed with Mia behind her. I looked away but our eyes had already met for a brief moment. I looked back. She was standing at the bar with Samantha and Chase and they were presenting their IDs to the barman. Now they joined our table, though they sat at the far end. Chase obviously considered it his duty to entertain Mia, asking her questions as though he were a talk show host and introducing her to the others one by one, stating their fields and sometimes a notable accomplishment: 'This is Isabel. She knows everything about early modern print culture. And this is Carlos. He's a medievalist. He just wrote a fantastic essay on Julian of Norwich for the *LARB*, which I recommend highly.' I hated to hear people talked about in this way, as though our personalities were identical to our achievements, and I began to imagine taking Chase into a pub full of bald Northern men and introducing them: 'This is Gaz; he's a bin man. This is Baz; he's a scaffolder. This is Big Phil; nobody knows what he does.' But now Chase had reached the far end of the table, where I was sitting. 'And this is Luca,' he said to Mia. 'Remind me what you work on, Luca?' The whole group fell silent. I was glad that it was dark in Daedalus because my face turned red with shame. He knew what he was doing. Nothing embarrassed me more than my failure to decide on a field of study. They were all looking at me now and I might have screamed were it not for Mia, in whose eyes I saw sympathy and understanding. 'I'm still figuring it out,' I said. Nobody smiled, nobody laughed. When Chase continued his round of introductions, I saw that Mia's eyes remained fixed on me.

I got up a few minutes later, squeezing past the others and making my way towards the back exit to smoke, hoping that Mia would follow me. I stepped out into the cold dark and lit a cigarette, waited, but she didn't follow. How silly of me, I thought, and I decided to get my bag and go home. Inside, Chase and Samantha were speaking across Mia, who leaned back in her chair and twisted her head towards me as I passed. Handing me her phone, she said, 'Can I have your email address?' I typed it in and said that it was nice to meet her, while Chase looked at me, his eyes full of contempt.

Back at home, I sat on the front porch facing the park,

looking up at the big white moon and refreshing my inbox. It was past midnight when she finally emailed. <No subject> 'It was nice to meet you tonight. I have some time before my bus tomorrow. Would you like to have a coffee?'

'He was dreadful,' Mia said of Fagan the next day. 'A kiss-arse of the worst sort. What an awful man.'

'Isn't he?' I said. 'I hate him so much.'

'Is he typical?'

'He's exemplary.'

'God. I don't envy you.'

'And in Maine?' I asked. 'Are they as bad?'

'I hardly see them. They leave me to my own devices. But no, from my interactions so far, I wouldn't say they're the same at all. They're sweet and wholesome. Liberal suburban. Unthreatening in quite a pronounced way.'

'Sounds nice.'

'Does it tire you here?'

'Terribly.'

'Then why are you doing it?' She sat back in her chair and folded one leg over the other. She had a habit of asking difficult questions directly.

'The honest answer?'

'That's up to you.' She took a sip from her mug of black coffee.

'I was pressured into it by a mentor. He did all his degrees here and he has strong connections. He held my hand through the whole process.'

'Who was that?'

'Jacob Solomon. Do you know him?' She shook her head. 'He was a kind of father figure, I suppose. He believed in me. I didn't want to let him down.'

I told her that after my dad died and I dropped out of

school, I had moved between a few cities, working odd jobs, drinking my wages, and getting used to the idea that I would lead a life of quiet despair, and that it was only when I belatedly went to university that I believed life could be anything more. Then I threw myself into my work in a way I hadn't known I was capable of. Ideas had made life meaningful again and I believed I had finally found my place in the world. So when Jacob invited me to his office during the first semester of my final year and told me there was a scholarship I could apply for that would pay for my first two years at Harvard, the master's years, and that if I could get through those – which he didn't doubt that I could – I would be able to stay and get my PhD, I felt that a moment I'd been waiting for all of my life had arrived: the promise of a sacred purpose.

Mia wrinkled her nose at this last phrase.

'I'm exaggerating a bit,' I said. 'But in essence it's true.'

'Do you really want to be here?'

'I thought so,' I said.

'Because you wanted to think and read and teach?' I nodded. 'And have you been here long enough to know that's not what it's about?'

I nodded again.

'It's a job,' she said. 'A good one in some respects. In others less so.'

'I just wanted to lie on a chaise and read novels.'

'That's what everybody wants. You can't truly have believed that's what you were signing up for, can you? You were canny enough to get this scholarship.'

'I lied in my application.'

'How so?'

'If I can be honest, I didn't think they would give it to

a white man of average talent unless he had another string to his bow – so to speak – so I made various allusions to my working-class background.'

'And that isn't true?'

'Well, I didn't think it was until I came here. In Manchester, I was middle-class.'

'But not here.'

'Coming here has made me re-evaluate everything. That's what I'm doing with my time here: re-evaluating my life. That scholarship interview was a turning point for me. I had to go to their offices in Kensington where I was interviewed by a panel of eminent professors, private school, Oxbridge types. I hadn't understood how people like that viewed me until that day. I hadn't understood what it meant to have an accent.'

Mia inclined her head to a guilty angle. 'I mentioned it yesterday when we met outside. It was the first thing I said.'

'It doesn't matter.'

'How old are you, Luca?'

'Twenty-nine.'

She squinted as though my answer confirmed a suspicion. 'Then you're probably going through your Saturn Return. Are you interested in astrology?'

'I'm open to many things.'

'Every twenty-eight years, Saturn returns to the position it occupied at the time of your birth.'

'Is that bad?'

'It can be. It's a time when people ask themselves difficult questions and make big decisions. It's a time when people can feel stuck, lost, frustrated.'

'How was it for you?' I said, and then realised that I

had slipped up. I only knew she was three years older than me because of my internet research.

She looked at me directly and without blinking, said, 'I realised that I was going to leave my husband.'

'But you didn't?'

'I waited. I requested that we do couples therapy. I wrote my second book.'

'But you did in the end?'

'Yes,' she said. 'I always knew I would, but it took time until I was ready. Everybody says that during your Saturn Return, you should resist the impulse to make rash decisions. That's what I did. But you should explore your fantasies and impulses. They can teach you a lot about what you want.' She paused here and deepened her focus on me. 'I think you're quite rash and impulsive. Am I right? Are you a Sagittarius?'

'I think so,' I said.

'When's your birthday?'

'December twentieth.'

She smiled, pleased with herself. I was enjoying myself, too. 'Do more,' I wanted to say, 'reveal me to myself.' I said, 'What time's your bus?'

She checked her watch. 'I've got time.'

'Another coffee?'

She raised a hand in firm refusal. 'But go ahead and order one for yourself.'

'No,' I said. 'I'm fine, not if you're not having one,' and she gave me a sceptical look.

'I'm going to Vassar College to look at the Bishop papers next month,' she said when we stepped out onto Mount Auburn Street and walked slowly towards the station at Harvard Square. The day was bright and freezing.

'Where is that?'

'Poughkeepsie, New York.' We stopped by a crossing while the traffic passed. 'Isn't it a pleasure to state the town and then the state?'

'Wilmington, Delaware,' I said.

'Duluth, Minnesota.' We crossed the road. 'Anyway, it seems there's no easy way of getting there without a car so I'll probably be passing through Boston.'

'Well. I'd love to see you again.'

I had surprised myself with that word but I didn't regret it because Mia now stopped at the entrance to the station, met my eyes, and said, 'Me too.'

We held each other's gaze for a moment. The look in her eyes seemed to ripple with possibilities. She looked determined, vulnerable, wary, horny, curious. Finally, we said goodbye without touching and she turned and walked down the stairs into the subway station without turning back. I went to the Harvard Book Store and bought copies of both her collections of poems, which I took back to my flat and scanned in bed with my hand down my pants, looking for some trace of our chemistry in the lines and finding nothing.

The light between the blinds said the day was long underway. The time on my phone read 11:28. There were no texts from Mia. Nobody was home. Tom had left a note on the kitchen counter that read: *Gone to work. Help yourself to brekkie stuff and coffee.* A set of keys with a fob for the automatic gates lay on top. From the kitchen window, you could see for miles over Salford and towards Prestwich: roads and train tracks, cranes, tower blocks, piles of red-brick houses and sandstone churches. I made some coffee with the Nespresso machine, slathered a toasted bagel with butter, and ate it standing by the window. It occurred to me that I had made several grave and life-altering mistakes. But it was too late to change them now, or almost too late, and rather than that final sliver of hope, it was inevitability that I wanted – it simplified things. Once I had burned all my bridges, I would have no choice but to move on from this embarrassing period of my life.

I had nothing to do and nowhere to be but I knew that staying in was out of the question – if I stayed in the flat, I was sure to become sullen – so without even washing up my plate and mug, I resolved to go out and keep myself busy.

I had once invested a lot into the notion that Manchester was an important, international city but each time I returned, it looked ever more stunted and provincial.

Returning from Cambridge only compounded this impression. The cracks and potholes in the roads, the litter in the street, none of it had really changed since I was a child. Then, it had been just like every other place in the North of England: poor, dirty, run down. You went into the centre to shop and then you got the bus home. You didn't hang around pretending that you were in Paris. If you ordered a coffee, you got Nescafé in a polystyrene cup, and if you wanted breakfast, you got bacon or egg on a buttered white barm. Now the centre was full of cafés, bars, restaurants, new apartment and office complexes. A tram network linked the centre with the suburbs, the vast housing estates built after the war, and the old mill towns that encircled the city. But none of these developments had addressed the poverty and hopelessness you saw everywhere; there were blankets and sleeping bags rolled out in every other shopfront.

I made it as far as Deansgate, where I ducked into a café and sat by the window, drinking an expensive coffee and watching the thick clouds above the old railway depot turn yellow in the sunshine. There, I realised that I had been wrong to leave the flat and that what I really needed was to rest. So I walked back to Tom's and was crossing the car park when his voice surprised me from the balcony above. 'Wait there,' he called.

'Why?' I called back but he didn't respond. For several minutes, I looked up at the tower block and the grey sky above it until Tom emerged from the foyer door. 'We're going for a drive,' he said.

'I'm tired. I was going to have a lie-down.'

'Doesn't matter.' We climbed into the car. 'We can't have you lying around doing nothing. You'll get depressed.' I didn't argue with him. What he said was true and I had often wondered whether leading a life like Tom's – a life that fully engaged the body – would cure me of my afflictions. Depression and anxiety, alcoholism, back pain, lethargy, financial insecurity: all of these could be put down to my decision to spend most of my life sitting in chairs or lying on sofas, reading and writing. There was a time, ten years earlier, when Tom had been prone to some of these same problems but he had solved them by committing himself to vigorous activity. He ran and lifted weights, worked long hours, and spent his money only when necessary. He saw the body as the source of mental unease and therefore kept his fit and active while I – though I had always known that physical activity lifted my mood – believed the ultimate causes of depression lay in society and history and, as I tried to understand them by reading books, drove myself ever madder. Tom by no means neglected his mental and cultural life. He often went to see performances of classical music at Bridgewater Hall, and in his spare time he read widely. He liked D.H. Lawrence, Rebecca West, and Ernest Hemingway, writers whom he believed had led lives worth chronicling. But reading, to him, was a treat that one earned by first dispatching the banal but necessary tasks that life threw up each day. He had never believed that literature would give him anything except pleasure.

'Where are we going?' I asked.

'Never you mind.'

I made an expression of annoyance at Tom's reply but, in truth, I was happy about it. I liked to be shuttled around without knowing where I was going. Indeed, on a larger scale, this was how I lived.

'How was the first morning of the rest of your life?'
'I slept.'
'All morning?'
'Most of it. I've got jet lag.'
'Jet lag. How big is the time difference, four hours?'
'Five.'
A light rain began to fall as we joined the ring road, where a white Mercedes cut in front of us, causing Tom to brake and beep the horn. 'Idiot,' he said. He beeped again twice, but the car was already speeding out of sight. 'I love beeping the horn.'
'You're in a good mood.'
'I'm happy.'
'That's good. Mel seems nice. You seem good together.'
'She's great. I've never been better.'
'I'm happy for you, mate.' I meant this in a sense and in another, I didn't. I took my phone out of my pocket to check the notifications. Even though it was still early in Maine and she was probably still writing with the office door closed and her phone in the bedroom, I hoped for a message from Mia and Tom must have sensed this because he asked, 'How did you leave it with Mia?'
'Unsure. Things got quite bad.'
'Bad how?'
'Bad atmosphere.'
'And you haven't spoken since you left?'
'No.'
'And when was that?'
'A few days ago. It's blurry with all the travelling.'
'Have you texted her?'
'Yes.'
'And she's not texted back yet?'

'No.'

'That's not great. You stayed too long. How long was it? Two weeks?'

'It wasn't two weeks.'

'It's madness to stay that long.' I felt annoyed at Tom for saying what I thought. For a passing moment, the whole situation felt like his fault. 'What's the situation then? When are you going back to Boston?' He flicked the indicator and we pulled off the main road onto a side street flanked by old factories with collapsing perimeter walls.

'I'm not.'

'What about the PhD?'

'I quit.'

'Properly?'

'Yes.'

'I thought you were just taking a break.'

'I told you I had left.'

'I thought you were exaggerating.'

'Entirely serious. I quit.'

'Fucking hell, lad. Why did you do that?'

'It was inevitable. I was floundering.'

'Did you read all the books?'

'I read some of them.'

'Even I know you have to read all the books. So, what are you going to do? Can't you just live in Boston anyway? Get a job there.'

'Any friends I made there, I lost the second I quit. You can't be friends with those people unless you're living in the same insane world as they are. When you run away from a cult, you don't stop by for tea a week later. Anyway, I don't want some office job.'

'Don't you want money? There's no money here.'

'I want freedom.'

'And how do you expect to get it without money?' We entered the car park of a small commercial unit. 'Bloody hell. And you've fucked it up with Mia too?'

'Not fucked it up. But yes.'

We pulled into a parking space and Tom cut the engine. 'So what are you going to do? Live here?'

'That's the idea.'

'Well,' he seemed caught off guard and hesitated for words. 'I suppose it will be nice to have you.'

'Good,' I said. 'What's this?'

'It's where I work. You know you can't live with me, don't you?'

'I know. I didn't picture it like this.' I nodded towards the industrial unit.

'I might know of a place you can stay a while.'

'Oh yeah?'

'Don't get your hopes up. You're always getting your hopes up.' He opened the door, said, 'I'll be back in a minute,' and left me alone in the car, where I watched an empty Doritos packet float around on the breeze.

Tom worked at a digital radio station called Mint Radio that played Manchester hits from the 80s and 90s. I had listened to it once or twice in America, only when I felt especially nostalgic. Two out of every three songs were by Manchester acts, so it was mostly New Order, The Stone Roses, Happy Mondays: all those bands from the city's late heyday in the 80s and early 90s, when a thriving music scene had grown out of the post-industrial decline of the 70s. Most of the DJs were veterans of that era, washed-up old geezers full of stories about Factory Records and the Haçienda. Tom had started working for them as an intern, shortly after he finished his A-Levels and decided not to go to university. At the time, I assumed the job would be temporary, that he would quit once he found a more exciting and fulfilling occupation or that he would move to Paris for a while, as he had sometimes discussed, but he did neither. While I moved around and did a series of menial odd jobs until I finally decided to go to university at twenty-five, he stayed in the same place and worked. He became a sound engineer and now he was in line to become a producer. When I had been admitted to the programme at Harvard, I had assumed that I would eventually ascend to a position of greater wealth and higher social standing than him, but that did not seem likely now.

Tom and I had grown up on the same street and our mothers had become friends. Mine had worked at the city council before she trained to become a schoolteacher while Tom's was a nurse. Because his parents had been thrifty and shrewd, his mother was able to give him a bit of money for a deposit on the flat, so long as he could secure the mortgage with his own means, whereas my mother had no money to help me out. However, because she and my dad had once tried to become academics – even though they had not ultimately succeeded – they had spent enough time in that milieu and absorbed enough of its codes and attitudes to bestow me with some of them, enough to let me move a bit more freely between different worlds. Though Tom and I rarely spoke about it, it was clear that one of our significant bonds, perhaps the one that bound us together despite the different choices we had made, was that we had both lost our dads when we were young. Tom had been seven, and his dad had died in a road traffic accident, whereas I had been fourteen and mine had killed himself. I always thought that Tom had it better because he knew that if only it wasn't for a drunk driver on the M60, his dad would still be alive and would love and care for him, whereas I had to contend with the idea that mine hadn't loved me sufficiently to stay alive. On the other hand, I'd had a dad for twice as long as he had and could at least console myself with the idea that he had chosen his own fate, whereas Tom had to live with the knowledge that one of the most significant events in his life had been senseless and arbitrary.

Tom emerged from the unit carrying a box under his arm. He put it on the back seat and then stood for a moment with his eyes closed, his head tipped up towards the ray of sun that was breaking through the grey clouds, breathing deep into his belly.

'What's in the box?' I said when he got in the car.

'None of your business.' He turned the radio on. 'I have to listen for a minute.' They were playing the first track from *The Return of the Durutti Column*. It began with a recording of birdsong and, hearing that sound as Tom started the engine, I imagined another place, perhaps another time, where it was warm and birds were singing early in the morning. I got my phone out of my pocket: no word from Mia.

'What will you do if she doesn't text you?'

'I'm sure she'll text me.'

'What makes you so sure?'

'A week ago, we were in love with each other. I thought we were going to live together and get married.'

'How do you know you were in love? Did you say it?'

'No.'

'Did she?'

'No.'

'Then you can't be sure. Anyway, things change. You've got to stay ahead of the curve, adapt to the new reality. You're unemployed, thirty, and single.' We slowed down behind a car as it waited for the automatic gates of an apartment building to open. 'Reckon you'd be crushed if you got caught in there?' He nodded at the corner where the gate closed onto a brick wall.

'Probably.'

'I reckon so. Crushed to death.'

On a residential street along the boundary of Greenheys and Moss Side, we parked between a gothic church and a red-brick church hall. 'We're going in here.'

'What is it?'

'It's where Mel works.'

'What for?' I got out and followed him around the corner.

'Just stopping by.'

It was a hall of the sort one finds all over Britain, used for hundreds of various purposes over the years, each of which had left a mark on its interior. Around the walls, beneath the tall frosted-glass windows, stood stacks of chairs and boxes. At the far end, where once there may have been an altar, there was a stage, though it was doubtful that a play had been put on in thirty years and it appeared now to serve as a storage space for sports equipment and dusty, bulging holdalls. Below this stage, a few elderly and middle-aged men were sitting in chairs while a woman of around sixty stood beside them, supervising their leisure and engaging them in conversation. At one side of the hall, a hatch opened onto a kitchen and Tom led us there. Two women in red aprons stood with their backs to us, working at the counter and talking in thick accents. Tom called through the hatch – 'Hello, ladies' – and my initial reaction was to cringe; I could not remember the last time someone I knew had used the word 'ladies'. But when the women turned around and saw Tom, they smiled and greeted him warmly: 'Hello, darling. How are you? Are you alright?' And he greeted them back in the customary way, saying, 'Are you alright?' without either party answering the question. 'This is my friend, Luca.' Tom pointed at me while I waved a hand. 'How are you, darling?' one of the women said. There was warmth in the way they greeted me and a touch of wariness. That I was now unused to these settings must have been clear from the stiffness of my posture. Tom asked where Mel was and the women said that she was in the back with a service user. 'No bother,' Tom said and when the women offered us a brew, he said yes and asked for coffee. One of them pointed a finger at me and asked if I would like one too and I said yes to milk and even to sugar because I was tired. They gave us mugs of instant coffee dissolved in water from a steel urn, a spoonful of sugar from a kilogram paper bag, and a splash of semi-skimmed milk from a large plastic bottle. Tom dropped a few coins into the biscuit tin on the shelf by the hatch and nodded towards the group sitting by the stage. 'We'll go and say hello.'

There were five people, three sitting, one standing, and one in a wheelchair. The woman standing diverted her gaze towards us as we crossed the room and smiled, though by continuing to nod, she made it clear that she was still listening to the man of around seventy who sat wearing a worn suit with a walking stick resting against his thigh. The others looked at the speaker or nowhere in particular, except for the man in the wheelchair, who trained his eyes on us as we crossed the floor. He was younger than the others and did not share the air of near-catatonic resignation that seemed to hang over them. His large, soulful eyes surveyed us as we approached. 'Hello, Tom,' the woman said when we drew near. 'Hello, Viv,' Tom said and the old man, realising that he had lost his audience's attention, allowed his speech to trail off. Another, a man in his sixties with large scabs on his hairless scalp, turned and regarded us with indifference. 'Hello, Edward,' Tom greeted the old man, who had now ceased talking, though his mouth made a few small after-movements as though to gesture towards what he might yet have said. 'Hello, Andy,' he said to the man in the wheelchair, who raised a fist for Tom to bump. Andy was heavyset and his head was big and round, but his high cheekbones and dark-brown eyes lent his face a subtle beauty. What I noticed first, though, was his strange animation; he blinked often and his whole body seemed to vibrate with impatience or excitement. 'This is my friend, Luca.' Tom raised a hand to introduce me to the group, who didn't seem very interested. 'He's just moved back from America.'

'Ooh, very nice,' said the woman, whom I understood to be a member of staff or a volunteer.

Andy, the man in the wheelchair, almost jiggled with excitement. 'I've been to America.' Our eyes met and his beamed with something so eminently human that my instinct was to shut it down.

'Have you?' My tone was patronising, but he didn't seem to mind.

'New York.'

'Did you like it?' I could feel that the eyes of the whole group were trained on us now.

'Loved it. Best country in the world.' He spoke with a slight difficulty, not quite an impediment but a kind of heaviness. 'Where did you live?'

'Boston. Well, just outside Boston actually. Cam—'

'Bawston.' He broke into a fit of laughter. He looked around for some recognition and found none. 'Have you seen *The Departed*?' he said.

I no longer saw the same look in his eye. In its place, was something pleading and earnest that I couldn't meet. I shook my head and smiled uncomfortably.

'You've not? What's wrong with you?' He laughed again. 'Are you going to be working here?' This question set off a complex and unpleasant response in me, a mixture of sympathy, fear and contempt.

'I don't think so.'

'You're always welcome,' the woman said and she and Andy laughed. 'Are you here to see Mel?'

'I am.' Tom's voice was firm and purposeful. He seemed to enjoy his role in this group, whatever it was.

'She's there now,' Andy said.

In the corridor we had come from, Mel was saying goodbye to a figure out of our view. Then she stepped into the hall, smiled when she saw us, and greeted the whole group as she approached. She was popular with them, I could see. They trusted her. She kissed Tom on the lips and the woman smiled approvingly. 'This is a nice surprise.' Mel said that she was already done for the day so we finished our coffees and said goodbye to the group.

'Bye, Tom,' Andy said. 'Bye, Mel. Bye, Luca.'

I laughed then. Why I found it funny that he remembered

43

my name, I didn't know. 'Bye, Andy,' I said. 'It was nice to meet you.'

My heart was pounding when we stepped out into the little yard at the front of the church hall and walked to the car. I had not been prepared for an encounter with people like that. I had always taken the suffering of others personally, as though it were me that were affected. This was not generosity but the opposite. I tended to take the pain of others so personally that I was hardly able to recognise that it was not my own. Furthermore, I never volunteered or otherwise gave my time to those less fortunate than I was because doing so tended to set my mood spiralling downwards. In a resilient mood, I could muster the strength to resist this, but I was not in a resilient mood today. Had only Tom been present, I would have chastised him for taking me there without warning, if only to let off some steam, but I stopped myself because Mel was with us. In front of her, I couldn't say what I wanted to say – Why did you take me to see those poor people? Don't you know how it affects me? – because I would have come across as horribly snobbish and self-involved or, rather, I would have revealed that I was those things. I closed the car door and sighed. 'How are you doing?' Mel said from the front seat.

'Just tired.'

'I bet you are.'

Tom started the car. He believed that I was too often tired without good reason, but he wouldn't say so now. He joined the traffic on the main road and drove towards the Asda. 'Andy liked you, didn't he?'

'Did he?' Mel laughed.

'Definitely. His face lit up when I said you'd just got back from America.'

44

'Aw. He loves America. He's always talking about his trip to New York. You'll have to come in again so that he can tell you all his stories.'

I smiled politely, but it was pointless because she couldn't see my face. 'What's wrong with him?' I said.

'How do you mean? Why does he use a wheelchair?'

'Yeah, I suppose.'

'He's got MS. Multiple Sclerosis.'

A heavy silence filled the car and I intuited that Mel had been made wary by my insensitive question and was wondering whether to say more, while Tom, who knew that my dad had suffered from MS, was wondering if I would now announce that fact to the car or if he should do it for me.

'My dad had MS,' I said. It was always more upsetting to announce such things in front of a person who already knew them.

'I'm sorry,' Mel said. 'Was it bad for him?'

'Very bad.' I suddenly felt very sad thinking about my dad in his last years, when he too had needed to use a wheelchair. Strong sensations like this were never available to me when I went looking for them. They only caught me by surprise and always passed as quickly as they arose. This one passed. Now a different question hung in the air. What had happened to my dad? Had the disease killed him? But Mel didn't ask, so I supposed that Tom had already told her.

I didn't follow Tom and Mel into the building when we got back. Their compassion was beginning to bug me, so I said I was going for a walk.

'You're not going to top yourself, are you?' Tom said.

'Nah.'

'Good stuff. I'll see you in a bit.'

I crossed the canal and joined the narrow path where the Irwell ran between the overgrown wharf and the rows of identical apartment complexes with names like Maritime Court and Merchant's Quay. I was in a bad mood now and I wanted to talk with someone, but the only person I felt would understand my situation was my mum, a thought that left me feeling maladjusted and lonely and made me think I would be better off walking alone until I discovered some resolve.

A light rain began to make little circles on the river's murky surface. 'Hello?' my mum said. There was concern in her voice. She would have expected bad news.

'Hey. It's me.'

'Oh, hi, honey. I was wondering when I might hear from you. We haven't spoken since your exam.'

'No.'

'So, how are you?'

'I'm in Manchester.' There was silence as she processed this news and searched for the right words.

'And are you feeling okay about that?'

'Yeah. I just got back yesterday.'

'Are you staying with Tom?'

'Yep.'

'Good.' She knew what had happened, I could tell. 'You know you can always come here and stay for as long as you like.'

'I know. Thank you. I think I'll try to stay here for a while.'

'You've talked about doing that. I think it's a good idea.' The wind off the river produced a distorted crackle on the line. 'Well, I'm on my lunch break.'

'Sure. It's starting to rain now anyway.'

'Love you, honey,' she said.

And I said I loved her too and hung up.

A few years earlier, my mum had taken voluntary redundancy from the college where she taught and moved to a resort town on the Costa Blanca, where the property prices had not recovered since the financial crisis and she could afford to buy a flat designed with holidaymakers in mind. There was a spare bedroom and she was out during the weekdays, teaching English at a local school. I had thought about flying directly to Madrid from Boston and going to stay with her for a while but decided against it. I was too old to go crying to my mother. I had done the right thing by coming here, to the only place where I could regenerate, or hoped I could.

When I got back to Tom's flat, I found a note that said they had gone to spend the night at Mel's so I could enjoy a day on my own. I was welcome to sleep in Tom's bed, it said, and to eat the leftover curry and rice in the fridge.

When I first arrived in America, I took a partially furnished apartment in the eastern part of Somerville, close to the Mystic River. It was only a twenty-minute cycle to Harvard Square but it lay well outside the cultural orbit of the university, in a less affluent neighbourhood trisected by Highway 93 and the fenced-off tracks of the Orange Line. It was a small one-bed for a thousand dollars per month – the price of a room in Cambridge or the southern parts of Somerville. I wanted to live by myself because I had been living with my girlfriend in London and I thought that if I had a flat of my own, she could visit and we might be able to live as though nothing had changed. I knew that our relationship would not survive my leaving and, deep down, I did not want it to, but I nevertheless wanted to make a show of trying so that I could forgive myself more easily when it inevitably failed. The other reason was that I was afraid of the new world I was entering and the people I would meet there. I believed that if I lived alone and further away, I could hold myself aloof from that world, arranging my life like a professional who moves to a new city for a job and spends his days working and his evenings in solitude. Only I didn't really want to live that way. Quite the opposite. I longed for connection and mutual understanding and wished to be absorbed so fully by my new surroundings that they would cleanse me of my past and make me somebody new. So, from the beginning, I resented the cycle home from the campus, which took me along the tree-lined streets where professors and other well-off people lived in large brick houses, through Inman Square, where graduate students lived in houses divided into flats and the cafés sold good drip coffee and espresso drinks prepared with oat milk, and finally beneath the highway bridges and over the train tracks, where the only businesses were auto repair shops, a Home Depot, and a retail park in the old premises of the Ford Motor Plant. With each stage of the journey, I felt that I was cycling away from the person I hoped to become and back towards the one I had always been.

I had arranged the rental through an agency before I arrived and although I had seen photographs from every possible angle and nudged around the neighbourhood on Street View, I had not thought to ask about neighbours. There were only two apartments in the building and we shared a downstairs hallway; one door led directly into my neighbour's apartment and another to the stairway up to mine. For the first few days, I neither saw nor heard any trace of the occupant but on the evening of the first Sunday I spent there, while I was winding down and preparing for the first day of term, I heard his door slam and felt his presence beneath the floorboards. He was moving between the three rooms, which I assumed mirrored mine: a living room with a kitchenette, a small adjoining bedroom and a bathroom. He had put on the TV or the radio and the sounds carried through the thin floor. After a while, I could discern a real human voice from among the recorded ones and I gathered that he was talking either on the phone or to himself. That in itself didn't bother me much, though I noticed that where I had relaxed, believing that I was

49

alone, I now stiffened, my breaths became shallow and quiet, and when I needed to go to the bathroom, I tiptoed. Then I thought that I was acting too strangely. I couldn't hide my presence and I had no reason to, so I flushed the toilet as loudly as I could and cleared my throat. I spent the rest of the evening reading on the sofa and if I wasn't completely relaxed when I went to bed at 9 p.m., that didn't stop me from quickly falling asleep. But then in the middle of the night I woke at the raised voice of the neighbour downstairs. The sound had made its way into my dreams so it scared me to open my eyes and find that a danger I thought was inside me was alive and outside of my control. He was cursing as though in frustrated rage. The modulations of his voice were clear, but the floorboards muffled the contours and made it difficult to discern what he was saying. I thought he could have been barking at the TV, talking back to the news, telling the anchors to shut up and stop lying, but the longer I listened, the more I was certain that no news was playing and the neighbour was talking only to himself.

The next day saw the beginning of a busy week of welcome talks, meet-and-greets, social lunches, and orientation events. These left me little time to think about the situation at home, but when the day's activities had drawn to a close, I was reluctant to set off and wished that I had taken a room in a student residence. So what if I was a few years older than the others? The embarrassment of living like a teenager would have been a worthwhile price to pay for safety and convenience. For a few nights, however, I only heard the sound of the television and an occasional groan or cry, so I was able to put the neighbour out of my mind until, on the Friday of that week, I arrived home from a trip to Trader Joe's and met him at the door as he was on his way out. He had taken up so much space in my mind – surely a great deal more than I had taken in his – that my heart sped up at the sight of him and I greeted him with a nervous, overenthusiastic 'Hi!', inexplicably setting my shopping bags down on the ground. Closing the door behind him rather than leaving it open for me to enter, he responded to my greeting with a curt nod and a sharp, indistinct sound, walking quickly past me and down the street without looking back. He was around fifty years old and more ordinary-looking than I'd expected. He wore a grey polo shirt and blue jeans and might have fit in anywhere were it not for his somewhat wild countenance and nervous gait. He was large in every sense, taller than me, broader, and heavier, but his keen, narrow mouth, and his snub nose made his round head, which was topped with a layer of thin brown hair, look even smaller than it was, just menacing enough that, although he was not the ogre I had envisioned, my fears still had a physical aspect to which they could attach themselves. I didn't hear him come back that night, but the next was the worst to date. He cursed and shouted and stomped around the flat. At one point, I thought I heard him sobbing. Later, during a fit of shouting, he smashed a plate or glass and then seemed to knock over a heavy object like a chair. This was Saturday and I had been invited to a house party by some British students in Cambridge. I hadn't especially felt like going but now I considered it just so that I would have a reason to leave, though in the end I felt too full of the strangeness of that flat to show myself in public.

I could more or less forget about my neighbour during the daytime – classes had begun and I was on campus from morning until evening every day – but I spent the nights in worsening states of worry. I calmed my fears by telling myself that although he was clearly unwell, he had not directed any of his violent behaviour towards me and so I had no good reason to be scared. Then I reprimanded myself for being selfish and thought that a better person would ask what they could do for *him*, whether there was a family member or friend who could be called upon for help. But whenever his raised voice reverberated through the floor, these thoughts were no match for the terror that possessed me, which was always worse when I was lying in bed. One night during the first full week of classes, as I was trying to fall asleep despite the sound of his cursing below, I found myself turning over a memory that had never returned to me with such clarity or so insistently. It was a memory of lying awake at night in the bedroom of my dad's house, listening as he sat up drinking, talking to himself, sometimes playing a CD and then stopping it abruptly, knocking things over whenever he got up to pour himself a drink, smoke a cigarette at the back door, or stumble up the stairs to take a piss, and of the fear and confusion I had felt over my inability to control or influence his behaviour and make him comply with my wish that he stop drinking and go upstairs to bed.

This was towards the end of the period when my dad lived in a house near the canal in Stretford, a fifteen-minute bus ride from where I lived with my mum. After several years in which he had endured a number of manic episodes, moved house every year, cycled through a series of brief relationships, and drank himself into hospital so frequently that my visits with him were brief and intermittent, things had started to go well for him again. He was on a new medication that stabilised his moods. He had resumed work on his thesis on 'Coleridge's Melancholy' and secured a temporary teaching job at a local university. He had a girlfriend, a graduate student at another university, and they had moved into the new house together. Whereas on previous occasions that I had visited my dad, he usually lived in austere rooms full of boxes he had not bothered to unpack, his girlfriend had decorated this house with framed pictures, candles, cushions, and other objects I was unused to seeing in his homes. They had a guest bedroom at the front of the house and I began to stay there one night a week, which meant I saw my dad more often than I ever had before. In the evenings, he cooked for me and his girlfriend and the three of us ate together at the kitchen table. In the mornings, he walked me to the bus stop and counted out thirty-seven pence to pay the driver. This was a happy time at first but it changed when, after several months of testing to determine the cause of his headaches and episodes of spasticity, he received a diagnosis of MS. Then he entered a deep depression and began to drink again. After his girlfriend left him, I didn't go to the house for a while and the next time I did, the walls were all but bare and the decorative cushions no longer adorned the armchair by the window where I liked to sit after arriving from school. A selection of his hardback volumes filled half the bookcase and left the lower part clear but for a thin layer of dust. In his room, there was nothing except a double bed and a small, antique dresser.

Although I was usually nervous as I walked from the bus stop to his house, it was not impossible, at the beginning of this phase, that he would be in a good mood when I arrived, and we might go out to take photographs of crumbling factories, brick walls topped with coils of barbed wire, and rusting fire escapes, or to look at the steam engines and spinning mules in the Museum of Science and Industry; this was well before his physical deterioration meant that he had to use a wheelchair, when he was well enough to walk unaided, only using his cane to counter sudden episodes of weakness in his legs. More and more often, though, he was grumpy when I arrived and he left me to draw or read while he worked on his thesis. He sat, striking his keyboard, muttering and smoking – little puffs of industry rising from his desk – while I lay on the sofa bed with a copy of *Kerrang!*, wary of his erratic movements and the sounds that arose from his strange communion with himself. Some evenings, he powered down the PC and when its fan whirred to a halt, he seemed to relax into the silence of the room and become present. His eyes would fix on me as though he hadn't seen me in years, and he would ask me how I was doing and what I was thinking about, as though the answer might be the figure of the angel in Rilke's *Duino Elegies* or a certain cloud study by Constable, rather than that I was vaguely imagining myself as the protagonist of an action movie. In these moments, I always sensed his disappointment that I was what I was – a ten-year-old boy in his last year of primary school – and not somebody older who could comfort and understand him. Some evenings, he smoked hash and then became peaceable and relaxed while we listened to music together, but if he had a drink, his emotions stirred and he was prone to tearing up during the Goldberg Variations. He would say, 'Shhh!' and hold a finger aloft, pointing at the faint sound of Gould's voice in the background of the recording as though it were with us in the room. Later, as his health worsened and his moods began to fluctuate more violently, my dad drank himself into increasingly unruly states and we no longer listened to music.

The scene that visited me as I lay in the bedroom in Somerville was from a particular night in this late period, when, against the wishes of my dad, who had encouraged me to stay up a while longer, I had gone to bed and was lying in the darkness when I heard the stairs creak and the sound of his slow step drawing closer. He murmured my name at the door and quickly repeated it more emphatically. Then he pushed open the door, took two stumbling steps towards where I lay and sat down on the edge of the bed. 'Luca,' he said, 'You're just going to sleep, aren't you?'

I didn't want to answer this question and for a moment, I considered pretending that I was already asleep but from the expectation in the silence I could tell he knew I was awake. 'Yes,' I said.

'Do you mind if I go down to the Dog for a bit?' He asked this question in an injured, pleading tone that I hadn't heard before. When I didn't respond, he said, 'It's just around the corner, you know. There's a bloke who always gets up and does karaoke on a Thursday. Neville.'

I didn't want my dad to leave but I was too afraid to say that, so after a moment I said, 'I'm scared.'

'Of what?'

'Being alone.'

'Nothing'll happen. I'm just around the corner.'

I didn't respond because I didn't know what else I could say. I was afraid of that neighbourhood, of the derelict house across the street, of the dark beyond the curtains in the window, and I desperately did not want to be left alone.

'Come on,' he said. 'Please.'

I remained quiet and drew the duvet over my face.

'Please. I'll just have a couple and then come back. You won't even notice I'm gone.'

'Please, Dad,' I said.

This appeal to his paternal responsibility seemed to irk him because he stood up in what looked like a fit of anger and walked out of the room, whispering to himself as he went. I heard him piss into the toilet bowl and make his way heavily down the stairs. For a moment, the house was silent. Then I heard the door slam shut and his footsteps on the pavement outside.

Although this was a sad memory, it was also a source of some comfort because it allowed me to reason that my reaction to the downstairs neighbour was irrational, rooted not in a sober appraisal of the situation and its risks but in my particular sensitivities, my past. If I could just remember that I was not really afraid of him but of something within myself, I could ignore the neighbour, especially as I was beginning to understand the pattern of his moods: a few nights of silence, a few nights of grunting and muttering, and then around once a week, a night or two of heavy cursing and shouting, never a threat directed towards me or, as far as I could tell, anybody else. But being able to explain the fear as irrational didn't really help. I was still afraid and I hated the feeling of not being safe in my home. I couldn't focus in classes or in the library and my mood was lower than it had been in years. How much this was because of the neighbour and how much was a predictable reaction to the demands of a new environment, I wasn't sure, but by October I had decided to cut my losses and move out, a costly decision that would have been impossible had the rental agency not granted me mercy after I visited the office in person and explained that I was losing my mind.

By November, I had left that flat – having avoided any face-to-face encounters with my neighbour except on that one Friday late in August – and moved into a flat in Inman Square with a balcony looking over the park, which I shared with two friendly graduate students named Kareena and Mar. Once I had unpacked my things, my new flatmates and I sat at the kitchen table to eat dinner together and drink a bottle of wine and I told them the story of the man downstairs. I took a lot of pleasure in their displays of empathetic shock, not caring much whether they were real because they helped me to establish that the incident had really happened and was strange at the least, which helped me to leave it behind.

But the memory of my dad's house lingered and I became more and more preoccupied with that time of my life. I was finding it difficult to keep up with my workload and I blamed my struggles on my immersion in the past. At the same time, I believed the explanations for my difficulties were to be discovered there and that I couldn't move forward until I understood them. It had been years since I had given any serious thought to this period of my childhood and now, in a sense, I felt that I was experiencing it for a second time, that it was more substantial than the world in which I lived. Sitting in a seminar room on the upper floor of Emerson Hall, looking out the window at the snow-covered grass in Harvard Yard, I would remember a time when it had snowed in Manchester and from the window of my dad's kitchen, which looked over the small backyard, you could see where the snow had gathered in an inch-thick sheet along the slanted coping of the wall.

A detail like this seemed to sing with significance and yet when I looked around at my classmates as they articulated their positions on the texts that lay open and annotated on their desks, I remembered that they couldn't give a shit about a bit of wall in Manchester – they had better and more important things to do, and so did I.

So, in a spirit of begrudging obligation, I set these memories aside and did what I needed to do to get through the semester with results that were acceptable, if below average. But when the winter holidays came around and all the other students went home, I stayed in Cambridge and summoned the courage to write to one of my dad's sisters whom I hadn't spoken with for several years:

Dear Aunt Siobhan,
I'm sorry that we haven't seen each other for so long and that I am seldom in contact. These days I hardly have time for anything except work. I hope this will change in the future. I have been thinking about my dad of late and I seem to remember that you had some notebooks of his. Would you be kind enough to scan any interesting pages and email them to me?
With love

She wrote back later the same day:

Dear Luca,
Lovely to hear from you darling and don't worry about us. I'm sure you're very busy and I know your da would be so proud of you studying in America – that was his dream! Send me your address.

A week later, I arrived home to find a bulky FedEx package sitting on the front porch. It contained two hardbound notebooks that my dad had kept when he was researching his PhD. The notebooks were full of quotations, aphorisms, and observations. Among them were jokes written in a vein of humour, sometimes dark, sometimes bathetic, that I could still link to the living person I had known. On one page, he had drawn a tombstone and written upon it the words: 'Non deerat voluntas sed facultas' – 'Twas not the will but the way that was wanting. On another, he had given an addendum to a quotation from *Samson Agonistes*: 'Be of good courage, I begin to feel some rousing motions in me which dispose to something extraordinary my thoughts. (He farts).' These made me cheerful not only because they revived my memories of him, but because they reminded me that he had not always been as unhappy as he was at the end of his life. But these happier details were outweighed by those that gave a picture of a gloomy, depressive, tediously self-involved person. Among those were Lacanian diagrams that he had copied out by hand and others he seemed to have invented, with points labelled 'The Real', 'Desire', '(big) Other', all connected with crisscrossing arrows labelled 'Semblance', 'Enunciation', and 'Castration'. Though I didn't entirely understand them, I felt there was something desperate about these diagrams, especially when he seemed to have designed them to explain himself. There were many memoranda, usually written in a spirit of pessimistic self-criticism: 'You have already wasted more than your allotted time.' 'When X, then Y. But I've already X and there was no Y.' And there were quotations and notes that demonstrated the suicidal ideation that, so far as I understood, he had always engaged in:

> Hard hearted parents both lament my fate,
> If self I kill or hang, to ease my state

The strange thing was that, although I had been so eager to get hold of these notebooks and to salvage whatever impressions I could of my dad and the parts of my childhood in which he had been involved, no sooner had I got them than I felt a powerful abhorrence. It was as though I had imagined they could bring him back to life and make the world that surrounded him vivid, and when they didn't, I hated their pages as though it were their fault. So I put them in a drawer and didn't look at them again until a few days before I left Cambridge, when I was packing up the last of my things and had thrown them along with my other personal effects into the suitcase that now stood at the foot of the sofa in Tom's living room.

Because I didn't have anything else to do or, rather, because I had too much to do and didn't know where to start, I unpacked the suitcase and placed the notebooks on the table. I was less interested now in the notebooks themselves than in the sheets of paper I had placed between their pages, a text I had been working on for several months and which, in a sense, had replaced them. I had written it for a creative writing course called 'Writing Selves', taught by an American author and associate professor named Regina Humboldt, who had written two well-received novels. Its focus was the 'vexed entanglements of selves, authorial, fictional and personal'. We met once a week in a slick new seminar room on the top floor of the Lamont

Library to read a selection of recent novels by authors whose narrators had come to be associated with their real-life authors – as well as a few short excerpts from Augustine and Rousseau in a nod towards historical context – and talked about whether this mattered and what it meant that these books had become so popular. Then we read each other's texts and discussed them in a workshop format. Soon after our email correspondence began, Mia had suggested that she might send me a poem to read and asked if I would share some of my work with her, but I had written nothing I was proud of, only the academic essays I had written for my courses, which, with their stiff, inauthentic style and their constant references to works I had only read in part, expressed nothing more clearly than my desperate desire to know more than I really did. So, against the counsel of my advisor, who insisted it was not a good use of my time, I had signed up for 'Writing Selves' and begun work on a novelistic text, in which I sought to recreate, with language, my dad and the world that surrounded him.

I began with a fictional account of his childhood in a suburb of North Manchester in the 1960s, a description of his large Irish-Catholic family, which focused on his fear of his hard-nosed father, a miner's son who became the manager of a biscuit factory and was a tyrant to his employees and his children alike. But I knew hardly anything about that time in his life. I was working backwards, surmising from my dad's unhappy adult life that something must have been wrong in his childhood, and though I could have asked any of his siblings, I had always been afraid of them, especially when it came to matters concerning our family, whose history was a point of ongoing contention. So instead, I tried to write an account of him at twenty-nine, meeting my mum while he was working on his PhD and following her to Chicago, where I was born just as their relationship was falling apart. But I didn't understand this period either – the chronology made no sense and I could never remember how it was that my mum ended up taking me to Manchester. I had asked my mum to explain the circumstances on a few occasions but only when I was so drunk that I couldn't remember them the following day, so the whole period was confused and indistinct.

The hardest lesson these failures taught me was that I could hardly remember what my dad was like. When you are young and a significant person dies, you have not yet finished distinguishing yourself from them and so they leave an amorphous impression; they become like the monsters you fear as a child lying awake in the dark, which are scarier for taking no definite form and for seeming to be everywhere at once. I decided that in as much as I possessed any solid traces of him, I did so in the form of my own habits and inclinations and so, finally, I wrote about myself.

I wrote about the morning in June when I found out he had died, the phone ringing downstairs and my mum's footsteps approaching my bedroom, the way I had run downstairs and opened the back door to gasp at the summer air. I described the anger that momentarily filled me as I realised what he had done and the way I directed this anger at the phone mounted on the kitchen wall, taking the handset and slamming it against the cradle before letting it dangle by the cord. I wrote about the funeral at Southern Cemetery, the buses splashing the long puddles on Barlow Moor Road as the mourners huddled under black umbrellas, the smoke from their cigarettes rising into the misty air, and the sense I had that it was his fate, too, to become diffuse, part of the essence of things, present everywhere and visible nowhere.

The problem was that I had hardly begun to process the events of these years and recollecting them turned out to be more difficult than I'd expected. Every time I wrote a few pages, I read them over the next morning and felt they were too obviously driven by an impulse to justify myself and account for my failings. I was embarrassed by that irrepressible part of myself that always wanted to say 'I' and found myself thinking that I would be better off seeing a therapist than trying to write a novel. As I skimmed the pages at the table in Tom's living room, I could only see the text as the death throes of a shoddily assembled ego and I felt ashamed when I remembered submitting it to the evaluation of my peers. I struck through sentences, paragraphs, and words until no word remained uncrossed. Then I ripped the documents into pieces, stuffed them into an empty shoe box, and emptied it with the rest of the recycling into the overflowing bin in the car park.

On Back Piccadilly, a dank alleyway lined with rusting fire escapes, gig posters on wooden hoardings, bins, pallets, and black bin bags full of rubbish, there stood a Pakistani restaurant named Marhaba Café, whose sign, unchanged in thirty years, was decorated with photographs of naan breads and kebabs so faded they had all but disappeared. 'Alright, boss,' the man behind the counter said to Tom, who entered first. 'Alright,' he said to me and Mel. A few plastic tables were arranged along the wall of the narrow space opposite the counter. An older man appeared from the saloon door to the hidden part of the kitchen and greeted us.

'What have you got on today?' Tom said.

The younger man removed the lids on the stainless-steel pots and lifted the serving spoons one at a time so that we could see their contents: 'Okra, chana, spinach, daal, potato, fish.'

Tom asked for rice with chana, potato, and fish with a naan bread. Me and Mel asked for the same. 'I'll get this.' I stood up and took my Bank of America card from my pocket.

'Cash only, pal.'

I looked at Tom, who shook his head and took some notes from his wallet to pay. 'I'll get you back.'

The younger man began plating up the food. His father sang quietly as he spun the naan dough with both hands.

'How's your new life going?' Tom said.

'Alright.'

'What did you do today?'

'I looked for work, looked at rooms.'

'Where?'

'The internet. Then I wrote a bit. "Only those who know the supremacy of the intellectual life – the life which has a seed of ennobling thought and purpose within it – can understand the grief of one who falls from that serene activity into the absorbing soul-wasting struggle with worldly annoyances." That's George Eliot.'

'Did you spend the day learning that by heart?'

'I have a good memory.'

'We can't have you coming around here and quoting George Eliot. Anyway, you think I don't know about

64

worldly annoyances?' With a firm motion he cracked open his can of mango Rubicon.

'What were you writing?' Mel asked.

'Nothing really. I've been tinkering with the opening of a novel to keep myself busy.'

'You can volunteer at the centre if you want to keep busy while you're looking for work. They always need people to help out, making tea and coffee, chatting with the service users, volunteering at the food banks.'

The idea of spending my time in the company of down-trodden people did not appeal to me, but I tried to give the impression I was open to the idea. 'That's a nice offer. Thank you.' I could tell that Tom knew I was only being polite but he didn't let on.

'You could just come a couple of hours a week if you like.'

'You can make friends with Andy,' Tom said. 'It'll be good for you.'

'He liked you,' Mel said.

'How do you know?'

'He mentioned you today.'

I made an expression of incredulity, looking from Mel to Tom and reading their faces for signs this was a joke they had prepared. 'Did he really?' I cared more than I might have expected.

'He asked me about you as soon as he came in. "Is your friend Luca coming back?"'

'No, he didn't remember my name.'

'He did,' Mel insisted. 'You made an impression on him.'

I tried to hide the pleasure I took in hearing this behind an amused expression. 'He seemed like a nice guy.'

The younger man began laying the plates on the counter

and signalled for us to collect them. 'Just be a few minutes for the naans, yeah?' We ate our curries in silence for a moment. They were rich and delicious and the taste reminded me of childhood, when the long lists of dishes on the menus of Rusholme curry houses – Dhansak, Korma, Rogan Josh, Pasanda, Balti, Bhuna, and Madras – had seemed to promise that life would be filled with pleasure and novelty.

'So,' Tom said. 'Are you going to tell us what happened? How did it all go down? How did it end with Mia? What happened with the PhD?'

I shook my head. 'Not ready to talk about it.'

'Did you misjudge the situation?' he asked. 'Did you think it was more than it was?' Mel now looked at Tom in a manner that implied he was crossing a line, but Tom kept his eyes fixed on me, though I could see that he was aware of Mel's expression.

'Maybe, yes. I thought I was finally getting what I wanted.'

He shook his head. 'You'll never get what you want. Tell us what happened.'

'I'll tell you once I've put my thinking straight. It's nothing glamorous.'

'Fair enough,' Tom said with a shrug. 'Fish is good.'

'Naans are ready,' said the man behind the counter. I stood up and handed the steaming naan breads over to Mel one by one. We ate in silence for a while longer. The naan bread was soft and buttery.

'What's this novel then?' Tom said.

'It's nothing yet. I'm batting ideas around.'

'It's not about you, is it?'

'I'm using the material I have at my disposal.'

Tom shook his head.

'What's wrong with that?' Mel said.

'You don't know him. He comes across as reasonable and level-headed but he's not. He lives in his fantasies. He'll do anything to avoid accepting the world as it is. Isn't that true, Luca?'

I chewed as he spoke, maintaining a neutral expression. It was my way of saying that although I did not disagree, I refuted the simplicity implied by his glibness.

'We need to get you down to earth. Taste the naan bread. Look around. You're back in the real world now.'

Outside, the rain began to fall heavily and the younger man moved to the open door, looking out at the narrow alley and the gloomy sky. The older man was in the back part of the kitchen, singing more loudly in what I assumed was Urdu. Perhaps he had forgotten we were there or perhaps he didn't care. He had a good voice. I thought the melody was full of longing and resignation but that may have just been me. 'A very Northern trait, that,' I said, 'insisting that it's somehow more real here than elsewhere.'

'It's true. This is real life: relentless, miserable, hard.'

'You don't think that,' Mel said.

'Life is much harder than Luca likes to believe.'

'It does feel like it's getting harder,' I said.

'We're getting older. The good times are over. It's a grind from here to the end.'

'It's not just getting older,' I said. 'Things are changing.'

'I'm with Luca,' Mel said.

'Baby!' Tom threw open his arms.

'Look at everything that's happened in the past three years alone. The world is changing, not just us.'

'I agree.' It was fun to side with Mel over Tom, who shook his head stubbornly and, having finished his curry, sat back with arms folded across his chest. 'It's true, isn't it?' I said. 'It's changed here too.'

'Four decades of neoliberalism and ten years of austerity,' Mel said. 'Every public service cut. Libraries, swimming pools, housing benefit, doctors and nurses. You can see it in the centre. People are desperate.'

'We're just getting older,' Tom said, 'so we're more aware of all that.'

At this, Mel rolled her eyes in a way that made clear she knew she was right and was only entertaining Tom's perspective out of politeness.

'What are you going to do for money?' Tom said, slipping his coat onto his shoulders and thereby announcing that the time had come to leave.

'I've still got a bit.'

'How much?'

'Couple thousand.' He smirked at this. 'What? I'll live frugally.'

'Live frugally off a couple of thousand for the rest of your life?'

'I'll find a job.'

'Doing what?'

'I don't know. Fuck off with your attitude.'

'All good, guys?' the younger man said as we laid our plates on the counter.

'Spot on, pal,' Tom said, zipping his coat up to his chin and pushing the door into the rain.

I didn't even consider writing the next day. The air was humid, the sky grey, and when I awoke at ten to an empty flat, I felt hollowed out by mortal fatigue. Tom's words had sobered me, too. My fantasies would not save me. I needed money, so I searched for jobs but found that I didn't know how to look for them. All the listings seemed fake, or else I couldn't understand the roles they sought to fill: bid writer, technical writer, medical writer, copywriter, SEO optimiser. The world had changed since I'd last needed a job. I made a cup of tea and smoked a cigarette on the balcony. It felt terrible, as it almost always did, but it was hard to stop nevertheless. I had been smoking since I was thirteen and I found it difficult to imagine that the future would be different to the past. The cigarette left a cancerous feeling in my mouth, so I went to the bathroom to clean my teeth. The face in the mirror looked haggard, skin splitting around the eyes, teeth stained yellow. I fetched a sponge and a bottle of spray and cleaned the mirror.

I gave the last of my cigarettes to a homeless woman sitting outside the Spar at the corner of Market Street and Deansgate. 'Thank you, darling,' she said. You're alright, love, I replied, rolling my Rs. I walked up Shudehill towards the Northern Quarter, where young people lived in new apartments, took their MacBooks to cafés in the daytime, and ate in restaurants at night. I wanted to walk among them, I wanted to feel like one of them, but when I got there, I didn't. They seemed to walk around happily, as though ignorant of the ugliness of this place and all the miserable lives it had contained, and so I thought the problem must be me. Then I remembered why I left Manchester and I wished I had not come back. I passed Afflecks Palace, the red-brick mill five storeys high where I had gone to buy posters, badges, and hoodies as a young teenager, and to lust after the goth girls who sat with their black-haired, dog-collared boyfriends cross-legged on the floor of the arcade. There were no goths anymore. The goths had grown up and nobody had replaced them. The ground-floor windows were bricked up and covered in colourful mosaic collages assembled from the detritus of Manchester history: portraits of Morrissey, Marx and Engels, George Best, and Oasis; Frank Sidebottom's big cartoon head, Danger Mouse; the logos United and City, Vimto, and Kellogg's – all the cultural heritage that had become the city's brand. The clouds had been gathering in thick black sheets and now a fine rain began to fall so I nipped into a café on Oldham Street, ordered a coffee, and sat on a stool by the window, watching raindrops fall on the slick paving stones. Once the rain stopped, I was about to slip outside when a face caught my eye through the window. My aunt Deidre, my dad's younger sister, was walking beneath an umbrella, her head poking out of a black anorak. I wanted to recoil but I steadied myself, lest she turn and find me trying to hide. She didn't turn, however, and so I was able to watch her from only a few feet away, so close that it felt cruel. She stopped right in front of me. I didn't divert my eyes. If she looked at me, I wanted to be smiling back as though I had only just noticed her, but she didn't look. She pointed her umbrella towards the road, shook it off and tied it shut, fumbling for a moment with the Velcro tag. She had aged considerably. Her eyes were sunken and her face was lined with wrinkles, the deep kind you only get from heavy smoking. I had seen her just once or twice since my dad died, and not for at least ten years. The sight of her made me think how my dad would have aged too, had he kept on living. He would be sixty now, his hairline would have receded into nothingness, and his skin would be cracked and frail.

Deidre packed her brolly away and stood for a moment, her eyes following a bus and then resting on the sky above Betfred, where the sun was breaking through the clouds. I remembered her as having a cheery disposition, but now she looked fed-up and downcast, though I supposed that all of us did when we thought that nobody was looking. She shuffled off towards Piccadilly Gardens, and I waited several minutes before I poked my head out the door and followed, my heart pounding and my gut twisted into a knot. With the image of my aunt's haggard face in my mind, the crowds moving around under the wet sunlight on Market Street appeared hostile and I had the sense that nobody could be more alien to me than these strangers whom I had cast as my people, wandering the streets of my imagination, none of them returning my gaze.

'Andy was asking after you,' Mel said when she arrived at the flat that evening. 'He was very interested when I told him that you were writing a book.' I didn't say anything. I felt angry at Mel for passing on this information, which I had shared in confidence, which I had hardly shared at all. I felt embarrassed to hear it said aloud – the absurd idea that I, a specialist in failure with all my hopes defeated, was going to write a book. 'Andy wants to write a book, too. He's been talking about it as long as I've known him. When he tells a story, he always ends it by saying, "It's going in my book." I think he wants you to help him write it.' Now I struggled to contain my annoyance. I wanted to tell her to leave my time alone. It might seem that I had nothing going on, but I had to put my life on track. I was thirty years old with no career, no money, and nowhere to live. I wasn't going to waste my time helping some hopeless wretch write his misery memoir. Before I could find a polite expression for my vitriol, Mel said: 'He's got some money to pay for it. Quite a lot, I think.'

'To pay for what?'

'A writer,' Mel said and Tom, who had been squinting at his laptop, now relaxed his face into a knowing smile.

'If he wants, I can help him find someone.'

'You wouldn't be interested yourself?'

'I don't think I'll have time.'

In some way, I meant what I said. I expected that a piece of good luck would befall me, but nothing befell me.

The next day, I received an email from the director of graduate studies at Harvard. She said that she had tried to contact me regarding my failure to respond to the several emails and letters that had been sent to me, inviting me to discuss my studies. If I didn't respond at the soonest opportunity, the board would be left with no choice but to terminate my position as a graduate student. I wrote a short email, informing her that I had left the US due to unforeseen circumstances in my personal life and would not be able to return. They should go ahead and consider me terminated. I wanted to take that conviction and write a similar email to Mia. Consider us terminated. But I couldn't send it. Because it was ridiculous – we already were – and because I wished it wasn't true.

The days of that first week passed with little variation. I woke up late, searched for jobs online, and applied to them without belief. I took walks along the canals in Castlefield or around Hulme Park. I looked for accommodation. My plan, in so much as I had one, was to find a temporary place until I made a plan for the future, but all the shadowy rooms in the adverts depressed me so I submitted these applications in the same half-hearted way I applied for jobs, believing that if only I held out long enough, an opportunity would come along. And, as it happened, Tom came home on the Friday evening of that first week with the news that some friends of his mother, Jem and Brenda, were celebrating their retirement with a three-month caravanning trip around Europe. They had left a week ago and were already in the Ardennes. Before leaving, they had been trying to find a house-sitter to mind their place while they were away but they hadn't found the right person. He had spoken with his mother and she had spoken with them. If I wanted to stay there while they were away, I was welcome to, free of charge. I just had to water the plants.

'What do you think?' Tom said.

They lived in Chorlton, the suburb a few miles from the city centre where we had grown up. It was a largely middle-class area, which Mancunians considered posh, though not even the sight of the organic food cooperative or craft beer retailer would have made a visitor from Earl's Court or Primrose Hill feel at home. Now, it was home to lawyers, doctors, and the new professional class who worked in city centre offices. At the turn of the millennium, our parents and their friends who lived there were teachers, social workers, trade union officials, counsellors, and nurses who had come of age in the 70s and 80s and were enjoying the relative prosperity and optimism of the late 90s, gathering on Saturday nights to drink red wine, smoke hash, eat breadsticks and dips, listening to Gomez, James and Buena Vista Social Club while we, their children, lay on the carpeted floor of an upstairs bedroom playing *Star Fox* and *GoldenEye 007* on the Nintendo 64.

We were there now, driving along Beech Road: past the launderette that my mum and I used to use, now a bar named Launderette, past Threshers the off-licence, now a French épicerie, past the empty lot where FREE TIBET had been spray-painted on a brick wall, where there now stood an apartment building and a mini-supermarket. We pulled into the street parallel to the one where Tom and I had lived as children in houses on opposite sides.

'It's this one.' Tom cut the engine and pointed to a narrow house overlooking a front yard two flagstones wide. 'We won't stay long,' he said, opening the door and disappearing into the kitchen at the back of the house while I stepped into the living room.

A small, framed watercolour of a Lake District scene hung to my left and on the perpendicular wall, a framed poster for a William Morris exhibition at the Whitworth Gallery. Below this was the TV, beside it the bookshelves: five rows of novels, non-fiction, and political biography, their quantity and quality suggesting steady, general leisure reading. I noted a shiny paperback copy of *The Corrections*, a fat biography of Robespierre, the diaries of Tony Benn. The upper shelf was shared by a row of cookbooks and a pile of board games in tatty boxes: Scrabble, Buckaroo, Mousetrap. By the window, whose net curtains were drawn, a Monstera stood potted. A lime-green Chesterfield sofa ran against the wall to my right, facing the television, and as I took it in, I felt a near-irrepressible desire to flop onto its plush cushions, kick off my shoes, and flick through the TV channels as though I were thirteen and had just got home from school. Something about the house – the lingering smell of vegetarian food and eco detergent, the particularities of its layout and decoration, but above all its air of permanence and solidity – reminded me of the period of my youth when life had been most comfortable, when I took it for granted that we were immune to history and circumstance and I imagined my mum would live in that house for ever. But this was no time to be sentimental, I told myself as I heard Tom's footsteps in the hall. In that world lay coiled the embryo of this one.

'Come on,' he called to me, and I closed the living-room door and followed him up the stairs.

There were two larger bedrooms and a small office to the rear.

'It's nice,' I said.

'Are you going to look after it?' He didn't give me a chance to answer the question. 'You can sleep in here.' We were standing in the middle bedroom, which had once belonged to one of the children and now stood half empty except for an unmade double bed, a pyramid of cardboard boxes stacked against one wall, and a yoga mat rolled out on the beige carpet.

'It's fine.' Tom gave me a disapproving face. 'It's perfect. Thank you.'

'You could use this time to your advantage,' he said as I followed him back down the stairs. 'Three months rent-free to get back on your feet. Come the end of it, you could have a job lined up and a place to live. You're lucky really.'

I poked my head into the middle downstairs room, which opened onto the kitchen and a small backyard.

Night had fallen when we stepped onto the street and got in the car to drive back to Tom's flat. The bars on Barlow Moor Road were already busy with people sitting under the heat lamps of their smoking areas and I wished for a moment that I could join them and drink pints until closing time, but I knew I would have to stop drinking for a while, or else this period might mark the beginning of a terminal decline.

'I'm serious, you know. It's a good opportunity for you to get sorted. How much money have you got left?'

'I told you: a couple thousand.'

'Dollars or pounds? How much exactly?'

'Does it matter?'

He was silent for a moment. 'It's not a bad thing to have a settled life. It costs you money, all this moving around. It costs you time.'

'Alright. I hear you.'

'Get yourself some work and a decent place to live. It doesn't have to be full-time. You can still do your writing and whatever else you want to do.'

'I'll do my best.'

The next day, I packed up my suitcase and Tom drove me back to Chorlton, stopping at Morrison's to stock up on pasta, rice and tins of beans. He took a last nervous look around the house while I began to unpack and then he bid me goodbye.

'Tell them I said thank you.'

'You can tell them yourself. I'll give you their numbers. See you soon. Get a job.'

'I will.'

'And don't mope.' He unlocked the car. 'Live in the present and plan for the future. Forget about the past.'

'Alright, pal,' I called from the doorstep. 'Will do.'

I tried to take Tom's advice and do as he would have. Every day, I went jogging along the muddy tracks of Chorlton Ees, nodded at the dog walkers, passed the old substation on whose wall the word *Death* had remained spray-painted for twenty-five years. I wanted nothing more than to wander between Chorlton's many bars, drinking myself into an insensitive stupor but I stayed home instead. I avoided the living room and preferred the office, where I wrote to-do lists on a memo pad and fulfilled them, signing off the last details on quitting the programme and finding a subletter for my room in Cambridge. But the lists were short and once I had crossed off the last items, the nothingness of those empty memo pages spread throughout the house and took over the days. I had believed that leaving the university and rooting myself in the only place I could feasibly call home would fill me with new ideas and boundless energy. Back in the real world, I would read widely and write from my heart; this reading and writing would be directly interwoven with the material activity of real people and all of it would cohere to give my life purpose and direction. But that didn't happen. I had never felt more out of place and alone in all my life. I hardly seemed able to do anything but look at Twitter and scroll up and down the homepage of the *Guardian*. What I really needed was to find a job, but all the applications I submitted were rejected without feedback and so finally I decided to apply for Universal Credit to tide me over until something good came my way.

At Rusholme Job Centre, I took a seat in the waiting area and picked up a damp copy of the *Manchester Evening News* that had been left on one of the green plastic chairs. A family was living through a never-ending nightmare after a beloved father was killed during a holiday in Benidorm. In Middleton, a man had been badly hurt in an unprovoked attack. A Newton Heath woman had been handed an unreasonable fine. A Viking-themed tapas bar was to open in the city centre. 'Luca Byrne,' a voice said, and I looked up to see a large man in a polyester suit, smiling over his glasses. After leading me to his office, he directed me to a chair, introduced himself as Phil, my work coach, and asked me a series of questions about my education (wasted), work history (no), criminal record (no new entries in nine years), military service (inconceivable), dependents (me), investments (no), and savings (also no). My life, forced into this moulding, sounded more incoherent than ever, and Phil responded to my efforts to be funny with a pitying expression that made me feel like a sad case. When he'd finished, he told me that because I had not been born in this country, my right to reside in the UK would have to be verified, which would delay my claim by several weeks. 'To be completely honest, it usually takes ages. But there's nothing to stop you from looking for work in the meantime. Any ideas what you'd like to do?'

'What do you recommend?'

'Aldi is always a good option in the short term. The pay is quite generous and you can usually start quickly. But a person with your education ought to be able to find something, let's say, more challenging than that. Have you thought about the civil service?'

At the end of our meeting, he told me that I would have to come and see him weekly.

'It used to be fortnightly,' I said.

'That changed a long while ago. You can thank Messrs Cameron and Osborne for that.' He handed me the pile of printouts and smiled warmly.

Back at my new house, I recovered the paragraphs about my teenage life that I had deleted a week earlier and tried to write, but while the world of my youth had seemed vital in America, now that I was again surrounded by its rain and smoke and brick walls, to describe this world was pointless. A representation could never compete with its overbearing reality. Besides, I kept thinking about Phil and the way he had grimaced as I described the trajectory of my life, as though he could see that I was heading towards disaster. I checked my bank account and saw that the balance had already dropped below $2,000. I had never managed to wholly let go of the idea that a thousand of anything was a vast amount of money and two almost incalculably large, but it did not seem like much when it had to last for ever. I closed the Word doc to search for work online, but reading the fathomless listings of jobs I didn't understand made me feel small and powerless. The bottom fell out of the day and it seemed my entire life was rushing through the house. One could die in a room like this, I thought, on a wet afternoon late in April, alone, without having finished a thing.

Later, when the rain had stopped, I sat down at the desk in the room upstairs and put on a hardcore punk album that Mia had once played for me. I had vowed not to fixate on the past but I wanted to feel alive again. The album began with a kind of lullaby, played on the high strings of a guitar. As the sweet notes filled the room, I pictured Mia, sitting in my bed at three or four in the morning, closing her eyes and restraining a smile, shaking her head ever so slightly as she mouthed the words. It was the way she pinched her smile at the cheeks. She wouldn't allow herself to laugh, because she was mouthing the words and it had to be done seriously, as everything she did had to be done seriously. A little thing like that can make you want to reach out and shake a person, say I love you; I love you and I don't know what to do with it. The music filled the room with this memory, sickening me to the stomach so that I had to press stop. The unbearable thought that took hold of me was that the richest times of my life were behind me and that I would never possess more possibilities than I had just thrown away. I opened a Word doc and tried to write about it. At least, I thought, my feelings had a kind of fluency that would make language come easily. But I couldn't do it. I could only think about money and the misery of not having any. Necessity pressed at my temples and my imagination felt as narrow as the dank alleyway behind the house.

The next morning, I texted Mel and said that I would write Andy's book if he still wanted me to. I had decided that I needed the cash if I was to get anything done in this sorry interregnum, but even more, I needed to lose myself in some activity that would keep my mind engaged and save me from drowning in myself. Mel texted me his number a few hours later. 'Give him a call this evening after five,' she wrote. 'He's expecting to hear from you.' So that evening, after returning from my jog on the Ees, I showered, dressed properly – putting on a shirt and tucking it into my jeans – and sat down at the desk upstairs to call the number. The ringing stopped almost immediately and I heard a clattering sound on the line. Andy requested to switch to a video call and when I hit the green button, his face appeared so close to the camera that I couldn't even see his whole head, just his eyes, nose, and part of his mouth.

'Is it Luca? The American writer?'

'It's me,' I said and he laughed. He seemed to be struggling to contain his excitement. 'Mel tells me you want to write a book.'

'A book about my life.'

'And that you need some help.'

'A lot of help.'

'How much have you written so far?'

He turned the camera so that one sombre eye filled the screen. 'Just notes.'

'And now you want to start writing?'

'I need you to write it.'

'I can do that.'

'I'll tell you everything that needs to go in it and you do the writing.'

'We can do that.'

'I'll pay you.'

'We can discuss that.'

Andy raised a thumb to the camera and said, 'Top one.'

'Tell me about your book.'

'You need to come here. I don't like talking on the phone. You'll understand me better when you meet me. Come here tomorrow. Eleven o'clock. I'll tell you everything you need to know.'

'Where do you live?'

'Four sixty Moss Lane East. Do you know where that is?'

'Of course. I'll see you at eleven.'

'Alright,' he said and the call ended.

I knew which was Andy's flat right away because of the wheelchair lift by the steps up to the front door. He lived on the ground floor of a large house off Wilmslow Road in Rusholme, the neighbourhood where my mother and I had lived when we first arrived in England and where my dad had spent much of his life. It was one of those villas built for a wealthy family in the nineteenth century, which had since been converted into three or four flats. A bay window looked across the street towards Whitworth Park: a grassy expanse surrounded by a rusting fence, a few paths leading to a disused fountain, a row of mature plane trees whose thick canopies kept the lush grass in shadow. I knocked on the door and heard a commotion on the other side: the raised voices of several people. A woman in her mid-forties opened the door. Her curly hair was tied up in a bun and she was wearing a pair of yellow rubber gloves. 'Are you Luca?' she said. I said that I was and she introduced herself as Val. 'Come in,' she said, as she left the door ajar and walked briskly back to where she had come from.

'Is that Luca?' I heard Andy calling from the front room while from the back of the house, where Val had gone, I could hear objects touching surfaces, cupboards being opened and shut. 'Come in,' Andy shouted, and I followed his voice through an open doorway into the front room. Photographs and memorabilia covered the walls and shelves and Andy was sitting in a leather recliner, wearing a look of eagerness one rarely saw on the faces of adult men. 'Luca.' He extended a hand and clasped mine with a powerful grip. His wrists and fingers were thick, his skin soft and smooth. 'Do you want a cup of tea?' Without waiting for a response, he called, 'Val, can you make Luca a cup of tea?'

Val appeared in the doorway. 'I can do you a coffee if you prefer?'

'Sit down,' Andy said to me.

'Give him a minute,' Val said.

'Sorry,' Andy said.

'He was up all night playing poker on his computer.' Hearing himself spoken of like this, Andy burst into a fit of childish laughter.

'Tea is fine, thank you.' I looked about to take in the many objects covering the walls. Large frames filled with many smaller photographs occupied most of the space, though some contained single pictures. Several framed T-shirts also hung by the windows. Various railings were fitted to the walls and cords dangled from the ceiling, lending the room an institutional atmosphere. A leather sofa ran across one wall, opposite a widescreen TV with a PlayStation and an expensive-looking speaker system. Above it hung a frame filled with ticket stubs and two Manchester City shirts, framed and signed.

'My memories.' Andy pointed to the leather sofa. 'Sit there.'

I sat down opposite Andy and continued to take in the room while he looked at me, breathing heavily. The curtains were partially drawn, obscuring the view of the park. The floor was of shiny laminate and an imitation bearskin rug lay beneath the coffee table.

'Here you are.' Val appeared from the doorway and set a cup of tea down on a coaster in front of me.

'Can I have a coffee?' Andy said.

'You've had enough coffee already.' She put a tray of pills down in front of Andy and said, 'I'll get you a glass of water.'

'Coffee,' he shouted as she left the room.

His eyes, when they met mine, were full of vulnerable optimism. Val returned, set a cup of black coffee down in front of him, and left the room while he began working through his pills. He was wearing a faded black cotton T-shirt printed with the famous Las Vegas sign, a pair of blue jeans, and no socks. His feet were pale and swollen. 'One second.' He swallowed and reached for his final pill with a muscular arm.

'Okay,' he said. 'Tell me why you're the right person to write my book.' The intonation of this statement led me to believe that he had made it on the advice of a friend.

'I'd need to know a bit more about the book before I can answer that question,' I said.

'It's my story,' he said. 'It's about a Mancunian boy who was born with nothing and still managed to lose everything.'

I asked him to provide me with some more specific details and he told me that he had been taken into care when his mother died. 'But I got through that and had a shop. Look,' he pointed to a white T-shirt in a frame, printed with the words Andy's T-shirts. 'That was me, my shop. I tracked down my dad and he didn't want anything to do with me. I thought my life couldn't get any worse and then I got diagnosed with MS. I was young and healthy. I wasn't sick. Look.' He pointed to a wall of photos. 'Go and look. I was a player.' I stood up and looked at some photos. My eyes landed on one of two young men with their arms around one another. 'That was my best mate, Brendan,' he said. 'He died. That was when I started smashing the coke. I was an alcoholic. The love of my life left me. I lost my shop. I had to be taken into hospital. Now I've got primary progressive MS. Do you know what that means?' I made as though to speak but couldn't get a word out before he carried on. 'It means it only gets worse. You can't walk or stand up. You lose your memory. Sometimes you can hardly speak.'

I felt suffocated by his overbearing emotion and didn't know what to say. When I realised that he expected me to reply, I said, 'That sounds painful.'

'It has been painful, Luca.' Our eyes met and his gaze intensified. 'It has been painful. But I don't want the book to be all doom and gloom. That's not what it's about. I'm not here to moan. I want to show people you can live through the worst and still have a good life. I want it to be entertaining. Funny. I've got a lot of good stories. A lot of people don't know what it was like anymore. Manchester in the 70s and 80s. There were a lot of good times. I want that to come across. Have I told you the title? It's *Chin Up*.' He took a sip of his coffee and his hand trembled as he held the cup to his lips. 'That was a piece of advice my dad gave me: chin up. That's how I live my life.'

'What are some of your favourite books?'

'I don't read that many books, Luca. Most of them don't do it for me.'

'Are there any you like?'

'*A Child Called It*. Have you read that one?'

When I said that I hadn't, he flexed his eyebrows and

raised his chin as though it were a mark against me. '*War and Peace*,' he said.

'Tolstoy?'

'Ricky Hatton.'

'The boxer?'

'One of my heroes. I met him once. Look.' He pointed to a photograph above the fireplace: he and the boxer were standing side by side, arms around each other's shoulders, bare fists raised for the camera.

'When was this?'

'While ago. Ten years. Around the time of his fight with Lazcano. The Homecoming. Did you watch it?'

'No,' I said. 'I suppose I was trying to ask, was there a book that made you want to write one yourself?'

'It's more the idea of it. My mates are always going, "You're an interesting guy, Andy. You should write a book." I always wanted to have a big family but I can't now. It's never going to happen. This book is my legacy.' I nodded as I began to grasp the scope of his ambition. 'What do you think?' he asked me.

From what he had told me so far, I considered Andy's project vain, self-indulgent, and unlikely to succeed, but I needed the money; more, I felt that in some way, I needed *him*, so I made a pitch for my suitability, one that I had planned ahead of time, in which I exaggerated the relevance of my literary experience. But as I described the plot of the one short story I had published and the thesis of a paper I had written for a course on autobiographical writing and the novel, his eyes began to dart around the room and his leg began to shake.

'I grew up around the corner,' I said to win his attention. 'On Lindum Street. Do you know it?' In fact, I had only lived there as a young child and we had moved to more affluent Chorlton when I was six.

'Of course,' he said.

'And I know what it's like. My dad had MS, too.'

That got his full attention. 'What happened to him?'

I hesitated to answer because I did not want to upset Andy. 'He died but not from the disease. He killed himself. The disease didn't help, but he had bipolar disorder, too.' As often happened, I began to speak these words affecting calm, as though I could accept what they signified with no feeling, but as I spoke, I remembered this was not the case. My voice began to crack.

'Same as me,' Andy said. 'I'm sorry about your dad.'

'It's alright,' I said. I was worried that what I had said would scare Andy but he seemed to be able to face it without flinching.

'It's a bad disease.' He was calmer now. 'It takes everything away from you. I've wanted to kill myself a lot of times too. A lot of times. What was his name?'

'Paul Byrne.'

It was only now, as he reflected on the name and I caught myself straightening up and waiting eagerly on his response that I realised I was hoping to get something from him too; I was not unaware that my dad's sudden disappearance had left me predisposed to fall under the spell of melancholy men, but perhaps Andy held the promise of something greater than resemblance. They were of a similar generation and, for a time at least, had been near neighbours at a time when neighbours still knew each other. My dad had not kept many friends, but there was a kind of silent, secret society among lonely, hard-drinking men. They saw each other as they made their rounds of the local pubs and though they didn't share tables and talk like friends, neither did they ignore one another completely – after all, the point of going to the pub was to have a break from yourself and be in the company of other people. I had more or less given up hope of knowing exactly what happened to my dad in the last years of his life, when his health declined quickly and there was a blankness in his gaze. But on the rare occasions when some new information promised to come to light, my heart sped up, my palms began to sweat, and I sought details as keenly as though it were my own fate I could discover. And so I wondered now if the pull I felt towards Andy – because there was one, I had felt it from the beginning, ambivalent though it was, mingling attraction with aversion – was the possibility of understanding what had happened to my dad.

'Where did he live?' Andy asked, as though he too understood what I was thinking and wanted to know if he could help me.

'He moved around a lot. Prestwich, Withington, Old Trafford. He ended up around the corner on Fleeson Street.'

'This is good.' He nodded as though in agreement with himself and the question of his acquaintance with my father seemed to vanish as quickly as it had come about. 'I think you will get it. My last writer didn't.'

'Who was your last writer?'

'Some writer. She didn't get it. She was posh, even posher than you. She wasn't from here. What will it cost?'

I had been waiting for this moment. I was no businessman and I had never set a price for anything but I knew that I had to find it in myself to strike a good deal. 'How long do you want the book to be?'

'You're the expert. How long's a book? A proper book.'

I looked away and squinted as though consulting an imaginary register. 'Seventy or eighty thousand words, give or take. Two to three hundred pages.'

'How thick?'

I held up my thumb and forefinger a few centimetres apart.

He closed his eyes and nodded. 'Alright. How much for that?'

'You know I can't print the book for you. I can write it but you'll have to find a publisher.'

'That's alright. A mate of mine knows a publisher. He says it will be no problem. I just need it written.'

I now explained to Andy the method I had devised over the weekend, combining the methods of psychoanalysis, creative writing, and home care: I would visit him five times a week and he would tell me his story in sessions lasting around one hour. This would save him from becoming exhausted and give him time to recuperate between sessions. I would record these interviews on my phone, make notes by hand, and, in the afternoons, work on his manuscript at home. After three or four weeks of interviews, I would be ready to write up the whole manuscript, which he could then read and annotate before I produced the final draft.

'How much for that?' he said.

'Are you ready to start right away?'

'I've been ready a long time.'

I took out my notepad and wrote down some numbers. I wanted to create the impression that I was in the business, that I was working out a rate according to the usual criteria instead of taking a punt on what I could get. Then I looked at him as directly as I could and said, 'Five thousand.'

'Fine,' he said.

I had expected it to be more difficult. 'You're okay with that?'

'Good quality costs money, Luca. I don't want knock-off. I want the real thing.'

'It's five thousand,' I said with new conviction. 'Two up front, two on completion of the first draft, one on completion of the final draft.'

'Deal.'

'Good,' I said. 'It's going to be good.'

'I know it is.'

'Do you want me to draw up a contract?'

'I don't do contracts. I trust you.'

'Okay. Then we'll start in earnest on Monday. Properly, I mean.'

I was grateful for the interruption of Val at the doorway, asking if Andy was ready for his lunch. With the difficult part of the conversation out of the way, I wanted to leave as quickly as I could. I began packing my things away and when I stood up, he reached out a hand for me to shake. He held my hand firmly and fixed his searching brown eyes on mine. I was about to say goodbye and leave when he said, 'Don't you want your money?'

'If you have it.'

He got up and began walking towards the TV. Halfway across the room, he placed a hand on the mantelpiece to keep his balance and I had to stop myself from turning away, so much did this action remind me of my dad. Andy didn't look at me and I sensed that he might have been embarrassed, which made the sight somehow more painful. Once he regained his composure, he took a few more steps forward. His legs wobbled and now I did look briefly away.

He opened a drawer and retrieved a biscuit tin from behind the television. Back in his chair, he removed the lid, pulled out several stacks of twenty-pound notes tied with rubber bands, and placed them on the table. 'Two thousand,' he said. 'I'm happy that you want to be my writer.'

Those words tightened around my chest and made me afraid but, at the same time, that constriction, that obligation that I feared, relieved me of another heaviness – of being nowhere and accountable to nobody. I got up and packed the cash into my rucksack just as Val appeared at the door.

'Are you off already?' she said. She was carrying Andy's lunch on a tray. 'How was he?'

For a moment, I wasn't sure whether the subject of this question was me or Andy. Then I realised. 'Oh,' I said. 'He was fine.' I said goodbye to Andy, but he didn't respond; his attention had turned to the lunch tray that Val had placed in his lap. I let myself out and set off towards Chorlton, glad for the three-mile walk along the run-down streets of Rusholme and Moss Side with their narrow terrace houses, vegetable stalls and halal butchers, across Princess Road and around the scummy pond in Alexandra Park, along the leafy avenues of Whalley Range, where the roots of sycamore trees broke through the pavements. I needed the time to process the conflicting feelings that Andy had provoked in me: of excitement and dread, of interest and boredom, a great compulsion to give him what he wanted and another to run away. The last was strong, but there could be no running away now that bundles of his cash were bouncing around in the bottom of my rucksack. At Morrisons, I peeled off a few notes to pay for the berries, chocolate, and soda bread that I had just laid on the conveyor belt, thinking about how the cash had already made things better, not only because it meant I could buy some decent food, but because it made life feel spacious again, because if there was one thing my education had taught me, it was that cash set the imagination free.

My correspondence with Mia began the day after we met for coffee and soon became my principal concern. Her writing was all compression, lightness, and agility. With a few carefully chosen words, she conjured the atmosphere of a rainy day at the condo she was renting in Orono, Maine, or the taste of the crab cakes at her favourite diner. Then I felt as though I remembered these details from a beloved novel. In my better moods, I regarded her descriptions as coded love poems and I longed to be the object of such careful attention. An email from Mia at night was as warm and sustaining as a bedtime kiss. A question – with her, never less than artfully posed – aroused in me a desire to make the messy, tedious stuff of my biography similarly artful. But in her ideas, she was nimble and seemed to move in unexpected directions while I felt one-dimensional and able to advance only by torturous increments. How compelling I found it to receive a private dispatch from her memory and how I loved to narrate my own life for her. I needed her questions for all the answers that were swirling around in my head. In my replies, I indulged in shameless confession and for my disclosures, I was rewarded with details from Mia's life.

I wrote that my dad had died when I was fourteen. When she responded, saying that her sister had died in a kayaking accident when she was eleven, I wasn't surprised; the young-bereaved spot one another like Freemasons. Her father was an aeronautical engineer from Halifax who had taken a job in Toulouse during the 80s. Her parents moved from there to Lyon, where she was born. Her father worked at the airport while her mother was a receptionist at the Swiss International School, which Mia was therefore able to attend without cost. She had hardly spent longer than a week in England before she went to York at eighteen, so she knew what I meant when I talked about a culture shock (she wrote). Yes, we liked to talk about feeling out of place; the subtext was that we were special and uniquely equipped to understand one another. Though I never lied, I ascribed outsized significance to some details and omitted others. I told her I was struggling to finish the last of the compulsory seminars while making headway with the reading list for my exams, but I was careful to create the impression I was meeting the struggle head-on, spending nights in the library, surrounded by books and papers. 'I forget too frequently why I'm doing this,' I wrote. 'I spend so much time asking what the point is, I don't have much left for the work itself.' She remembered that feeling, she replied. She'd had the same one. 'I think it's good to keep asking why,' she wrote. 'I found the trick was to channel that curiosity into the work and not let it be an excuse for procrastinating.' 'You've inspired me,' I replied, but she had scared me. I was now beginning to dream frequently that I was back in school and had to retake the GCSEs that I had failed at sixteen. I suspected that in the deeper recesses of my mind, I was preparing myself to let go. But there was bargaining to be done. If I were to quit, as my parents had done before me, what was to stop me from ending up like them? I couldn't share these thoughts with Mia. They were too dark and alive. They would have repulsed her like a bucket full of maggots. So, in my emails, I tried to assemble a persona who was altogether lighter.

Dear Mia,

You describe the strangeness of your childhood so evocatively. I went to Lyon once and also found it a strange place, beautiful but somehow lacking a soul. You might say it's the opposite of Manchester in that respect.

You say the cold weather has given you a new focus and I am glad for you. I wish that I could say the same but I feel as though I'm rubbing two damp sticks together and hoping for a fire. Everything I'm reading and writing seems to happen at such a high level of abstraction that it all seems to become one big mess and I have a headache by lunchtime. I'm reminded of a line from a poem I read recently: 'They preferred the name of the tree / to the taste of the apple.' I worry that I'm an apple man in a world of names. Do you know this feeling? Sometimes I think the whole enterprise of literary criticism is not just parasitic but also pointless and I want to write a text that comes right out of life the way juice comes out of oranges.

Fruit on the brain – I must be hungry. It's cold and bright here, my favourite weather. I hope the sun is shining in Maine, too. I'm looking forward to seeing you again.

I wrote too much, couldn't hide that I was bursting at the seams. And what was this fruit stuff? I deleted half the email, read it several times for spelling – I was always afraid of revealing to Mia that I remained at heart the half-literate schoolboy I had once been – and hit send, wondering as soon as the email whooshed away why it was that I only wanted to write about myself while my peers had attained a level of objectivity that enabled them to write about all manner of subjects. Was I so diminished that I had constantly to recreate myself? What was the cause of this solipsism that made me alternate madly between blathering and hiding? These questions were no good because they only led to more introspection; so long as I kept asking who I was and why, I would only wander further away from those established fields of study in whose fertile soil an intellectual life could grow.

Mia's poems suggested that she did not share the same inclination or that, if she did, she had found a way to circumvent it. Since buying both of her collections, I read them nightly, trying to assemble a fuller picture of her with little success. Sometimes, I thought that I had sniffed out an autobiographical clue:

> She flickers with intention
> to infiltrate
> the water's platinum

Reading this stanza alongside Mia's emails, I wondered if the 'She' of the opening line referred to her sister, if the water referred to the lake where she had drowned and her 'flickering with intention' to the quality she had acquired in Mia's memory, retrospectively, of seeming ready or destined to die. But in the next stanza, the subject became the 'he' who had painted the woman in the first stanza and the poem went on to describe the composition in a cold, technical language that seemed to indict the painter for creating a woman from surfaces and artifice. I wrote an email to Mia in which I cautiously expressed my enthusiasm for the poem and received a reply the next afternoon:

That's sweet of you to say. To be honest, I no longer feel at all like the person who wrote that collection and I wouldn't publish that poem today. Your email sent me back to it for the first time in years. I was twenty-five when I wrote it and I feel it betrays the vagueness and hesitancy that characterised my thinking then. Gosh, I was quite sombre, the final year of my PhD. I am trying to be much more objective and precise in my new work, as you may have noticed when I read at Harvard. I might send you something soon if that would be okay? And you mentioned you were working on a prose text? I would love to read it if you wanted to share.

When I looked again at the piece I had been writing about my dad, I saw that it had none of her work's agility or wit. The worst thing was its transparency. As I read it through Mia's eyes, I could see that all of its desperate wishes lay plainly on its surface. Whenever it posed a question, it did so as though it really expected somebody to answer. I never sent it.

It didn't matter. Mia came to visit on her way to Poughkeepsie, shortly before the Christmas break and we met in a bar in Central Square. Our correspondence had seemed to create a sense of intimacy between us but now that we were sitting opposite one another, that intimacy didn't seem to count for much. We talked about books and writers and these topics did not lend themselves to good or honest conversation. We were wary of one another and when I briefly touched her thigh in a gesture of emphatic agreement with a statement she had just made – an affected gesture, half-consciously intended to gauge our situation – the look she gave me made me shrink with shame and led me to believe that I had got everything wrong. But then we stepped out into the cold to smoke and it seemed as though our awkwardness might just have been the result of our sitting opposite each other. She smiled and her aspect softened. We finished our drinks and walked in the snowfall beneath her umbrella to another bar where the lights were dimmer and the staff wore black. She ordered an Old Fashioned and when I said that I found whiskey disgusting, she looked offended or at least unimpressed. 'I don't like too much sweetness,' she said and cast a disdainful glance at my Negroni.

'Can I try it?' She pushed the glass along the bar towards me and I took a sip and winced.

'You don't like it?'

'I do.'

'Don't say you like it if you don't,' she said.

'But I do like it,' I said, though I didn't.

We took an Uber back to my apartment and no sooner than we'd started kissing in the living room, she got up and went to my bed. Neither of us said so – we had fallen into a delicate silence that neither of us wanted to disturb – but I sensed from a distance in her manner that, like me, she hadn't been with anyone else for some time, maybe since she left her husband, and that she was in a place that made sexual intimacy if not difficult then not easy, that her desire was in tension with an instinct to protect herself.

She closed her eyes when she came, as though she didn't want the reality of the situation to interfere with the greater pleasures of her imagination, and I assigned myself the duty of keeping this fantasy alive and enjoyed that rare moment of escape from myself, of feeling that it didn't matter what was in my head. We had sex three times, hardly spoke a word in between, and fell asleep in the last hours of darkness. I put an arm around her as we fell asleep, but she did not soften at my touch, nor move closer towards me. After a few minutes, I removed it and she rolled away.

The next morning, she inspected my books while I made coffee. 'There aren't many,' I said.

'No.'

'I move a lot. It's not worth letting them pile up.'

Her head was cocked to the side and her eyes were running down a stack of spines. I had hidden most of my favourite novels in a drawer and replaced them with serious works of philosophy and political theory that I'd borrowed from my flatmates' rooms.

I walked her down to the front porch, where an Uber was waiting to take her to the bus station. She looked at me with a blank and serious expression and I leaned forward to kiss her pursed and unresponsive lips. She got in the Uber and did not look back as it drove away. Was that it? I wondered. My heart was sinking into my stomach as I climbed the stairs. On the kitchen table, her empty cup stood browned with coffee in an oblong of morning sunshine. I lay down on my bed, looked at the bulb dangling from the ceiling, and was about to mope when I reached for my phone and saw that she had already sent an email: 'Thank you for a nice time.'

The Christmas break came and Cambridge emptied out as the students flew back to their warm family homes. I stayed, trudging up and down Kirkland Street between my deserted apartment and the library. The freezing air blowing in off the Atlantic was so cold it made my ears burn. I had smoked so much with Mia that my lungs were burning. I caught the flu and I was horribly, helplessly in love.

When the new semester started, I took a reduced course load so that I had time to make my way through the reading list ahead of my exams, but my thoughts were still so full of Mia that I could hardly read a page without drifting into reverie and then checking my emails, hoping that I might have one from her. A few long weeks went by without a word. I hoped that she would visit me on her way back to Maine from the UK but when I finally heard from her, she was already back at the condo. She said that it had been good to spend time with me (the ambiguity of this phrase alone was enough to precipitate an early lunch break). She described the neat lawns of Vassar College and the view of the dark Hudson, mottled with frost on a cold afternoon. Then she described the strangeness of returning to London, the way that, after a long time abroad, one sees familiar things as though for the first time. I read her off-hand observations more voraciously than I did any of the canonical novels I was supposed to be studying. A special place in my psyche seemed to have been reserved for a person like her. Forces were gathering in me that needed a form, a face, a voice to speak on their behalf and in her, they found what they were looking for. She became the addressee of all my private thoughts, so that any words that passed through my mind as I walked back and forth from the campus, walked the dark corridors of the library stacks, smoked in clandestine corners, took the form of preparatory drafts for the next email I would send to her. She became the eyes that watched me and the voice that criticised me. If I arrived home after an anxious afternoon in the library and looked to entertainment for some relief – if I streamed football on my laptop or listened to some inane podcast – I saw her reproachful face. *This* is what you're doing? it seemed to say. This is how you choose to spend your time? One afternoon, passing through the skate park on my way home, I even imagined performing a kick-flip while she looked on admiringly. Oh, it was so pathetic. So transparent. And yet there was nothing I could do. Even when I chastised myself, I did it to prove to her that I was trying to change.

I was not so oblivious to my own machinations as to never ask what compelled me towards obsession and everything pointed towards the image of my dad: distant, inscrutable, difficult to impress. It was my desperation that led me to sign up for a course of free CBT therapy, but the therapist was not interested in my pseudo-psychoanalytic conjecture. 'When she visited me,' I told him during our first session, 'I took her to see the statue of John Harvard.' His patient gaze remained unblinking. 'Even though I hardly feel a connection to this place, no sense of belonging, no ownership of its name. We looked at it together in embarrassed silence. Don't you see? I showed her an erection that was not my own.' This didn't seem to impress him. 'I'm trying to fulfil the ambitions of my dead father,' I added.

'That's a neat idea,' the therapist said. 'I can tell that you're very creative. But we're not really interested in that way of thinking. Why don't you tell me about some of the day-to-day problems you're experiencing?'

'I had a dream,' I told him, 'that I became president of the United States.'

The therapist couldn't restrain his smile.

'Journalists were going through my history and printing stories about my misdeeds, saying that I wasn't cut out for the job. Everyone could see who I really was.'

'Is that something you worry about often?'

'What?' I said.

'Social anxieties. Being perceived as inadequate.'

I sighed. 'When I said, "Everyone could see who I really was," you could have replied, "And is that a fear? Or a wish?" That's the kind of thing I'm after.'

He raised his open palms and gave me a look full of benevolent frustration. 'Which is it?'

As I shifted my body in the crimson armchair, crossing one leg over the other and folding my arms across my chest, my limbs yielded a memory of sitting in another armchair long ago, speaking, a few months after my dad's death, with a grief counsellor – a grievance counsellor as I had called him then with no knowledge of my error – whom I had similarly tried to frustrate and perplex. The thought that fifteen years had failed to change me was enough that I said, 'Go on, tell me about Activity Scheduling.' Back at the flat, however, when I sat down at the desk in my bedroom and examined the worksheets under the lamplight, I felt that the questions addressed a subject determined to improve themselves and succeed, whereas all I wanted was to set fire to everything I had made.

'I was born in Stepping Hill hospital on the fifteenth of August 1971.' Andy began our first interview, speaking as though from a script he had memorised. His speech was somewhat laboured and he was prone to elongating the vowels in longer words. 'My mum's name was Anne Marie Docherty. She was the youngest of eight siblings. Big Irish family. My dad's name was Frank Barton. He was ten years older, from London. He met my mum while he was working at Kellogg's in Trafford Park.' He was sitting in his big armchair and I was sitting opposite him on the leather couch, recording everything on my phone and taking notes by hand. 'I don't know why he was there. He just was. They met at the Twisted Wheel. It was the heyday of Northern Soul.' Andy nodded at my notebook when he said this to indicate that it was important. 'To be honest, I think it was a one-night stand. They couldn't have been together too long because my dad was already out of the picture when I was born and he didn't visit my mum when she was in the hospital. I was a healthy baby.'

'How do you know all this?' I said.

'Medical records.'

'What about the other stuff? How your mum and dad met, who told you that?'

'My dad did.'

'You're in touch with him?'

'I met him once. I tracked him down and wrote to him. I went to London to meet him.'

'But you didn't stay in touch?'

'He didn't want to. He's dead now anyway.'

'I'm sorry. Let's get back to where we were.'

'My mum's family didn't want anything to do with me. My mum was homeless for a while. I'll never know what happened in the first year of my life. In 1972, my mum got a flat in the Crescents. We were one of the first families to move in. My first memories are there,' he said.

'What were they?'

He shrugged. 'Just memories.'

'Tell me what you remember.'

'There was a stain on the ceiling over the bed shaped like a rhino's head. And I can see my mum watching TV and smoking. I can see the big concrete balcony outside the flat. I can see the grass outside. A kid from one of the other flats climbed out onto a ledge and fell off the balcony.'

'What happened?'

'He died.'

'Shit. Do you remember it?'

'Sort of. After that, they decided the flats weren't safe for kids. In 1976, we were relocated to another block in Salford.'

I asked what his mum was like and he said he didn't remember. 'She was just like a mum.'

And what was that like?

She was impatient, Andy said, always telling him to stop doing whatever he was doing. She lost her temper a lot. She had headaches and if he made any noise or tried to talk with her, she screamed at him. He felt she didn't like him very much. There were a few different men who came over. Some of them talked to him and some didn't. He remembered playing on the living-room floor. He had a set of marbles but if he rolled or dropped them, his mum told him to stop because the sound drove her mad. 'She got me a Mr Potato Head for Christmas and I smashed it with a hammer.' He laughed, though his eyes were full of sadness. 'She went mad at me.' He didn't like school and he got in fights with kids in his class. But he wasn't there for long anyway.

'Why not?'

'Because my mum died,' he said with a hint of incredulity, as though I ought to have known already.

'How did she die?'

'Heroin overdose.'

It had happened once already, he said. He was at school, in a classroom at the front, looking out onto the street. It was almost the end of the day. The head teacher took him out of the classroom and told him his mum had been taken to Salford General Hospital. When she recovered, she would be transferred to a psychiatric ward. He was collected from school and taken to a foster family in Stretford. He hardly remembered anything about them, only that they lived by the Bridgewater Canal and he could see it from the window of the bedroom he shared with three other kids. Then he was taken without notice and placed with another family in Moss Side.

'They were nice. The Baileys.' He said he spent the first day hiding in his room but when he came out, they welcomed him warmly. They were a married couple in their sixties, a woman from Scotland and a man from Jamaica. All of the kids called the foster parents Mum and Dad. They cooked rice and beans or fish stew with dumplings and the whole family ate together around a big table in the kitchen. While he was there, his mum was discharged from the hospital. She visited him a few times and met his new brothers and sisters. He thought he was going to go back to live with her and then one day, he heard the phone ring in the living room and his foster mum took him aside.

'I remember it like it was yesterday. She said, "Your mummy has passed away, sweetheart."'

'How did you feel?'

'I was confused,' he said. 'I didn't even know what she meant. I think she had to explain it to me.'

'Remind me how old you were.'

'Seven. It was the third of February 1979.'

'You remember that?'

'I've got the records. Everything that's on record, I've found.' He turned towards the back of the flat and shouted, 'Val.'

'What?' she called back.

'Can you bring my box of letters?'

'Give me a minute.'

'Keep going,' I said.

'After my mum died, I stayed with the Baileys and started at a new school, Holy Name on Denmark Road.'

'Here.' Val appeared at the door holding a shoe box. 'That's one of them.'

Andy began leafing through the box and it was clear as he did that he knew its contents intimately, knew the letters from the shade of their paper alone.

'Look.' He handed me a yellowed sheet. The heading read, 'Certified Copy of an Entry: Death.' A table below stated that in the registration district of Greater Manchester, in the sub-district of Salford, Anne Marie Docherty, born 1950, unemployed, of 404 Blacksmith Court died on 3 February 1979. The causes were given as 1. Pulmonary aspiration and 2. Poisoning by drugs (diacetylmorphine).

'She choked on her own sick.'

I had finished reading the certificate but felt callous when I thought of handing it back. I sensed that Andy revered his box of documents. He had fallen silent in its presence and was watching me closely as I read, holding it with the tips of my fingers, as I had been taught to handle rare manuscripts. When I thought that I had looked at it long enough, I handed it back.

'I think it was deliberate,' he said. 'I think that when she saw I was happy with the Baileys, that they were nice to me and I had brothers and sisters, she thought I didn't need her anymore so she went where she wanted to go.' Val was standing in the doorway, nodding, and I felt guilty that I didn't see it the same way. It seemed to me more likely that Andy's mother had died accidentally and that Andy's version was a consolation. But I didn't say that. I asked if she was right to think that he didn't need her.

'No,' he said. 'She was my mum. I needed her. It would have been better if she'd stayed alive.' Now he began to cry.

'Sweetheart,' Val said. 'Your mummy loved you, didn't she?' When Andy covered his face with his hands and continued to cry softly, she turned to me and said, 'Would you like some lunch?' I declined as politely as I could manage. I felt sick when I thought about eating Andy's food. 'I'll bring yours through now.'

He had taken a tissue from the packet that sat beside his chair and was drying his eyes.

'Maybe we can leave it there for today,' I said. 'What do you think?'

'Good idea.' His eyes were red.

'You've done well,' I said.

'Do you think so?'

'I do.'

Val came back and set a tray down on the table in front of Andy. On it stood a glass of squash, a tray of pills, a bowl of soup, and a ham sandwich. I stood up and was about to say *bon appétit* when I thought better of it. People didn't say that here and it would make me sound like a snob. I tried to remember what the Northern equivalent was but I couldn't. 'Enjoy your meal,' I said, which was also wrong.

At home, I listened to the recording of our interview through my headphones and typed up a transcript. It didn't come out well. Once I had deleted all the grunts, the repetitions, and my own nervous interjections, there were only a few hundred words of raw biographical facts and a couple of half-interesting details. As I read over the unpromising draft, I considered for the first time that it might be impossible to give Andy what he wanted.

Still, each morning that week, I sat on his couch and listened as he recounted his memories. His moods changed quickly – he was in turns excitable, melancholic, distracted – and with his moods, his capacity to coherently recall events from his life also fluctuated. Sometimes, gripped by sudden agony, he could not continue his story. Sometimes, he returned to a moment we had already discussed and attempted to add some elusive detail. There was a man who rode a motorbike, a stray cat named Buxton, a party for the Queen's silver jubilee. To Andy's visible exasperation, I often struggled to see the significance of these impressions and place them correctly in the timeline of his life. At other times, he was more lucid and I tried to extract as many words as I could before his attention dropped off again. Why he was like that I couldn't be sure. To what extent did his MS, his bipolar, his ADHD – for he'd told me he had been diagnosed with all of these – affect his capacity for recollection? To what extent was his disordered and incoherent

thinking simply the outcome of his disordered and incoherent life?

After these visits, I returned to my empty house, ate
lunch at the dining-room table, and then lay down until
my nerves had recovered from sitting with Andy. His cease-
less self-inquisition reminded me of what I most disliked
in myself, but even more troubling were the symptoms of
his illness, his spasms and tremors, sudden headaches and
episodes of tiredness, all of which revived in flashes the
memory of my dad, especially of a certain bewildered look
of his that I had long forgotten – a lonely look of terror
at the things that were happening inside him that he did
not understand. Only after my nerves had calmed did I go
up to the office and work slowly on the beginning of Andy's
manuscript.

Though I possessed a few vivid impressions of Andy's
life, I found it harder to imagine how his voice could take
a literary form. 'My name is Andrew David Barton and I
was born on the fifteenth of August 1971,' I wrote. What
was wrong with that? First of all, it didn't sound like him.
Secondly, it had no character. In effect, it said little more
than 'I was born', which was the least that could be assumed
of anyone. But if I left the transcripts unedited, they hardly
amounted to anything. Then what were books made of? I
tried to start with a memory:

In my first memory, my mum is smoking a cigarette
and watching TV. The year is probably 1973 and we
are at home in our flat in the brand-new Crescents
Estate in Hulme. The flats are a bold, ambitious
project and the new tenants are excited to live in them.
Where is my dad? I don't know him yet and I won't

meet him for almost twenty years. It's just me and Mum here.

That was very bad. The tone was all over the place. It didn't know what it was trying to be or from what position in time it was speaking. I deleted what I had written and started again.

By the time I was born, in August 1971, my father had already left town and when my mum walked out of Stepping Hill Hospital, holding her new baby to her breast, she was entering an uncertain world. Her parents wanted nothing to do with her illegitimate child. She had no job and no place to go. How did she survive? I wish I knew the answer. All I know is that by the winter of the next year, we have a flat in the newly opened Crescents Estate in Hulme. This is Manchester in the 1970s. The factories are closing. Life is tough. And for me, Andrew Barton, it's not about to get any easier.

Was that better? Perhaps. But it didn't capture the world I pictured when Andy spoke.

'I left school just before I turned sixteen,' he told me in the last session of our second week, 'and got my first job at the Boddingtons brewery in Strangeways. I hated the smell. The air made me sick. The first few days, I could hardly stand it. It was all the nitrous oxide.'

'But you got used to it?'

'I didn't get used to it. I just had to deal with it. My job was washing kegs. I had to remove the snap rings and then clean the inside with a pump and bucket.' At the weekends, he went into town and walked around, looked in the underground market or the Corn Exchange, listened to some records in HMV, just seeing what was out and about, hoping to bump into someone he knew. Eventually, he found the courage to go back to the Baileys, where he had lived before he was taken to the care home. His old foster dad had died, but his mum was still there. She gave him the address of one of his brothers, the one he'd been closest with, and Andy went to see him at home. The first time he went, nobody answered the door but he went back the next weekend and he was there. He lived on Yew Tree Road in Fallowfield, miles from where Andy was living, and since he had to save every penny he made, he walked, which took him two hours. He still remembered the moment Brendan opened the door. He didn't look at all surprised to see him. He said, 'Alright, Andy, how are you?' and invited him inside for a brew. From then on, he went to Brendan's every weekend. He shared a flat with two other lads and they always had girls over. Andy beamed, 'They used to dote on me.' He impersonated this doting and it was a somewhat grotesque sight, this middle-aged man attempting to imitate a twenty-year-old girl's flirting. I tried not to wince. It was around this time, he said, that they started going to the Haçienda.

'What was it like?'

'Amazing.'

'Describe it in detail,' I said.

'It was just mint.'

'What did it look like?'

'It was massive. The best club in the world.'

'Tell me what you remember.'

'Nothing.' He laughed. 'I was off my head all the time.'

'Do you remember the first time you went?'

'It was 1988. I was with Brendan and a bunch of his mates. They were all saying how great it was and how I was going to love it. When we got there, it just looked like a warehouse. It looked like the brewery where I worked. I thought it was going to be shit.' When they went inside, Andy said, it was like nothing he had seen in his life. A wall of smoke and flashing lights, people dancing, house music. He'd never heard acid house until he walked into the Haçienda that night. But what made the deepest impression on him was the way that everything felt easy as soon as you stepped inside. Everyone was happy. Everyone was dancing. You could be best mates with anyone. If you bumped into someone, they were more likely to hug you than punch you in the face. It took him some getting used to because it was so unlike everything he'd known. All week, while he was hosing down kegs in the dank brewery in Strangeways, he would be thinking about the Haçienda, on Monday and Tuesday about how good it had been and then from Wednesday, about how good it was going to be. He thought he'd found his place in the world. He wanted to stay in the Haçienda for ever. 'There should be a lot about it in the book,' he said.

Back at the house, I pressed play and skipped through the interviews. Andy was describing the sense of belonging he felt at the Haçienda. I had been moved by that part. It was how I felt when I started university. But I struggled to imagine how we would dedicate a substantial section of his book to nights at the Haçienda. It wasn't just his lack of detailed memories that concerned me. The material also did not seem promising from a narrative perspective. I understood it had felt special to be there, not only for

Andy but for the countless people whom I had heard recall that era. But it was just people dancing in a club all night long. I copied down a few utterances, verbatim except for minor corrections to the grammar, in which Andy attempted to describe the experience of being high on ecstasy without great success. It wasn't working.

After failing for several hours to assemble an immersive and lively description from Andy's remarks, I went frustrated to the kitchen to make a cup of tea and, as the kettle boiled, I took a copy of *Moby Dick* from one of the bookshelves in the dining room. I had not felt like reading novels since quitting the PhD. The mere sight of them filled me with dread. But I wanted some trace of the outside, some words that were neither mine nor Andy's. I opened the book at random and read a sentence. 'It was nearly six o'clock, but only grey imperfect misty dawn, when we drew nigh the wharf.' A feeling of stillness and distance came over me. Yes, I thought, the grey imperfect misty dawn of a New England wharf in the middle of the nineteenth century. Here was a setting alien to me and yet when I read those words, I knew it. And surely it went the other way too. I could take one of Andy's stories and surround it with weather to give it a sheen of reality. After all, a life was a life. There were differences between people but these did not stop us from recognising the experiences of others. And if I could imagine the weather, I could also interpret Andy's silences, the gestures he made with his shaky hands, the moods that moved like clouds across his eyes. If I gave myself permission to imagine all of the details that had fallen between the cracks of his memory, recreating a scene at the Crescents or Haçienda did not seem so impossible. So, I went upstairs and began to write in a more novelistic style about Andy and his friends taking pills and dancing in the Haçienda, about the lights and the smoke and the cold as they left in the early morning and waited for the bus on Oxford Road. With this approach, I produced the first paragraph of Andy's book that I felt proud to put my name to.

During the hours when I wasn't occupied with Andy and his book, I was busy fending off the sense that my whole life lay in disarray, awaiting my attention like a stack of dirty dishes too large to begin. It didn't take me long to remember why I had always wanted to leave this city; I was not strong enough to stop its depressive moods from permeating my own. I took every scrap of litter, every moribund apartment complex, and every street fight personally. When I walked past the bars by the Metrolink station and saw the middle-aged alcoholics drinking their pints of ale and smoking roll-ups, I felt their loneliness in my own heart. When I walked around town and saw a couple of men my age, vaping outside the phone shop where they earned their money, shoulders sagging as though they had accepted that life could only alternate between work and want, I was full of pity on the one hand and on the other, a scornful feeling like contempt, an urgent need to hold them at a distance for fear that we were not as different as I liked to believe. There were bars and clubs and people going out to be merry in them; areas that had been all but abandoned ten years earlier had been developed beyond recognition, their factories and mills turned into luxury flats and restaurants, but I could take no pleasure in those scenes because I did not believe the city had really changed, only that it had been fitted with an artificial smile.

It was embarrassing to realise that I had returned in search of a world that no longer existed, mistaking my childhood for the city where it happened to have taken place. My mum had left, taking with her the last of that era's warm glow, and the house we had lived in had been sold to a family richer than we could ever have become. Even Tom with his stable income could no longer afford to live in the area where we had grown up. I needed to make a plan and find a place to be but I didn't know where to begin, so when Tom texted to say his football team's centre-back had fallen off a roof while installing a solar panel and asked if I could play in his absence, I said yes not only because I was beginning to feel lonely but because I craved discipline and organisation; I wanted men to bark instructions at me and point towards the places I needed to go.

Tom picked me up from the house and drove us to the sports complex at Platt Lane. He parked the car, got out, and stretched his quadriceps. Other men were getting out of other cars. They wore shorts and long socks and carried their keys in their hands. From the pitches came the sound of shouting and boots making contact with footballs. I followed Tom around the perimeter, where men stood in small groups, stretching and bantering. At the far side, three men in their thirties wearing red and white striped jerseys were passing a ball back and forth in the strip of unused surface between the pitch and the perimeter fence.

'This is Luca,' Tom said as we drew nearer. 'Our new signing.'

'Hiya, pal,' said one of the men. He was bald and ruddy.

'Paul.' He extended a hand for me to shake. 'We've signed you from Major League Soccer, haven't we?'

I never knew what to say to these kinds of men so I smiled and muttered a yes.

'Where do you play, pal?' said another of the men, short, strong, and hairy.

'He's going to play at centre-back with me,' Tom said.

'I'm Ste,' the hairy man said.

A goal was scored in the game taking place directly next to us and one team erupted in a cheer. I began to stretch and my teammates cast subtle glances in my direction. You could tell a lot about a person's background from the way they behaved on a football pitch and I could see that my new teammates thought I was posh. There was no way of hiding it. My frame indicated a life of little physical labour, my movements a childhood with little football.

'Hiya, pal,' a third man said, having finished his warm-up routine. He was pulling on a pair of goalkeeper's gloves and, having strapped the Velcro around his wrist, extended a gloved hand for me to fist-bump. 'Neil,' he said. 'Is it Luke?'

'Luca.'

'Luca. Where's that from?'

I shrugged. 'My parents liked it.'

'Fair enough.' He looked up towards the car park. 'Here's Kyle.'

Kyle was tall and fat and walked like a dancer. A clump of mousy brown hair lay atop his large head, bouncing as he walked behind the goals and around the corner flag. He carried a gym bag over one shoulder. 'Alright, lads,' he said when he arrived. 'We're going to need to be better than last week to beat these. They're top of the league.'

He pointed to a group of young men standing ten metres further along the pitch, wearing plain black jerseys and shorts.

'Let's go, boys,' Tom said, clapping his hands together. We assembled in position: Neil in goal, me and Tom at the back, Paul and Ste ahead of us and Kyle up front.

The ref blew his whistle.

The opposition kicked off and passed the ball with a fast tempo around their defensive half. 'Push up,' Tom said to me and we stepped a few yards forward. One of the opposition midfielders looked up and saw their forward was running into the space behind me.

'He's gone!' shouted the opposition keeper.

'Follow,' shouted Neil. 'All the way.'

The opposition forward tried to nip beyond me so I stuck a leg out and tripped him to the ground.

'Fucking hell, you little dickhead,' he said as he got to his feet. 'What the fuck was that?'

'Easy,' Tom said quietly behind me.

The opposition's shortest player stepped up and clipped the free kick onto the bar. Our keeper collected the ball and looked for a pass. 'Movement,' he said. 'Who fucking wants it?'

'Come on, boys,' shouted Kyle. 'Fucking get it together.'

'Stay,' Tom said to me. I hadn't yet had a touch of the ball. Paul blocked the throw-in and the ball deflected off his shin and rolled towards me. Before I could retrieve it, the short opposition player sped across and brought the ball under control.

'Quicker there,' Kyle said and I raised an apologetic hand.

The opposition tried another through-pass. This time,

I intercepted the ball and passed it to Tom, who passed it to Paul, who turned and looked for Kyle but was tackled.

'That's better,' Ste said. 'Triangles.'

The opposition keeper kicked the ball out high and their forward dashed passed us, brought the ball under control, and took a fierce shot. Neil dived to his left and parried the ball wide. 'Switch on,' he shouted as he got to his feet. 'Follow your fucking men.'

'Tuck in,' Tom said.

A choppy few minutes followed, where neither side controlled the ball for long. Then the ref blew for half time.

'We're doing alright,' Tom said as we gathered by our goal.

'We're taking too many touches,' said Kyle. It was clear that when he said 'we' he meant you, especially me. I sipped my Lucozade and stared at the pitch's radiant, artificial green. I was out of breath and seeing little spots of light in front of my eyes, whose constellation reminded me of a painting by Paul Klee that I had seen with Mia at the Met.

'You alright, Lucas?' Neil said to me.

'All good, mate.'

The ref peeped his whistle and we made our way back onto the pitch.

We kicked off. Kyle passed to Paul, who passed back to me. I tried an ambitious pass towards Kyle and kicked the ball out of play. But the opposition took a poor throw and the ball fell to Ste. He steered a powerful cross towards Kyle, who nodded the ball onto the post, drawing a general groan.

'That's more fucking like it,' Neil shouted, thrashing his gloved hands together.

Now the opposition keeper booted the ball upfield and into the path of the opposition's forward. I chased after him but I was too slow. He opened his body, feigned once to send Neil sprawling on the floor, and chipped the ball over him and into the net. The opposition cheered while I looked at the artificial surface and panted. A hot flush of shame engulfed me. The goal was my fault, though nobody chastised me.

'Come on, lads,' Tom said. 'We're still in this.'

We kicked off. Kyle passed to Paul, who passed back to Tom, who passed to Ste.

'Push,' Tom said to me.

There followed another period of attrition, in which neither side could complete a series of passes.

Tom recovered possession on the wing and passed inside to me but I was caught flat-footed. I adjusted my body shape and tried to control the ball, but I was being charged down by the opposition's lanky midfielder, who swung an elbow into my abdomen as we both challenged for the ball. I landed hard on the ground, winded, while he walked off without extending a hand to help me up.

Tom took the free kick while I got to my feet. I was hurting and distracted and the pain was turning into a sadness so consuming that I didn't notice we had conceded possession until the opposition forward was again running past me with the ball. Unchallenged, he slotted it into the bottom left corner.

I looked at the ground but from the corner of my eye, I saw Kyle shake his head and mutter some words to himself while Neil kicked the goalpost in anger. There was only time for a short string of passes before the ref peeped his whistle and the game was over, lost 2–0 thanks to me.

'Did you enjoy that?' Tom said in the car.

'I was culpable for the goals.'

.

'We were all to blame for the first one,' he said. 'The keeper shouldn't have been allowed to bypass the midfield like that. You switched off for the second one and we got punished. They were a good side. You did well in the rest of the game.' He was focusing on the road, which made it hard to gauge the sincerity of his remarks. I looked out the passenger side window as we drove through Fallowfield. Dusk in springtime: a melancholy stillness hanging over the evening. 'You made some good tackles,' he said. 'Are you keeping busy? You're not spending all your time with Andy, are you?'

'Feels like it.'

'How often are you over there?'

'Once a day for an hour or so.'

'Well, remember to keep a bit of distance. He's had a tough life and I know what you're like. You'll get too involved with him.'

That night, as I lay in my empty room, replaying my footballing mistakes and trying without success to fall asleep, I noticed a subtle modulation in the light. My phone, which lay face down on the dresser, had lit up with a notification. Though I was beginning to accept that I would probably not hear from her again, every time I heard the ping of a text or email, I still thought that it might be Mia and my heart swelled. I got up and went to the dresser. My lower back and legs were stiff and aching and I had a sore spot on the upper part of my shin. It was a text from Andy. 'Hi Luca,' it said. 'What do you think about having a bit at the beginning where you meet me as I am today before I go back in time a bit like I'm telling a story by a fire.' He began typing again. It took him a long time to write his message but finally it appeared: 'There could be other bits in between when it comes back to today.'

'A good idea,' I wrote back. 'Sleep well, Andy. I'll see you on Monday.'

Mia had hardly been out of my thoughts the whole time she was in London for the winter holidays and all my worries turned to elation when she suggested we meet in New York in February. I was having a good week with work and when I set out that Friday morning, I couldn't stop smiling; I was a graduate student, in America; I was to become an expert on modern literature and critical theory – the field was too vague and I didn't know what I would write my thesis on, but I still believed there was time to clarify my thinking. I had my own desk in the stacks of Widener Library with postcards on the bulletin board and cereal bars in the locker: little possessions that meant the place was, in some sense, mine. Next year, I would be teaching undergraduates and would be able to pepper my conversation with the phrase *my students*, as my peers did with such glee. I was riding the Red Line to Boston South Station to catch a train to New York City and I was going to spend the weekend with the woman I was falling in love with, who might have been falling in love with me, too, and that woman was Mia Knight, the poet and academic. I desired the person I was getting to know and the body I had kissed and touched, but these desires could not be separated from my desire to live a life like hers, to which she seemed to offer me safe passage.

When I got off the subway at South Station, I bought a

copy of the *New York Times* from a kiosk because I'd had the idea that we would lie in bed together and do the crossword. My fantasies had crystallised around this image; under the duvet, propped up against the headboard, she would lean her naked body on mine, rest her head on my left shoulder, and recall some obscure fact from the dim stacks of her memory while the pen in my right hand filled in the squares. I took my seat on the train and read some of the headlines but I couldn't concentrate, or didn't want to, and instead, I rested my head against the window. I thought of the house in Maine where Mia was living, where I had never been but which I had dreamed of. I imagined myself reclining in a posture indicating financial and personal security, imagined Mia smiling at me, imagined us walking into a literary party in New York or London, arm in arm. For once in my life, I believed that my fantasies were not clues that, if properly examined, could reveal my current unhappiness, but ideas that extended naturally and easily from my situation, images of the future towards which I was travelling. The cup of Dunkin' Donuts coffee on the tray table, the view through the train's small windows of the sparkling Atlantic between Providence and New Haven, a text from Mia saying she'd landed at JFK and would meet me at the hotel: these details conspired to make me believe that I was finally, really living. As though in some rare solar event, my situation and my desires had aligned.

Mia had mentioned that she was busy so I'd booked us a hotel, one close to Madison Square Park. I had no taste in such matters and, afraid of seeming unworldly, I had booked a nicer place than I could really afford. It was a sunny day, warm for February, and as I walked along

Broadway, I thought – and just to be thinking while walking along Broadway was novel enough to make me grin – of all the times in my youth that I had turned up in some big city without a destination and had felt crushed by the scale of the place and the indifference of its people. This couldn't have been more different. I had a place to go, there were more than two thousand dollars in my bank account – as far as I was concerned, I was rich – and Mia had texted to say that she was having a drink in the hotel. I saw her through the window as soon as I arrived. She was sitting at the bar with a glass of white wine, looking over the tables of people eating lunch with an expression I took for contented absentmindedness, the look of a person who finds themselves unoccupied for the first time in a while. I went inside and joined her and she got off the stool to hug me. The smell of the conditioner in her hair reminded me of the nights we'd spent together on our first visit and filled me with a desire that I was able to enjoy now that the possibility of rejection and disappointment felt small enough to be a part of the fun. We separated and looked at one another. Her eyes were bluer than I'd remembered them, brighter, and animated by a playfulness that I'd only glimpsed before, and which I loved straight away. It was like alcohol: from the first sip, I wanted it to be endless. I wanted more of it than I could ever have.

The lift to our room was crowded with other guests and as I looked around at their unmoving faces, it occurred to me that from their perspective, Mia and I looked like a couple. Our relationship had so far progressed slowly, from a distance, and with the gentlest of movements. Now it had a momentum of its own, and I responded to this thought with a sense of dejection. It wasn't that I didn't want for us to be a couple – on the contrary, I wanted nothing more – but that I guessed Mia didn't want that in the same way and I felt that the eyes of the guests weighed heavily on her. We didn't make eye contact as the lift went up and her neck was stiff, her eyes fixed upon the red debossed letters of a cautionary sign on the wall. When the door opened on the tenth floor, she pulled the handle of her suitcase and it remained stuck in its retracted position. I watched, not knowing what to do, while she struggled. I didn't want to intervene and risk seeming not to understand the line between chivalry and sexism, but then one of the other male guests in the lift grabbed the suitcase's handle. Seeing him do this, I thought that I ought to have acted sooner, and so I grabbed the handle too, and now both of our hands were on it, and we wrestled it together out of the lift, while Mia looked on, harried and dismayed. The man walked in the other direction and an uncomfortable silence hung over Mia and me as we made our way along the corridor to our room. I became too aware of that aspect of our relationship that we couldn't escape: she was older than me, more sophisticated, successful, smarter, richer. I glowed when she directed her affection towards me, but without it, I felt like a person wearing a T-shirt in winter sunshine who feels suddenly freezing when a grey cloud obscures the light. Much too conscious of this, I tried to feign nonchalance, opening the door with the key card and throwing my rucksack onto the bed. Then I stood by the window in the corner, which had a view, partially blocked by the neighbouring building, of the street far below and the white roof of a passing bus. I wished that I could find the words to address our situation, clarify it, break the tension. I wanted to name everything that hadn't yet been said, but I couldn't think of a word to say.

'How's the view?' Mia said behind me and her voice on my shoulder felt much lighter than my thoughts.

'Unremarkable.'

'I've seen worse.' I turned to meet her eyes and she smiled at me with a touch of inquisitive concern.

'Shall we go out? While the weather is good.'

Without our luggage, descending in an empty lift, our situation felt simpler. A gust of wind swept through the sunlit street and a car horn honked. I took a packet of cigarettes out of my inside pocket and opened them towards Mia, the way I did the first time we met. She took one and I lit it before lighting my own. She regarded hers, pointing the lit end towards herself as though to inspect it, and when she looked up again, I thought about putting a confident arm on her waist and drawing her towards me for a kiss, but I couldn't be sure the arm would be confident, and so I didn't.

'Let's walk this way,' she said, 'to the East Village.'

When we walked beside one another, I never knew what to say, and I did not find our silence comfortable. It did not feel to me like the contented silence of two people who are pleased simply by one another's company but like a constant impasse. I scrutinised the tops of the buildings as though one of them might offer inspiration, but when you are looking for anything to say, nothing will do.

'I like those flats,' I said eventually.

'Do you?'

Then I wasn't sure. 'In a way.'

'I don't.'

'No. I didn't think you would.' She looked taken aback,

as though my comment had sounded barbed. By way of a retraction, I added, 'I'm not sure I like them either.' It was a disaster, I thought. We don't have anything to say and we're stuck together for a weekend. But soon, Mia led us off the main street and onto a quieter one. It must have been East 22nd or 23rd Street. The sky was still clear and blue but the sun had disappeared behind a tall tenement building across the street. 'Nice time for a drink.'

'I was thinking the same,' Mia said and we hurried into the first place we came across, a cocktail bar on an idyllic stretch of street, opposite a basement record shop and a colourful apartment building with balconies decorated by flowers in hanging baskets, like a Hollywood depiction of New York. We sat at the bar, as was becoming our tradition, and eyed the server desperately, because we both knew that as soon as we were drinking, things would get better. I ordered a Negroni, Mia an Old Fashioned and our server placed the drinks on the black napkins in front of us. I sipped on my thin straw and half the glass of Negroni was gone. Mia provoked the ice in her glass and took a sip. The atmosphere loosened. When we drank, it was easy between us. It wasn't just that we talked with less inhibition, as everyone does, it was also that when we were drinking, we seemed to be fulfilling the need for which each of us had brought the other into their service: to enable a kind of fantasy life that we both needed, a suspension of everything that terrified us and a deferral of every difficult lesson we would have to learn about ourselves when we were done playing around. We didn't talk about her divorce, nor my failure to work. We talked as though neither of our personal situations existed, though of course, both of us knew they did, and it was this delicate arrangement that the alcohol helped us to maintain. No, to enjoy – because we did enjoy it once we got going. We got light-headed and drunk, ordered more and more cocktails, and went out to smoke cigarettes in the cool air.

Evening had fallen when we left the bar. We swayed into one another as we walked and, each time our arms touched, a charge passed between us. If we had stopped and allowed our eyes to meet, our bodies would have followed and we would have kissed. How I wanted to stop and kiss. 'Look at this place.' Mia pointed to a seedy-looking entranceway on the street level where a pink neon sign in the small window read, *Psychic*. Beneath that, another sign hand-painted on white cardboard read, *Raya: Clairvoyant, Healer, Spiritual Advisor. Past, Present, Future. Palm Reading, $10. Tarot Reading, $30.*

'Have you ever had a tarot reading?'

'Never. Have you?'

'I draw a card every morning but I've never had a reading.'

'We should go for one.'

Mia stopped. 'Shall we do it now?'

'We could.' I wanted to say no. I wanted to go back to the hotel room and have sex, not to satisfy a physical desire but to draw us into complicity, but I also liked the idea that the reading would become part of our shared mythology and bind us closer together.

'I don't mind.' Her tone implied that it was some practical thing that would have to be done sooner or later.

'Come on. Let's do it.'

We pushed open the door and stepped into a cramped vestibule, where a small, bald man was sitting hunched on a chair and looking at a television. The bright light shining on his face told me he was watching a cartoon. The air was thick and warm and smelled of weed. 'What can I do for you this evening?' The man turned off the television and tidied things away from the table as we entered and told him that we wanted a reading. 'Amazing,' he said. 'Why don't you decide who would like to go first and come through when you're ready?'

Mia turned to me and I had the same feeling I'd had in the lift, the discomfort of being cast as a couple before the proper time. We were not supposed to make any decisions together, only to indulge in pleasure.

'I'll go,' she said and I shrugged in response. I no longer knew what I thought about what we were doing. I wanted to treat it as a joke, but it seemed to have become serious. The man went behind a low counter in one corner of the room and fetched a pack of cards while I stepped outside.

The air was cold now, the street quiet. There were no benches in sight so I stood a few metres away from the door and smoked a cigarette, which hurt my throat and lungs. The buildings opposite were tall, built from red brick, and decked with steel fire escapes. They looked like the buildings in the centre of Manchester, and I remembered that years ago, I had been walking along Dale Street when I came to a section that had been closed for a film set. A small crowd of locals watched from behind a barrier, though nothing was happening, and the members of a camera crew were conferring with one another and adjusting their equipment. I approached one of the security staff to ask what they were filming and I laughed when he said *Captain America*, but he wasn't joking. With the camera positioned in the right way, the Northern Quarter was an adequate stand-in for Manhattan, a laughable idea because Manchester was a dying place while New York was alive. That I was in the latter, that home had never appeared smaller and further away, seemed evidence that I was no longer a prisoner of my personal history and I was free to make my own fate. I never had to go back. I wanted Mia to come out. I was flush with manic, euphoric feeling and I wanted to drink more, smoke more, fall deeper in love. I wished we hadn't agreed to do the reading. I wanted to stop pretending. But another ten minutes passed before the door finally opened and Mia appeared, looking relaxed and a touch giddy. It was clear that I had no choice but to follow her. 'Was it good?' She nodded and angled her head towards the door as though to say, your turn.

The clairvoyant was sitting at the low table, shuffling his cards. He had lit an incense cone and the smell of sandalwood hit me as I entered. I lowered myself into the chair opposite his and he handed me the deck. 'Hold the cards,' he said, 'and press your energy into them. Imagine that you are filling the cards with your energy. Like that. That's good. One last press. Give them everything you have.' Then he took the cards from me. 'What's your name?'

'Luca.'

'Okay, Luca. He dealt the cards into a column on the table. 'You don't live in New York City.'

'In Cambridge, Mass.'

'You're a thinker of some kind.' I suspected that he was simply making an educated guess based on information Mia had given about herself, but I was flattered anyway because he was telling me what I wanted to hear, and embarrassed that I was so easily flattered. He looked up and regarded me, though his attention was not focused on my eyes. Rather, he seemed to look past or through me, and the disconcerting effect was like looking at a person speaking into a video camera: his gaze looked at mine but didn't meet it. 'You're smiling in your face,' he said. 'But you're not smiling in your soul. I see a lot of grey in your aura.' He dealt another two cards next to the others, tilted one of the cards towards himself, and raised an eyebrow as he considered it. I tried to read the card he had looked at. It depicted a man with some swords. 'You are lost.' He looked towards me again. 'You have taken the wrong path.' He dealt three more cards in rapid succession. 'Did you lose someone?'

'My dad.'

'As a child.'

'As a teenager, yes.'

'I see sadness. It's like a fog. I can hardly see.' He squinted as though a real fog had filled the room. 'It was a bad death.'

'Suicide.'

The clairvoyant drew a sharp inhalation of breath, took the incense from the table, and waved it once as though to clear the air. 'His spirit is restless.' Then he inclined his head again as he dealt another three cards and scrutinised them. I tried to tilt my head to read them, too, but I struggled to distinguish one from another. Some faced me while some faced him. I saw a sun, a moon, a man hanging from a tree. 'You will live a healthy life,' said the clairvoyant. 'And you will be wealthy. I see a house with a garden.' He dealt more cards. 'You are not supposed to move from one relationship to another and have many lovers. You have one true love. What is her name?'

'Mia?'

He closed his eyes and squinted. He shook his head. 'I

131

don't see a Mia.' Then he fixed his eyes on me again before dealing a final set of cards. 'You're lucky, but you are alone. You've lost your way on a dark and winding path and you are far away from home. How will you find your way home?'

'I don't know.'

He sighed and shook his head. 'I do not see disaster in your future, but I see sadness, and soon there will be change. What will change?'

'I don't know.'

'You know in your soul. But your mind has wandered far away from your soul.' He held my gaze for a long time, looking at me as though I might respond. Then, when he saw that I wouldn't, he finally said, 'Do you have any questions about what the cards have told us today?'

I shook my head.

The clairvoyant exhaled, 'Okay, Luca. It was my great pleasure.' His tone was suddenly breezy as he showed me towards the door. 'I wish you a fabulous weekend in New York.' I was about to wave him goodbye when I realised he was looking at me with expectation. I took three twenty-dollar bills from my wallet, wondered for a moment whether one had to tip a clairvoyant, thought yes, and because I had nothing but twenties, gave him eighty dollars.

'How was it?' Mia said when I stepped outside.

I linked arms with her and we walked west along whatever street we were on. 'Fuck, I don't know,' I said. 'Weird? Bad? How was yours?'

'What did he say?'

'He said I was smiling in my face but not my soul.'

'Really? Mine was good. He said most people have one guardian angel but I have eight.'

'Eight? That seems like a lot. He didn't mention guardian angels to me. He just said I was alone.'

'He said my aura was blue.'

'He said mine was grey.'

Mia stopped to laugh. Then she looked at me and said, 'Did it upset you?'

'No.'

'It did.'

'It didn't. It was just strange, to have someone look at you like that and make an assessment of your character.'

'He wasn't assessing your character.'

'He was. Of course he was. He was just judging my vibe and pretending to look at the cards. He said I'm sad.'

'Well, you are a bit sad, aren't you?'

'Am I?'

'It's upset you,' Mia said. She tried to put an arm around me but I brushed her away.

'Are you in a mood?'

'No.'

'You are.' We came to a small park. 'You're in a mood,' she said.

'Just let me process it. What else did he say to you?'

'He said I would have a very creative phase soon, the most creative phase of my life.'

'Good for you.' I thought I meant this as a joke, but as I spoke, I heard its malicious intent. 'What about health stuff?'

'He said I would be healthy. Did he say you would get sick?'

'No, he said I would be healthy, too.'

'That's good.'

'I know. But he said I would be unhappy.' I wanted to

ask Mia what he had said to her about love. Was she in love with me? How everything could have changed if she had told me right then that she was in love with me. I sat down on a bench in the park. 'I'm sorry.'

'I don't mind.'

'I just need a minute.' Mia remained standing, looking up and around at the tall buildings that surrounded the park, while I pressed my face into my hands and tried to force myself not to cry. Then, after a few minutes, I stood up and said, 'Okay, I'm fine now.'

We went for another cocktail but the mood had changed. I couldn't get the clairvoyant's words out of my head. I kept thinking of the eighty dollars I had spent on paying for us both and feeling like an idiot for spending my money on a scam. After our drink, we went back to the hotel room. The tarot reading had created an atmosphere of heaviness that precluded real sexual excitement, but we pretended that it hadn't and we lay on the bed and kissed. Although our sex had always been somewhat cold and dispassionate, an aspect of our relationship I had found exciting because it was novel to me, the way we had sex that night in the hotel room was merely disengaged. As I lay on the pillow, looking at the dark ceiling, I thought that our relationship was already over. I could tell that Mia was not asleep either and I thought about speaking to break the tension, but before I could think of the right words I was asleep, and then it was morning, the sun was shining through our window, and Mia was on top of me, kissing me awake and grinding her body on mine. One hand clasped my shoulder and with the other she touched herself until she came, her eyes closed as though she were somewhere else, her lips appearing almost to move as though with some private language. Then she lay for a minute with her head on my chest before getting up and going into the bathroom while I remained in bed, listening to the sound of the shower and looking out the window at a corner of blue sky above the rooftops, full of a sense that the world, rather than shutting down, was opening up.

Two days later, we were back in Cambridge, strolling around the Natural History Museum as I tried to explain to her that I was not really doing my work. I hoped that a confession would bring us closer and help us to avoid lapsing back into that unpleasurable distance. But I didn't want her to know the real extent of my inactivity, so I couched every confession with a qualifier and ended up speaking to myself while she looked at the samples of rock laid out in their glass cabinets. We entered the taxidermy hall and Mia's eyes darted around. A smile broke out across her face. 'Do you like it?' I said.

'Very much,' she replied.

I talked some more about my situation and her chest seemed to move as though with a sigh. Without diverting her eyes from the elk she was scrutinising through its glass case, she said, 'When my PhD students tell me they can't find the focus to complete their work, I always tell them to write about why they wanted to do it in the first place.' She took a step to the side and met the glassy eyes of a stuffed roe deer. 'It's strange how many have never asked themselves.'

'How did you end up writing about Elizabeth Bishop?' I asked her.

'Because I like her work, in the first instance. And because the money was available. As a matter of fact,

Bishop didn't have all that much to do with Maine. She spent a few summers on North Haven towards the end of her life and wrote one poem about it. But she's one of these writers whose work has given rise to a small industry and it's in the interest of the university to have a stake in it. They made some money available. I applied and I got it.'

'You make it sound so simple.'

'I was lucky in this case.'

I was always trying to get us out, to some place where we'd be distracted, into a bar, where we could drink and go outside to smoke, but that evening Mia suggested we stay home. We lay in bed together, propped up against the headboard, the duvet warming our legs, drinking cans of beer, and we talked for the first time about some intimate topics we had so far avoided.

'When did you and your ex-girlfriend break up?' she asked me.

'Not so long ago.'

'Before you moved here?'

'We tried to keep it going for a while.' She looked unmoved. 'It was over a long time before that,' I added. But this wasn't exactly true; I was no good at letting go. 'What about you and Henry?'

'What about us?'

'When did you separate?'

'In the summer, before I moved here.'

'Don't you ever wonder if you'll get back together when you go back to London?'

She shook her head. 'I make clean cuts with the past. I'm not very sentimental.' We got up to smoke on the porch and she asked if I had anything warm that she could borrow.

I gave her my sweater and smiled when she pulled it over her head. 'What?' she said.

'Sorry.' I knew what she meant. I was looking at her as though it meant that she was mine now.

She forgave me. It wasn't always awkward and stuttering. When I gave up my busyness and stopped thinking of her as someone I needed to impress, her eyes fixed on me with a disarming openness that drew me out of myself. In bed, she rested her head on my chest and asked if I wanted to take a train somewhere, in the summer.

'I love trains,' I said.

'Me, too.'

She slept in my arms for the first time that night.

'Will you visit me in Orono?' she said the next morning.

'I would love to.'

'I'm busy for the next month or so. I have to write this article. But when that's finished.'

'I'm busy, too. I won't be able to come until after my exam. Then I'll be free.' I saw her to the front door and, this time, she kissed me back. We kissed for several minutes, running our hands over each other's bodies, and the meaning of this seemed to be that we wanted more – more of this for as long as we could have it.

Snow covered the skate park, filled the sandpit, caked the lawns in Harvard Yard. There were four weeks exactly until my exam and, with the deadline so close, I stopped bothering to leave the flat. I read the introductions to a pile of books about medieval poetry, restoration drama, the novels of Samuel Richardson, and various other subjects that I would not have time to read directly. It was all just information and my job was to process it. There was no time for the experience of reading, only for the systematic accumulation of facts. The important thing, I had learned from observing my peers, was to be able to speak about everything, so I spent the days prostrate on the bed writing clichés onto index cards.

'You look happy,' my flatmate Kareena said when she came home on the first Friday of that month and spied me through the open bedroom door.

'I'm getting organised.'

'Great,' she said. 'Look at you.' Kareena was in all respects better adjusted and better integrated than me. She worked hard and had a community of bright and engaging friends. 'I'm going to a party tonight.' She was boiling some water in a pan on the stove. 'Why don't you come?'

'What sort of people?'

'They're nice.'

'Nobody from English?'

'No. They're from Comp Lit and Classics. It's my friend Juliana. She's Canadian. It will be fun.'

'All right,' I said. 'I'll come.'

After I'd showered and dressed, I texted Mia to say that I was going to a party tonight. She appeared online and wrote. 'Jealous!' Then she sent a photo of her slippered feet resting on a pouffe by a television, on which I recognised a scene from *Gilmore Girls*. 'My Friday night,' she wrote. 'Have fun at the party.'

Kareena and I stepped out into the frosty air in our coats and scarves and it was so good to be in love in the USA, to be going to a party on a snowy Friday night in Somerville, walking through Union Square with the snow crunching beneath our feet. 'Got ID?' said the man in the liquor store. I did: a Massachusetts ID card bearing my face and my name, confirming that I was a person who had torn themselves away from home and made their life a novelty. The man nodded gruffly as he handed back the card. Up the hill from Union Square, behind the houses with their clumsy wooden porches, the moon lay on the glazed snow of the backyards. We arrived at a big colonial house with spongy window frames and a creaking gate, pushed open the front door and caught a wave of warm air, the clean, neutral smells of the young and healthy. The atmosphere was welcoming and I did not feel ashamed or out of place. Even when Kareena rushed off to say hello to a cast of smiling white teeth and bright eyes, I did not feel alone. I recognised a man with whom I had been in a seminar and he introduced me to two of his friends. 'What do you work on?' they said and I confessed that I hadn't yet figured it out. 'Sounds relatable,' one said. So comfortable was I that when the host, Juliana, invited me to join her and a few friends on the porch for a cigarette, I was compelled to tell them all about Mia. 'I'm in love with a poet,' I said. The group nodded in recognition. I was about to carry on when a man stepped out the side door and joined us. He was tall, shaven-headed, and the cut of his jeans and long coat suggested that he was not American.

'Do you know Michael?' Juliana asked me and I said that I didn't.

He offered me a hand, friendly but with a touch of reluctance, just enough to acknowledge that the custom of handshaking was imperfect but not yet redundant. We shook hands. 'Nice to meet you,' he said and I could hear in his accent that he was English, perhaps even Northern.

'Luca was just telling us that he is in love with a poet,' Juliana said.

'Oh?' Michael raised an eyebrow and smiled with a not-unkind amusement.

'There's not much more to it than that, I'm afraid.' I didn't want to go into it in the presence of another man.

'Come on,' Juliana said. 'Of course there is.'

'Does she love you too?' her girlfriend asked.

'I don't know. We just spent the weekend together. In New York.'

The whole crowd made a noise as though to say, well, then there's no doubt.

'Does she live in New York?' Michael asked me.

'She lives in London. But she's on a residency in Maine.'

'Have you been to visit? It's beautiful. My partner and I went to Mount Desert Island in the fall.' The others began to talk among themselves, leaving me and Michael in a one-to-one conversation. 'I loved it,' he said. *Loved*: he said the word from the bottom of his throat, his tongue dipping to fish out the low, broad vowel.

'Did you grow up in the North of England?' I asked him.

'I did.' He smiled with a touch of hesitation, perhaps out of fear that I might start up with some tribal banter, rather than shame about his origins. 'I grew up in Manchester.'

That was why I recognised him. It must have been something about the way he held himself. 'I did, too.' I met his eyes to say that I considered it significant, that I considered us bonded by our common home and privy to a certain perspective not shared by the rest of our company, but his eyes did not say the same thing to me. 'Where did you grow up?'

'Failsworth,' he said. In bleak North Manchester, then, where men fished with magnets in the filthy canal for shrapnel and old grenades. I asked him what school and university he went to, because I had to understand how he had got here, if he had been one of those kids whose parents send them to a private school and then to Oxbridge so they can get away before the city has a chance to leave its mark on them. He hadn't. What did he study?

'History,' he said with confidence. He studied the history of trade union movements in Britain. He was more or less finished. Then he would adapt his thesis into a book to be published by Duke University Press. He was currently on the job market. 'What about you?' he asked me, and I could tell the question was born of politesse; he was not as hungry to know about me as I was to know about him.

'I grew up in Chorlton,' I said.

'I meant, what do you work on.'

'Oh, English. I'm in my second year.'

'How are you finding it?'

'Hard sometimes.' I searched his face for a sign of recognition, a cue that I might say more and be understood. I was about to ask him what his parents had done for work when another man stepped outside and joined us. Michael turned around, saw the man, and made a small gesture whose exact meaning was illegible to me. 'This is my partner, Jameel,' he said. Jameel shook my hand and we introduced ourselves. He looked cautious, I thought, but perhaps he was just shy.

'Luca's from Manchester,' Michael said.

'Are you?' His eyes widened. 'We go every year to visit Michael's family. It's a fantastic city, so vibrant.' Was I doing a PhD too, he asked me and I said that I was. Every single person at the party, every person in this cursed city, was doing or had done a PhD. 'Are you almost finished?'

'Second year,' I said and I felt a distance open between us. I was their age and yet so far behind them and this slight deviation from the order seemed to unsettle him. Now Juliana asked Jameel a question about a person I didn't know, someone called Greg or Craig who had recently taken a job in Florence. I stood listening for a while and then slipped away, walked into the kitchen, where two women I didn't know were talking by the fridge, and I excused myself as I reached in to get a drink. I snuck out to the front porch to smoke a cigarette alone. I could hear the others conversing on the side porch: the voices of Michael and Jameel, of Juliana and her girlfriend, and now of Kareena. The sound of their laughter echoed around the yard while the cold bit my ears and I thought of Mia, the only person I wanted to be with.

I couldn't remember getting home that night and lost the whole subsequent weekend to a bad hangover. The week did not go as well as the one before it. Milder weather melted the snow. The skies were fine and cloudless, but the days left few traces on my index cards. The exam kept moving closer but I remained as I was: stuck, unable to focus, and wondering why I did not have the proper appetite for success. Mia didn't appear online for several days and I was disturbed by the ferocity of my longing for her correspondence. When she re-emerged, she told me that she had taken a day off to mark the anniversary of her sister's death – as she did every year – and sent a picture: a ginger cat standing on the long ramp descending into the water of the harbour in a town called Stonehaven.

Though I thought of nothing else for a week ahead of

the date, the exam nevertheless seemed to come all of a sudden. I woke up one morning and found myself pushing open the large oak doors of a seminar room in the English department's basement, where three professors were arranged in a line behind a row of tables. The scene brought to mind an old memory: entering the youth court, the condescending faces of the magistrates behind their high desk. They found me guilty of the charge of shoplifting and ordered me to pay a fine of £80. I shook off the memory, bowed, and made my way towards the chair that sat before the panel. I had not been notified in advance of the professors who would comprise the panel and I was disappointed by the result. The only one I knew personally was Gladys de Rijke, whose class I had taken in my first year, and she had not liked me at all. I gave her a familiar nod but she did not return it, only gazed at me over the rims of her glasses as though she had never seen me in her life. She wore a scarf, though it wasn't cold in the room. In the middle was Maynard Choate, one of the most senior and conservative faculty members, well known for having published several influential books on Milton in the 70s. Most students, except for those in his small clique of disciples, regarded him as a mean-spirited patrician. As I made my way towards the chair, he looked down at the lap of his olive-green suit pants as though he were ashamed of my presence. On the right sat Jared Dresser, the youngest tenured professor on the faculty, a specialist in modernism and the 'Digital Humanities'. He wore a shirt and tie and an expression of discomfort as though his face were too tight for his skull.

'Mr Byrne,' Professor Choate said.

'Call me Luca,' I said.

'Thank you for joining us, Mr Byrne. Before we begin, I will briefly explain how the proceedings will unfold this morning. My colleagues and I have prepared a series of questions that we will now pose to you. The time allotted to us permits expansive answers. We will not ask you about any texts not included on the list provided to you, though you are, of course, welcome to draw on any that you like, so long as you deem them appropriate. I will be asking you questions on the literatures of the medieval period and the Renaissance. Professor de Rijke will question you on the literatures of the eighteenth and nineteenth centuries. Finally, Professor Dresser will discuss with you the literatures of the twentieth century. The examination will last around seventy-five minutes. Do you have any questions before we begin?'

I shook my head.

Now Professor Choate began to speak. At first, his speech followed the syntactic and tonal patterns of declaration and so I nodded along accordingly as he spoke about political turmoil in the late fourteenth century. Then his inflexion began to rise and suddenly he had posed me a question about Chaucer's *Canterbury Tales* and Langland's *Piers Plowman*. Silence filled the wood-panelled room.

'I'm sorry,' I said, 'could you repeat the question?'

Would I care to address how the prologues to these poems addressed the political and religious conflicts of the day? he asked me.

I had read both prologues, though I could hardly remember a thing about either apart from the famous opening lines of Chaucer's, which reminded me of a trip I had taken with my ex-girlfriend to see a friend at the University of Kent. As we approached Canterbury and the cathedral spire appeared on the horizon, I read the prologue aloud in an exaggerated Middle English. I could picture her laughing as she steered the car. But I had nothing to say about the prologue other than that I liked it and that was not a suitable answer. I sat silent and still while the piercing, intelligent eyes of the panel looked at me, seeing things I could not understand, understanding me better than I understood myself, placing my failure to speak in a historical context that I had not even begun to grasp.

'Can we circle back to that one?'

'Very well,' Professor Choate said and he began with a second question.

It was well known that no general exam passed without a discussion of Shakespeare so I was somewhat prepared for the next question, which concerned the theatricality of Shakespeare's plays. What did Shakespeare's plays have to say about theatre? I liked the angle and I could even think of a few starting places: the theatrical production in *A Midsummer Night's Dream* or the play-within-a-play in *Hamlet*. But perhaps those were too obvious – perhaps the question was intended to gauge whether the student could find a better point of entry – and I had nothing to say about those plays anyway. I was mute. My face began to move and I became aware of the muscles on either side of my mouth and nose. I seemed to want to speak but couldn't.

'I'm really sorry,' I said. 'I'm nervous. I'll come back to this one too.'

Profs de Rijke and Dresser were making notes while Professor Choate turned a page and began to ask another question. This one concerned Renaissance humanism and its interest in heresy, evil and the demonic. That was good. I had written an essay about *Paradise Lost* and theodicy whose argument I could regurgitate. But first I had to steer the question in that direction and make it sound as though the answer I planned to give was the only natural one. A sequence of words now escaped my open mouth. I was trying to sound eloquent, but one cannot imitate eloquence and so I began to feel the way I did in those dreams where I was speaking a language I had never learned. I manoeuvred to the topic of *Paradise Lost* and recited the argument of my essay in a mechanical fashion that did not succeed in disguising my method. But I was glad that I had at least managed to speak. Then Professor Choate began to respond to what I had said, taking issue with my argument and even quoting from the poem itself. To this, I had nothing to say except to acknowledge that yes, he was probably right. 'You're the expert,' I said.

Professor de Rijke took over, asking me about the emergence of the novel form and the works of Daniel Defoe, Coleridge and Wordsworth, lyric poetry and society, and the novels of Charles Dickens. I was able to provide a short answer to each of the questions, though in every case I was horribly aware of every book I hadn't read, of how my attempts to smooth over the gaps in my knowledge were always evident, of how far I was from anything resembling expertise. As I spoke, I began to see myself through their eyes and hear my voice with their ears: I was a product of the poorly funded state school system, of a broken home, of the age of the post-war university with its relaxation of entry requirements. I was not of the calibre they were used to. I retreated deep into myself and all I could think of were the words 'give up'. I was free to give up if I wanted to and there was nothing more appealing than the freedom I associated with this idea. These words seemed to spawn two more: 'go home'. Where home was didn't matter. It was an idea more than a place. The important thing was that I find some way to go home as soon as possible.

'The novel of development, the Bildungsroman, has a long tradition coming out of the eighteenth and nineteenth centuries. What are some of the conventions of the novel of development, and how are they employed by, say, James Joyce and Virginia Woolf? Maybe you would like to speak about a third novelist of your choice. I'll leave that up to you.' This was Professor Dresser speaking. He spoke in the polished, nasal voice that was common among American academics his age. I answered the question with reasonable success and managed to answer the questions that followed, on T.S. Eliot and modern poetry and the novels of Toni Morrison. At this point, the tension in the room began to relax. I had already failed and now I only needed to fill the silence until the time was up. There were a few more questions from Professor Dresser and a final question from Professor de Rijke, inviting me to take a synoptic view of the matters we had discussed, which I declined.

'Thank you, Mr Byrne,' Professor Choate now said. 'The panel requests that you excuse yourself for fifteen minutes while we discuss your performance. We will inform you of our decision upon your return at,' he consulted his watch, 'half past eleven.'

I stood up, thanked them, and left the room. Sweat was soaking through my shirt at the armpits and my heart was racing. I took the wide steps to the ground floor, walked the red-carpeted corridor to the big double doors and stepped outside. The sun was shining with the first warmth of spring. I was standing in the courtyard where Mia and

I had first met five months earlier. I lit a cigarette and smoked it within seconds. Then I lit a second and turned on my phone. I had a text from her. 'Good luck with the exam today. I think you're going to do well.'

'It went badly,' I wrote.

The word *online* appeared within a few seconds and it soon became the word *typing*. 'Badly how?' she wrote first and then, 'How badly?'

'Terribly,' I wrote.

The *typing* pulsed once and then rested. 'Oh no!' she wrote.

'I think I am done here.'

'Done how?'

'I want to see you.'

There was a pause. The dots moved, stopped, moved again. 'I have to finish my article for PLMA.' I waited. 'So I can't go to Boston.'

'How's it going?'

'But, you can come here?'

'That would be nice,' I wrote. 'You sure?'

A pause. 'Yes!'

'Okay!'

I flicked my cigarette into the shrubbery and checked the time. There were more than ten minutes left to go before I could go back inside, but I decided not to go back at all. I already knew the result and I didn't want to see the professors' faces again. I wanted nothing more to do with this place. I wanted to go to Maine. When I checked the timetable, I saw that I was about to miss the day's only bus and the next one didn't leave until 12 p.m. the following day. So I went to Widener Library and stripped my carrel of its decorations, emptied the contents of the locker into my bag. Decision propelled me home, past the William James building and the Swedenborg Chapel, past the big clapboard houses with their white picket fences. The placid streets looked alive in the way that places do when one rediscovers the finitude of things. Nobody was home. That was to be expected. I always got home first because my flatmates worked harder than I did. I put on The Fall's *I Am Kurious Oranj* at a high volume and quickly drank a beer on the porch. Down in the park, the parents were rooted in their lives, drinking takeaway coffees while their kids in the sandpit spoke with one another using words and grammatical structures exceeding the norm for their age group. The air was alive with the sound of birdsong and clattering from the skate park. I flicked my cigarette into the bucket, went inside and started packing up my room, singing along to the title track. I laid my suitcase open on the floor, threw in some T-shirts, my football boots, my raincoat. I piled the library books into a tall uneven stack on the desk. Into a cardboard box went my tie, the satchel, a copy of the *Harvard Gazette*. Into the box went folders, papers, pages of notes, throat lozenges, batteries, paperclips, pens, all the little trappings of a temporary life. Into the suitcase went a fistful of novels. I unpinned the postcards from the wall – postcards I had bought at the Met and the Boston Museum of Fine Arts with Mia – and tossed them in. 'What are you doing?' Kareena asked, surprising me from the hall.

I turned the music down. 'I'm going home,' I said. 'I'm making a pilgrimage.'

She looked concerned as she scanned her memory for an explanation of my strange mood. 'Oh my god – your exam. How was it?'

'It was good.'

'Oh yay.' She put a hand to her heart.

'It was good in the sense that it went so badly, I was able to accept that the time has come for me to move on.'

'Luca,' she said.

'I'm serious.'

'It wasn't good?'

'It was among the most shameful experiences of my life.'

'Come tell me about it. Stop doing this. Let's go for a drink.'

'I could drink. Just let me finish packing.'

'Why packing? You hate England. Where will you go?'

'Manchester or London. I'll have to see.'

'See what? Luca, this sounds like a bad idea. I don't think you've thought it through.'

'I'm going to Maine first, to see Mia.'

'Really?' Kareena said. 'Now?'

'Tomorrow,' I said. 'Maybe we'll travel together, I don't know.'

'And you're sure she's the person you want to be with right now? You seem a bit manic. You might freak her out.'

'She is the person I want to be with at this moment of profound clarity, yes.' I threw some socks into the suitcase, some into the box. 'You'll be fine,' I said, referring to Kareena's own exams, which were coming up in a few weeks. 'You've done your homework. Shall we go out?'

We picked up a six-pack of beers from Inman Wine and Spirits and headed towards the park, where I tried to describe to her how the exam had gone, but I was too embarrassed to recall the details so my account was rambling and full of omissions. We had taken a seat near the skate park by the time I got to the end.

'Oh, sweetheart,' Kareena said. 'Don't go to Maine. Go back tomorrow and try to fix things. Tell them you're not well. Your behaviour indicates that you're unwell.'

'But I'm fine,' I said. 'I'm not supposed to be here. I don't want to waste my life failing to become an adjunct professor. I want to ride the Greyhound to Maine and walk in a forest with Mia.'

'What will we do about the Haçienda?'

'We can skip over it for now. I can work with what you've given me.'

'I don't want to skip over it. It's important.'

'Just for now. So that we can keep moving forward.'

'Call Darren Walker. He's got a good memory.' Andy took his phone from the table and began to unlock it.

'Andy,' I said, but he ignored me. 'Andy,' I repeated more sternly than I'd intended, as though I were speaking to a child. I expected that he would protest but he said nothing. The phone began to ring but nobody answered. It rang ten or eleven times before he finally hung up. 'Andy,' I said, 'Things will come back to you. We don't need to get it all right now.' He looked at me blankly. For some reason, he couldn't or didn't want to let it go. He appeared distressed as I sought to reassure him that the memories would not simply disappear, that we could leave that episode open and return to it whenever we liked, but that we shouldn't get stuck revisiting the same few impressions unless he really thought they would yield new insights. For ten or fifteen minutes we sat in near silence. I watched Andy as he scanned his memory. His eyes darted left and right. Sometimes he emitted a soft groan or sigh. He said a few words: 'Jennie's cousin.' But my attempts to coax more out of him came to nought.

The next morning, however, Andy greeted my arrival with clarity in his eyes and an impatient rapidity in his movements. No sooner had I sat down than he launched back into his story exactly where we had left it two days earlier.

Back in the office that afternoon with the blinds pulled over the windows to keep out the sun, I listened to Andy's voice through my headphones and wrote:

I left my job at Boddingtons after a year. One of the girls that hung around in Brendan's flat owned a vintage clothing shop in Afflecks Palace and she offered me a job. The money was less than I'd got at the brewery, but life was better. It was a cool young crowd that worked at Afflecks. At lunch, you could go up to the café on the top floor and the girls working there would chat with you. The whole idea behind Afflecks was that for not much money you could rent a space on a weekly contract. That meant you could get a small business up and running without getting into debt. I had been saving up some money to buy a TV since I first moved out but at some point, I realised I no longer wanted a TV so I kept saving until I had a few hundred quid. With this money, I bought a heat transfer press and paid the first four weeks' rent on the cheapest stall I could get, deep inside the maze of corridors on the third floor. I started out by getting old T-shirts from the vintage shop and printing them with a simple design: a smiley face, a Playboy bunny, a Rolling Stones tongue and lips. Nobody cared about copyright. The whole building was full of bootlegged CDs, cassette tapes, VHS tapes. I started by selling these T-shirts and slowly added new lines. After a while, I could afford to buy the blank T-shirts new, wholesale, from a guy in

Ancoats. I started doing band T-shirts. Every few weeks, I'd go to HMV and look at what the top-selling albums were. If any of them had an eye-catching cover, I'd make a T-shirt up and sell them in the shop. I did Nirvana's *Bleach*, Morrissey's *Viva Hate*. I did A Tribe Called Quest and Public Enemy. I didn't have a sign or a good idea for a name so I printed 'Andy's T-Shirts' on a white shirt and hung it up at the entrance to my stall. That became the name of my business: Andy's T-Shirts. After a year or so, I was making more money than I had been at the brewery. It still wasn't much but it was enough to pay the rent and the bills, eat three meals a day, and go out at the weekend. In those days, that was all anyone wanted. My big break came when I started doing T-shirts for gigs. Whoever was playing, I would make up a load of T-shirts with their album covers on the front and sell them outside to the punters coming out of the venue. I did a few in the spring of 1990 and they brought in good money. When Prince played Maine Road in the summer that year, I sold three hundred quid's worth of T-shirts in a night and I could have sold more if I hadn't run out. As time went on, I had more and more T-shirts in stock in the shop, all folded and mounted on the walls. I did the concerts when I could and I started renting a unit in an old mill in Beswick, where I did my printing and kept my stock. Soon, I had to start paying people to help me out. If a load of printing needed doing, I paid someone to look after the shop while I did the printing at the mill. I didn't have any full-time staff and there were no contracts, no tax stuff. It was all informal, laidback, cash-in-hand. 'Would you look after the shop for us on Friday while I do some printing? I'll give you twenty quid.' 1991 was a good year for the concerts. Snap! played GMEX in the spring. Blur played. Nirvana. All the punters wanted T-shirts. You couldn't sell them for much because the quality wasn't as good as the shirts you could buy inside – they were a quid to begin with, two quid, three at most – but you could sell a lot, and steadily. There was never any trouble. Sometimes, a couple of policemen would walk around Afflecks but they were making sure that nobody was selling drugs or guns. They didn't give a shit about bootleg T-shirts. At some of the bigger gigs, big bands playing the arena, where the money was, the police would tell you to move on from time to time but never before you had the chance to sell a load of stock. As the night went on, we lowered the price and whatever we couldn't sell, we sold for next to nothing to clothing companies who could recycle them.

I loved to be busy, loved leaving the shop in the care of a mate and passing between the stalls at Afflecks and their displays: mannequins in vintage clothing, dolls' heads draped with colourful wigs, army surplus gear, the door of a Soviet military plane, earrings, beads, necklaces, arcade games from the 60s, latex and leather, bongs, grinders, lighters, posters, records, dildos, stamps, cigarette cases, a model yeti two metres tall standing in a glass case. I greeted the shopkeepers as I passed, knew them all by name. 'Alright, Frankie; Hello, Tara, darling, how are you?' Some had red hair and lip piercings, some of them were just normal blokes making a bit of money. All of us were in it together; all had each other's backs. I loved walking up Oldham Street, across Great Ancoats Street, and between the mills of Ancoats, most of them empty and disused with windows broken, doors covered in metal panels, outer walls covered with graffiti, because this was 1991 and de-industrialisation had run its course, decimated the city, and the big-money regeneration had not yet begun. The city was falling apart but I loved it because it was mine. I loved to walk along the Rochdale Canal. Even better if it was a crisp winter day with a glazing of frost on the cobbles, a scarf around my neck. I loved the hiss a cigarette made as it hit the thin sheet of ice floating on the canal's surface. I loved to swing my keys on my finger as I crossed the courtyard of Brunswick Mill and climbed the stairs to my floor, walked the dank corridor, let myself into my unit. On the concrete floor, I had lain an old rug by the printer to keep the cold off my feet. The brick walls were falling apart. There was a window of six small panels covered in grime that was a hundred and fifty years in the making and could never have been cleaned. I had a table, upon which stood a kettle, a mug, a tin of coffee, and an ashtray full of butts. I liked to think about all the work that had been done in the room long before I was born, when it was full of spinning mules, where people stood for twelve hours at a time, spinning cotton, building the city I loved and where I now stood, bent over the transfer press, printing Simply Red T-shirts for a gig at GMEX in January 1992, getting richer with each one I printed and closer to my dreams: my own house, a family, a life that was all mine. I liked to think that the workers who span the cotton would be happy if they could see me pressing the Simply Red logo onto a T-shirt, if they knew that Central Railway Station was now a gathering place for thousands of people who would dance and sing along to music. Could they ever have imagined it? I felt like the future belonged to me, to my generation, and the things we cared about: music, dancing, doing shit our own way.

In the summer of 1992, I met Kelly Hooper, the love of my life. Just before my twenty-first birthday, I moved into a flat on Tib Street. In the 80s, nobody wanted to live in the city centre and hardly anyone did, but now stuff was starting to happen again and living in town seemed exciting. I had a flat above one of the sex shops, a two-minute walk to Afflecks and a ten-minute walk to my unit in the mill. Kelly spent a lot of time at the flat and made it feel like a home. I wanted more than anything to have a big family. I would have had ten kids if I could have and I wanted them to grow up in a big house with food in the cupboards and a mum and dad who loved them. Kelly wasn't against the idea but she wasn't ready yet. I had grown up too fast whereas she was still young in her heart. Everything else was set, I had never been happier, and I decided it was time to track down my dad.

At that point, all I knew was his name and that he lived in London. I'd always wanted to know who my dad was. I believed it was possible that he simply didn't know I existed or else that he did and had no idea how to find me. I had looked him up in the phone book but there were so many Frank Bartons in London and even if I decided to call every single one, how would I determine which was the right one? Being a man about town as I was in those days, I knew all kinds of people and one weekend, I was drinking in the Albert in Rusholme the evening after a City game when I was introduced to a private investigator named Dennis Aspinall, a Brummie with a mane of white hair and a goatee, who said that he would be able to track down Mr Barton easily and, because I seemed like a decent bloke, would do so for a reduced fee of a hundred pounds. That was no small sum to me, even now that I was making steady money, but in truth, I would have paid much more. I agreed, paid this man half the fee upfront, and never heard from him again.

Now Val's voice interrupted the recording: 'Are you telling him about the one who stole your money?' There was some clattering as she placed our sandwiches on the table. Cheese and butter on white sliced bread with some crisps and lettuce on the side and two glasses of purple squash. In the office at Jem and Brenda's house, I took a sip of my tea.

'What a scumbag,' she said.

'Scumbag,' Andy repeated.

In the recording, I thanked Val for the sandwiches and Andy carried on speaking, chewing a sandwich as he did, which meant that I had to keep pausing and rewinding, listening to everything he said several times before I could understand. He went on:

'After that, everyone knew that I was looking for a private investigator. Darren Walker's brother introduced me to one and he found my dad. It took him less than a week. Darren came to my shop with a bit of paper that said— wait, I've got it.'

An extended period of rustling and clattering followed, interrupted by a loud tapping when I touched my phone, probably to check my notifications because I was bored or anxious; usually, I was both. Andy had opened the shoebox on the table and from it, produced a sheet of paper torn from a telephone pad branded with the logo of the Grafton Hotel, on which was written: Frank Barton, Flat 77, Granville Court, N1 5SP, London. 071 724 2441. I could hear my pen copying the words.

'What did you do?' I said.

'I called the number.'

'And what happened?'

'He answered the phone and I said, "Is that Frank Barton?" And he said, "Yeah." I said, "This is your son." And he said, "Which one?" I said, "One you don't know about. Andrew."'

'How did he take it?' I asked.

Now he imitated the sound his father made, a weary, apathetic sigh that I struggled for some time to render in words. I said I wanted to meet him, Andy went on, and he said okay. I would have to go to London. He said he didn't have any money and I said I didn't mind. I just wanted to meet him. I said I could come the next weekend and he said, alright, can you meet me at Alfredo's café on the Essex Road? Half past twelve on Saturday? We'll have lunch. I said yes and that was it.

The next Saturday, I left Kelly in charge of the shop and took the train from Piccadilly to Euston. I was more nervous than I'd been in years. I kept going to the toilet to piss and to check myself over, make sure that I looked smart. Each time I opened the door, I was surprised to see myself wearing a suit – I had bought it in the Corn Exchange the day before – and my own face freshly shaved, which made me look so young that I felt an unexpected tenderness towards myself. I chain-smoked throughout the whole journey and had to buy another pack of cigarettes when I stepped off the train at Euston. Overwhelmed by the commuters and traffic on Euston Road, I took a long time to find the right bus stop and when I found it, I suddenly needed to shit so badly that I had to run back into the station and find a toilet. When I finally stepped onto the

73 bus, I asked the driver to give me a shout when we got to Essex Road. 'Where on Essex Road?' the driver said and I said I didn't know. I expected to see landmarks I recognised but I didn't see anything, just busy roads, shops, pubs. Wherever I stood, I seemed to be in someone's way and when a seat finally became available, the driver shouted that we'd arrived. I stepped off the open section at the back of the bus – how novel even in these circumstances – and asked an old lady if she knew where Alfredo's café was. She said, right there, love, and pointed across the street. As I waited to cross at the lights by Islington Green, I remembered that I was going to meet my dad and my stomach lurched.

I pushed open the door and looked around. At one table, four builders were eating sandwiches and talking at a high volume. At another, two old ladies were sharing a pot of tea. A few smaller tables were occupied by lone men reading newspapers over empty plates and I examined them carefully. 'Are you alright, love?' the waitress asked. My mouth was so dry that I could hardly sputter out the words. I ordered a cup of tea, sat down at a small table, and resumed my looking at one of the lone men. He wore a baby blue shirt with the top few buttons undone and he was making notes in a diary or address book. I looked at him until he looked back and as soon as he did, I looked away. It wasn't my dad. I watched the door, my heart rate shooting up every time it opened and after fifteen long minutes, my dad walked in. It was his cautious way of looking around that first gave him away – it was clear that he didn't know who he was looking for – but then I saw the resemblance. His jaw was stronger and wider set than mine, but he had the same high cheekbones and the same brown eyes. Only he looked weaker, less sure of his step. He was wearing a shabby brown suit and thick-rimmed glasses. His hair was thinning. He looked like the sort of bloke you saw hanging around at the greyhound track in Belle Vue and he was much older than I had imagined. My heart was pounding so forcefully that I thought I wouldn't be able to speak. My dad walked across to the table and said, 'Is it Andrew?' We shook hands and my dad sat down.

'My name is Andrew David Barton,' I said. 'My mother was Anne Marie Docherty and I believe you are my father.'

'Right,' Frank said. He was breathing heavily as though the walk had tired him out. 'Well, my name is Frank Barton and yes, that sounds like it could be right. I remember Anne Marie. She was a lovely girl.'

'She passed away,' I said.

'Oh, dear. That's unfortunate. Bless her heart.'

I asked Frank what he could tell me about the circumstances of their meeting and he said that he would try to remember as much as he could, but that perhaps they should order first as it could take a while for the food to arrive on Saturdays. He caught the eye of a waitress and ordered a full English breakfast. I ordered the same.

'We met at the nightclub there by the cathedral,' Frank said.

'The Twisted Wheel.'

'Right, that's the one. I remember we had a dance together and then she spent the night at my place.'

'Was I conceived that night?'

'Well,' Frank said. 'I'm not quite sure. We saw each other a few times, see.'

'Were you an item?'

161

'I wouldn't say that, no. We saw each other four or five times.'

'Why did it end?'

'I don't quite remember,' Frank said. 'Sometimes it just does, doesn't it? Do you have a girlfriend yourself?' I showed him the picture of Kelly I kept in my wallet and he made an approving noise. 'I wish I could remember more.'

'Did you know she was pregnant?'

'No. I don't believe I was aware of that. It probably wasn't long before I came home anyway. When were you born?'

'Fifteenth of August 1971.'

'Right, yes, well. I moved back to London in March of seventy-one.'

'Why did you leave?'

'I was offered a better job,' my dad said. 'I was working on the production line for Kellogg's up there and a friend of mine said he could get me a job at Wall's sausages on almost twice the wages so I packed up and moved. What about you? How has your life been?'

I told him that my life had not been easy. I told him about my mum dying and about being taken into foster care. I told him about working at Boddingtons and then moving to the vintage shop but I stopped myself before I said anything about the shop. Instead, I summed up my story by saying, 'I'm on my feet now. I've got my own place and I'm financially independent. Don't worry, I've not come to you looking for handouts.' My dad laughed off the remark and turned away, perhaps bashfully, I thought. What led me to say this must have been the same idea that had caused me to keep my mouth shut about the T-shirt business; namely, that my dad might have agreed to meet up because he wanted money from me. The thought had not even crossed my mind before but now I gave it strong consideration. This man did not look well-off and there was a weakness about him, though it pained me to recognise it. If I had met him in another context, I would not have had a good impression.

'I'm sorry to hear that, son,' he said.

'Son?' I said on the recording. 'He called you son?'

'He called me son,' Andy said. 'I didn't know if it was just what he called younger people, you know how everyone used to. If an old feller spoke to you, he called you son.'

'How did you feel?'

'Emotional. I said, "It's alright, Dad. It's not your fault." And he said, "No, I suppose not."'

'Wasn't it?'

'I don't know,' Andy said. 'What could he do? He didn't know about me.'

There was a long silence on the recording – only room sound and muffled traffic from Moss Lane – before I said, 'What happened next?'

'He asked me what I was hoping to get from seeing him. I said, "First of all, I want to know who my dad is. Second, I want to have a relationship, if you do as well."'

'I'm afraid I might not be much good for a relationship,' my dad said. 'I'm quite poorly, see.'

'I don't mind. If you want to be my dad, I'll be your son.'

'That's very kind of you, Andrew.'

I asked if he had any other children and he said that he did, four in fact. He said that he didn't see them very often and I asked him why. 'They don't want to for one reason or another.'

'Do you live with anyone? Do you have a wife?'

'No,' Frank said. 'It's just me now.'

I asked my dad to tell me about my family history. Who were my parents, who were my grandparents? Frank said that the Bartons were Londoners and had lived and worked in the East End for as long as anyone could remember. The same was true for the Drapers, his mother's family. His parents had both passed away and he wasn't in touch with any of his brothers and sisters, though he did have some and, as far as he knew, they were still alive. As I took in these details, a sense of horror crept over me. All week, I had been steeling myself for a combative encounter where my dad refused to answer my questions. If this happened, I'd promised myself I wouldn't waver. I would demand answers. But my dad answered all my questions willingly. There was just nothing there. I had always believed that although I felt alone in life, somewhere a family was waiting for me; a dad was longing to know about me; brothers and sisters were waiting to take me in and treat me as one of their own; perhaps two grandparents were even waiting for another grandchild who would join them for Sunday dinners. I had not prepared myself for the eventuality that my dad would be even more alone than I was.

The waitress brought us two breakfasts of sausage, egg, bacon, beans, tomato, mushrooms, and four rounds of toast. As she set his plate on the table before him, the steam rose up and clouded Frank's glasses and when he removed them, I saw myself in my dad's face. From the nose upwards, this man had the same face as me, not only the contours of my cheeks but the same animation. I couldn't take my eyes away from this face that was more like my own than any I had ever seen. What did it have to tell me? Something about who I was. My dad looked away as he ate, chewing methodically, swallowing with discomfort. I myself had no appetite at first but then, when I began to eat, I realised that I was starving. My dad remarked on the quality of the food and I agreed that it was good. Otherwise, we said nothing until both of us had finished eating. Even then, we were silent a while longer.

'What have you got planned for your trip to London then? Have you been down before? Need any tips?'

I asked him what he recommended, though I had no interest in sightseeing. I was only trying to conceal my disappointment.

'I don't get out and about so much anymore,' Frank said. 'But of course, there's Buckingham Palace and the Houses of Parliament. Trafalgar Square. All that stuff.' The waitress cleared our plates and we sat a while longer. Frank lit a Benson and Hedges. 'It was good of you to get in touch. If you have any more questions, I'll be happy to answer them to the best of my abilities.'

'But you don't want to have a relationship?'

'I don't think I have it in me.'

We shook hands on the street outside. He must have been able to tell that I was feeling sad because the last thing he said to me was, 'Chin up, Andrew.' I didn't go sightseeing. My visit to London lasted a total of three hours and I caught the train back to Piccadilly feeling sick to my stomach, feeling as though the bottom had been taken out of me and everything was sinking limitlessly and would keep sinking for as long as I lived.

'Maybe that would be a good place to pause for today,' my voice now said on the recording, which I was listening to for the fourth time today. 'We've done a lot.'

There was a long pause, perhaps because Andy was chewing. 'Fine,' he said.

This was followed by the muffled sound of me packing things into a bag and saying goodbye before the recording stopped.

'Do you think it will be a good book?' Mel asked me that evening. We were sitting at the table by the window, watching the reflection of the sunset in the new skyscrapers across the roundabout while Tom prepared dinner in the kitchen.

'I had my doubts at first. I was sticking closely to everything he said and the text read like a transcript, but the more time we spend together, the freer I feel to put my own spin on it. So yes, I do.'

'I'm glad to hear that,' Mel said. 'I wasn't sure whether it would be a good fit. But he seems really happy. He was in this afternoon, telling everyone about it.'

'You saw him today? What did he say?'

'He said he was writing his book and it was going to be a bestseller.'

'Did he say anything about me?'

'He said he likes you. I asked him what he thought of you and he said, "He's sound," and gave me a thumbs-up.'

'Was that it?'

'Yeah,' Mel said. 'He seemed happy.'

Tom set the table with three bowls of gazpacho, a dish of ceviche, a warm salad of squash and brown lentils, some buttered sourdough bread, and a bottle of cold white wine.

'Nice stuff.'

'He just got a pay rise,' Mel said.

'Did you?' Tom sipped some soup from his spoon and nodded. 'Congratulations.'

He went to pour me a glass of wine and I stopped him. 'Not drinking?'

'Haven't had one since the night I came home,' I raised a glass of mineral water. 'Something had to change.'

'Good decision,' Tom said. 'You're a pain in the arse when you're drunk.' As we clinked glasses, Tom looked at me forcefully as he always did, as though it fell to him to remind me that I was supposed to look him in the eyes. It was a constant point of contention between us that I thought he observed rituals and customs too closely, while he thought that I didn't observe them closely enough.

I sprinkled salt into the cold soup and wondered how much money Tom was now making. A few years ago, I'd always had a rough idea, but not anymore.

'It's good,' Mel said.

'It is.'

'Any thoughts about what you're going to do, workwise?' He placed the stress on *you're* as though our talking about his work offered a natural segue towards my own situation.

'What do you mean?'

'How are you going to make a living?'

'I'm writing this book. I hope that it will lead to more opportunities.'

'What, do all his mates want books too? Will you become a bestselling ghostwriter of misery memoirs?'

'There's probably decent money in it,' Mel said. 'People love reading books about overcoming childhood trauma. And people want to talk but feel they can't. I bet there are thousands of people like Andy who want to tell their stories. They would never go to therapy because of the stigma but they still want someone to listen to them and recognise what they've been through. You could set it up as a business. They tell themselves they're writing a book but secretly they're doing therapy.' She laughed. 'I mean, obviously it would be better if they saw a qualified professional rather than you, but you would be better than nothing.'

'The problem,' Tom said to Mel, 'is that he thinks he's above it. He loves the working classes in theory but not in practice. He holds these kinds of people and their tastes in contempt and he wouldn't be able to hide it.'

'Andy's not working class,' I interjected. 'He doesn't have a job.'

'Irrelevant. You would want them all to write experimental, modernist novels and then sulk when they didn't want to. Isn't that true?'

'No. It's not.'

'It is,' he said.

'Not anymore. I'm beginning to see things from a new perspective.'

'The perspective of a person who can no longer afford to consider themselves above the concerns of regular people?'

'I understand the point you're making,' I said. 'It's a good materialist argument. I approve of it.'

'You know what he wants, don't you? Have you ever read a footballer's autobiography? Have you read a celebrity hardback?'

'I know what they're like.'

'You don't.'

'I do. Anyway, why does it have to be like that? Has he told you that's what he wants? He's paying me to help him find the appropriate form for his ideas and experiences. That form might turn out to be more interesting than a celebrity autobiography.'

'See,' Tom said with a self-satisfied smile. 'You can't help it. You want to teach him, don't you? Have you got him reading bits of *Ulysses*?'

'Why don't you just ask him what he wants it to be like?' Mel said.

'Of course. In the end, I'll be guided by him. I'm going to give him some samples to look at.'

'Like carpet samples?' Tom said.

'Yeah.'

'I think it's a good idea,' Mel said. 'You take the samples to the new customers and say, "You can have your life story in one of these styles." Can't you see it?' she said to Tom.

'I don't see him starting a business full stop.'

'I can see it,' she said while Tom took the dishes to the kitchen.

He returned a moment later with a tub of ice cream and three bowls. 'I forgot to defrost this,' he sat down and dug out a few rock-hard balls. 'You won't see us for a couple weeks now. It's my dad's day on Sunday, so we're getting together with the family.'

'Then we're off to Wales, aren't we?' Mel said.

'Cousin Jake's caravan in Anglesey,' Tom added for my benefit.

'What do you do on those days?'

'Which days?'

'With your family.'

'Well, I visit his grave. Then we all get together at my uncle's house and remember him, tell stories, have a lot of food.'

'Right.' I grimaced as the cold ice cream hurt my molars. I thought of Tom's big family getting together and then of Tom and Mel spending two weeks in a caravan in Anglesey and I didn't know whether the sensation that took hold of me was jealousy or disdain. Would I have liked to spend two weeks in a caravan with a partner? The thought seemed impossible and perhaps it was the sense that my life had drifted away from those of everyone I knew that caused my bitterness.

Mel might have noticed this because with an empathetic tone and a cautious glance away from her ice cream, she said, 'Do you think you'll try and meet someone?'

I didn't know what to say in response. Of course, I didn't want to be alone for ever, but I felt that my personality had fallen into a state of disrepair and that putting it back together would take a long time. Before I could answer, Tom raised an eyebrow as though a thought had just occurred to him. 'Have you heard from Mia yet?'

'No,' I said and Tom shook his head. 'What?'

'Poor conduct.'

'I'm no better. Anyway, she's getting her head together.'

'No excuse.' Tom dug his spoon through a tough chunk of ice cream and seemed glad of his judgement. The sun had set and the sky over the city had turned to streaky black.

'Luca,' my dad says, leaning on my arm more heavily than he means to. 'Look here now.' He reaches across my small body to place a finger on the window and his breath is hot and heavy with the smell of alcohol. 'Look.' The window is too condensed for me to see anything but diffuse streetlights streaking the darkness. 'You can't see anything. Can you stop?' he says to the driver. 'Stop, please.'

'You want me to stop here?' The driver has already slowed the car down and is twisting his neck to call back to us.

'Yeah, if you wouldn't mind. Just for a second so I can show him this.' The driver pulls in beside the kerb and keeps the engine running. He checks the rear-view mirror, but the street is deserted. My dad, leaning across me all the while, fumbles with the control in the door handle until the window lowers all the way in one motion and the cold air comes blowing into the taxi. We're looking across the street at the front of the Church of St Francis, whose gothic arches are so deep that I can't see the doors within them, only blackness. 'Tilt your head,' my dad says, returning to an upright position in his seat. I lean forward and tilt my head until I can see the tall stained-glass windows between the flying buttresses leading up to the spire, which sits obscured by darkness several hundred feet above. Then I sit up and turn to face him, smiling because the height of the building has impressed me somewhat and I want him to see the look on my face, but as soon as I lock eyes with him I understand that the height of the building is not the point. He places a hand on the empty seat in front of him and says, 'Thank you, mate.'

'All good, boss?' the driver says.

'All good,' my dad says as the driver pulls out and shifts through the gears. 'I just wanted to show him that.' He slurs the final word. Now he looks at me and says, 'The people who communed in that church in the 1870s had a spiritual connection to the world that nobody in this city has today – except for maybe the Muslims by your grandmother's house and the Orthodox Jews up in Crumpsall and maybe a few artists and musicians, but I doubt even the best of them can match the depth of feeling that you would have found in a parochial church on a Sunday in 1875. It's not even the most beautiful building. Go to Cologne, go to Ulm, go see the Alhambra. They make that church look like the Arndale centre. But it's not a question of beauty. It's about remembering there was a time when people took their lives seriously and didn't scoff at everything that strived towards something bigger than themselves. And it was left to go derelict. Some wankers bought it and said they were going to turn it into flats for other wankers but they just pillaged it for scrap and then left it for the junkies. They sold the organ for scrap. Can you imagine sitting in there and listening to the St Matthew Passion on the original Wadsworth? I would have liked to have shown you that.' He has lost himself in his monologue and now seems to remember that I am listening. 'You're not bothered, are you?' he says. 'You're not bothered.' He shakes his head and appears to become preoccupied, but

I can't tell whether he is disappointed with me for being too young to understand or if he's embarrassed with himself. Both of us look ahead as we join Ashton Old Road. There is no traffic and the driver accelerates towards the city centre. 'Busy tonight?' my dad says.

'Quiet,' the driver says. 'Very quiet. Cold. Week before payday.'

My dad ponders this remark with a stoic expression, as though to allow its profundity room to breathe. 'Your Aunt Deirdre's full of shit sometimes,' he says to me. 'You have to take what she says with a pinch of salt. She knows as well as I do that your grandad was a selfish cunt but she likes to defend him. Your Uncle Darragh's the same.'

We join the traffic on the Mancunian Way and he falls silent, though I can tell that he is brooding, turning things over in his head, and I clutch the door handle and keep my back straight, my eyes on the traffic ahead of us, as though it will reduce the chance of my annoying him. A few minutes later, I sense that his mood has softened and as we approach the Deansgate Interchange, he turns away from the side window and says, 'Do you mind if we stop at Boozy Busters?'

'Yeah, no worries, boss,' says the driver and the indicator begins to tick as we approach Chorlton Road.

'Do you want something, Luca?' my dad says when we pull up outside the off-licence. He seems to be in an appeasing mood. I say no and he opens the door and clambers out, using his walking stick to support his weight as he stumbles towards the door. Through the shop windows, between the shelving units and posters, I can see his figure moving around as he gathers his purchases and chats with the man behind the counter. Then he emerges with a packed carrier bag dangling from one hand. 'I got you something just in case,' he says when he climbs back in. I look at the bag between his feet but I can't make out the contents. 'Anywhere here is fine,' my dad says when we pull into his street. 'I'm just before that wheelie bin.' He hands the driver £10 and tells him to keep the change. Then he gets out with his walking stick in his left hand and the carrier bag in his right, fumbles with his keys for a while, and lets us into the house.

It's cold in the hallway and the air is damp. My dad flicks the switch on the wall and the bare bulb dangling from the ceiling fills the hall with harsh light. He puts his walking stick down by the door and loses his balance right away, his legs wobbling, I think, with spasticity rather than drunkenness. He places his right hand on the wall until he's steady and then proceeds to push open the door to the living room. 'Let's go in here and get comfortable, shall we?' I follow him in. A print hangs on the wall above the fireplace, a reproduction of a sombre historical painting. 'That's new,' my dad says as he falls heavily onto the sofa and begins unpacking the contents of his carrier bag onto the coffee table. 'It was looking a bit bare in here.' He takes out a litre bottle of Bombay Sapphire, a bottle of tonic water, a twenty-pack of Marlboro Lights, and two bottles of Blue WKD. 'They're for you,' he says. 'There's a bottle opener in the kitchen. Can you get me a glass while you're there? And some ice.'

I go to the kitchen, fetch a glass from the shelf and the bottle opener from the top drawer. I open the freezer but the ice tray is empty. 'It doesn't matter,' my dad says when I return to the front room. He pours himself a large measure of gin and tops it up with tonic water. Then he picks up one of the bottles of WKD and opens it for me. It's sweet and artificial with an aftertaste of ethanol that lingers on my tongue and seems to exert a pressure on the top of my head.

'Shall I make a fire?' my dad says. He begins to lower himself to the floor, where he takes a few pieces of wood and arranges them on the grate, before stacking some coal from the scuttle and laying it on top with some more wood and then stuffing the structure with kindling and scrunches of newspaper, looking strangely steady and sober all the while. When it's done, he takes the box of Cook's matches from the hearth, strikes one, and lights an end of paper. A tall flame climbs the scrunch and disappears beneath the kindling, where it turns to smoke. My dad watches as the pile catches light and takes a sip of his drink. 'Do you like that?' he asks me, nodding at the drink in my hand. 'Here, let's put some music on.' He appears to consider standing and instead chooses to drag himself to the corner where the CD player stands. 'What shall we listen to?'

'Green Day?'

'No, no. There's a time and a place for that but it's not now.' He picks up a stack of CDs and examines them one by one: Beck, Radiohead, Alabama 3. 'Let's listen to The Smiths,' he says. 'It's about time you got into The Smiths.' He replaces the CD in the player with *The Queen Is Dead* then heaves himself onto his feet, loses balance, and places a hand on the wall as the voices of the music hall intro begin to sing. 'Don't laugh,' he says.

'I was laughing at the music.'

'Don't laugh at the music.'

The kindling has caught fire and flames lick at the wood. My dad stops to look at it for a moment. 'Here,' he has regained his balance and is making his way towards the sofa, where he falls heavily and tops up his drink with more gin and tonic. 'Wait. Now.' He points to the CD player as the drums begin. 'This is a masterpiece,' he says, slurring the long word. 'I'm going to roll a little spliff.' From the biscuit tin on the table, he takes a packet of king-size Rizla, spreads some tobacco along one, and sprinkles it with weed from his zip-lock bag. He does all of this with deft, easy motions and rolls the contents into a tidy-looking spliff. 'Look at that,' he says, holding it up for me to inspect. 'Do you want some of this?'

I shake my head.

'Go easy on that.' He points at the drink. 'It's not pop. You're supposed to sip it.' He puts the spliff in his mouth, lights it and exhales. 'That's nice. We should have just stayed home and chilled out tonight, eh? Listened to some music and ordered a curry. What do you think of this?' He points to the stereo and I shrug. 'You'll get it when you're older. Listen to that guitar.' Now we listen in a concentrated way, him pointing at the stereo, me looking. 'This came out a few years before you were born. I was living in a squat on the Holloway Road and working on my PhD. I had a great little record player in my room. I must have listened to this a hundred times in the first month alone.'

'Like me with *Take Off Your Pants and Jacket.*'

'Exactly. Imagine that but better. Because this is a better album. I know you don't think so now but when you're older you'll agree with me. I'm not being a dick. There is objectivity in aesthetic matters. The Smiths are ten times better than Blink-182, Mendelssohn is seven times better than The Smiths, and Bach is seven times better than Mendelssohn. The numbers aren't exact but the spirit—'

He takes a long drag on the spliff. 'And better because I was twenty-five and all day I was reading Coleridge and Wordsworth and Goethe and loads of fucking great stuff, and in the evening, I was in my room with a girl, sharing a smoke and listening to this masterpiece. It doesn't really get better than that.' He leans back into the sofa and looks into the fire, which is crackling and spitting and beginning to warm the room, and for a few minutes we listen to the music.

'Are there any girls you like in school?'

I make a show of embarrassment.

'Go on,' he says, 'you can tell me.'

'There's one,' I say. 'Georgina.'

'Georgina. That's a nice name. What's she like?'

'She's nice.'

'Is she pretty?'

I nod. He stubs out the spliff in the ashtray on the table and says, 'You know what's happening to me, don't you? This disease. Can I tell you about it?' He picks up the remote and turns the volume down, so that his voice doesn't have to compete with the music. 'I want to tell you about it so you understand. The disease attacks the central nervous system. The simple explanation is that we're full of tiny, connected nerve cells and life – basically all of this, everything we know and feel and do – at least from one perspective, is just electricity travelling up and down these cells, sending images and sensations and sounds and all kinds of information. That's not the way I used to think about it, but I sort of have to now. Most of these cells, a lot of the most important ones, are in the brain and the spinal cord. They all have little covers that control how fast the information travels and for some reason, in my case, those covers are damaged so the nerves inside them are exposed. These things are so small you can't even see them. They're just part of the mush inside us, but they're important. I'm still trying to get my head around all this. But it means I'm not myself. There's a lot happening inside me that I don't understand and can't control. And it affects everything. Not just movement. It's going to affect my memory and maybe my speech one day. My mood. Is that alright? I wish I could do something about it but I can't and I want you to understand.'

I say that I understand and that he doesn't need to apologise.

'Thank you,' he says. 'Thank you.' He takes a Marlboro from the packet and lights it. 'I love you,' he says.

'I love you, too.'

We stop talking and listen to 'I Know It's Over' in silence. 'If you ever start thinking I'm too much of a miserable bastard,' my dad says, 'remember Morrissey and be grateful you didn't end up with him. Do you promise me you'll do that? I'm sorry I'm such a miserable bastard. I wouldn't be if I could help it. But at least I'm not as bad as him.'

'You know I wasn't always this way? I was happy for a time. I wish you could have known me then. When I was in my late twenties, when I was working on my thesis, around the time I met your mother. The first year we spent in America was the best of my life. It's easier to be happy in America than it is here. Nobody's really happy here. I was teaching and writing my thesis and we were living in your mum's studio flat. That was before the little Person from Porlock came along.' He looks at me with a teasing smile. 'I'm just pulling your leg. It just wasn't the best time for your mother and after she quit her doctorate she didn't have any money, so we had to come back here.'

He nods to the fireplace. 'You can put some more wood on that.' I go down on my knees and drop a few pieces onto the burning pile. 'Not too many,' he says. 'That'll do.' The wood is burning brightly and the coals are beginning to glow. I stay by the fire and warm my hands. A nervous excitement spreads through my skull, though I don't know whether it's because of the alcohol, the sugar, or the second-hand smoke. 'Nice, isn't it?' my dad says. 'That fire is my favourite thing about this house.' When the next track begins he picks up the remote and skips forward. 'I love this song.' We listen together. 'You know the cemetery he's singing about is the one near your mum's.'

'Really?' I say.

'Really, but the poets he's singing about aren't buried there. Keats is buried in Rome and Wilde is buried in Paris. I don't know where Yeats is buried, probably in Ireland. You could do a grand tour of Europe just visiting cemeteries. Would you like to do that?' I say yes, though I find it hard to imagine because we have only been on one trip together, to Blackpool. 'Once I get this disease under control and before it gets too bad, if I can get some money together, we could do something like that. We could go to Venice. The most beautiful cemetery in the world is in Venice. It's an island all of its own and you have to go by boat. I went out there alone, early one morning in the summer of 1981. When I die, see if you can smuggle my body out to St Michael's cemetery in Venice.' The song ends and my dad picks up the remote and presses pause. 'That's where the first side of the vinyl ended. Now you would just hear the needle until you got up and flipped the record over.' He raises a finger as though we could hear the sound together, but there's only the crackling of the fire.

'Shall we go and see Jerome across the street?' I don't know what to say. I had thought that I might soon go to bed, but now he pauses the music and stands up, his body full of excitement as it always is when we are going out. He goes to the hallway and stumbles back into the living room wearing his leather jacket and carrying his walking stick. He puts his smoking materials into the pockets and picks up his bottle of gin. 'Come on,' he says. I put on my jacket and shoes and follow my dad out the door. He pulls it to and then pushes it to make sure it's locked. We walk along the middle of the street and I look into the front window of the derelict house opposite my dad's while he walks a few paces ahead, towards the dead-end of the cul-de-sac where Jerome lives. When we get to the door, my dad presses the doorbell and knocks three times. A moment later we can see Jerome through the windowpanes in the door.

'Hello, Paul,' he says when he opens the door. 'Hello, Luca. How are you, mate?'

'We were just wondering if you fancied a smoke,' my dad says.

Jerome looks somewhat surprised but shows us an accommodating smile and says, 'Yeah, sure, why not? Come in.' As he opens the door more fully to invite us inside, he looks at me again and sees the open bottle of WKD in my hand. His eyes widen with alarm and he hesitates for a moment. 'Come in,' he says again and we follow him through the hall and into the living room. The ceiling light is on so the room is brightly lit and a large television stands on a unit by the window. 'I'm watching the snooker,' he says, picking up the remote to turn the volume down. 'Have a seat, guys.' He points to the sofa, which is covered with a patterned throw. 'I was just making a brew. Do you want one?' We both say no and my dad asks for a glass. Jerome walks through to the back room, where the kettle is boiling. My dad has sat down on one end of the sofa and is watching the snooker on the TV with an absent look. I sit down next to him and a moment later Jerome returns holding a cup of tea and a glass of ice for my dad. 'Do you like the snooker?'

'My dad played snooker,' my dad says. 'I'm prejudiced against it.'

'Did he, yeah? I don't really follow it. I just have it on sometimes. I find it weirdly relaxing.' He laughs warmly.

My dad has taken his tobacco and papers out of his jacket pocket and says, 'Shall I roll one?'

'Yeah, sure,' Jerome says. 'Use mine if you like.' He points at a margarine tub on the table and my dad dismisses the offer with a wave. He looks at the bottle in my hand. With a strained smile he asks, 'How old are you now, Luca?'

'Eleven,' I say.

'Is your daughter around?' my dad says. He is concentrating on his rolling and seems not to have noticed this exchange.

'She's at her mum's this weekend.' He watches my dad struggling and says, 'I can roll it if you like.'

'Go on,' my dad says. 'You make them nice.'

Jerome takes the materials from his hand, rolls them into a spliff, and hands it back to my dad to light.

'How are you, Jerome? What's going on?'

'Nothing, nothing.' He leans back for a moment with

his hands cradling the back of his head. 'I've just been working all week and then taking it easy.' I can tell that he is feigning an easy manner, that he is preoccupied by our presence, but my dad doesn't seem to notice. He has closed his eyes as he drags and exhales.

'What about you?' Jerome says.

My dad passes the spliff to Jerome. 'We were at my sister's in Gorton. He was playing with his cousin.'

'Have a few drinks?'

'We had dinner, had a few drinks.'

Jerome takes a few short, shallow drags and passes it back to my dad. He looks at one of us and then the other, back and forth.

'We were listening to The Smiths just now. Do you like The Smiths?'

'Not really.' Jerome smiles. 'Not my cup of tea. He always seemed like' – he gives me a naughty look – 'always seemed like a bit of a knob. Not for me, let's say. Did you like it, Luca?'

'It was okay,' I say.

'Okay,' my dad says with a tut. He shakes his head at Jerome conspiratorially. My dad tops up his gin and, for a few minutes, we all pretend to watch the snooker.

'Do you mind if I use the lav?' My dad gets up with difficulty and wobbles on his feet.

'No, of course,' Jerome says as my dad makes his way towards the hall, using the doorframe to steady himself. 'Will you be alright on the stairs?' Jerome calls to him but he doesn't respond. We can hear him going up slowly, using his hands as well as his feet. When he reaches the landing at the top and closes the bathroom door, Jerome turns to me and says, 'Is your mum at home?'

'I think so.'

'Do you know your phone number?'

I recite it for him as he takes the cordless phone from the windowsill. He asks me to repeat the number and then walks into the back room. After a minute, I hear his low voice speaking into the phone. My dad flushes the toilet and begins to make his way down the stairs. He and Jerome reappear at the same time. 'Shall we go home, Luca?' my dad says. 'Leave Jerome to watch the snooker.' He doesn't seem to notice the cordless phone in Jerome's hand. Jerome insists that we don't need to leave, but it's clear that he feels relieved. 'No, we don't want to overstay our welcome. Come on, son,' my dad says and I follow him into the hall.

'Good to see you, guys,' Jerome says. He is looking at me and seems unsure of what to say.

'Good to see you,' my dad says. 'Take care of yourself.'

He is stumbling heavily now, holding the gin bottle in his left hand and using the walking stick to keep his balance. 'I don't think he was in the mood tonight,' he says as he hands me the keys to open the front door. In the living room, the coals emit a gentle light. 'Would you get my tonic water from the fridge?' my dad says. 'There's bread and cheese and stuff if you're hungry.' When I come back, he hasn't turned the lights on and is sitting on the floor by the stereo, leafing through a pile of CDs. 'Here, I've been wanting to play this for you.' He places *The Queen Is Dead* face up on one speaker, and replaces it with Philip Glass's *Metamorphosis*. It seems that he is about to stand up but he changes his mind, choosing instead to rest against the wall as the two, low alternating notes begin. 'Can you pour me a drink?' he says and, while his eyes are closed, I fill the glass with tonic and just a splash of gin. 'Listen,' he says as he takes it from my hand. He wants me to hear the sad, high notes of the motif. 'Listen to that.' We listen. 'It's based on a story by Franz Kafka about a man who wakes up one day to discover that he's an insect. Before that day, his whole family had depended on him to work and pay off their debts. Now they're ashamed of him. He stays in his room and tries to speak with them through the door but they can't understand him. They don't understand what he's saying. When they see him, they're disgusted. They can't understand what's happened to him and he doesn't understand it himself, but he has to live with it. He has no choice. His boss comes and tries to get him to go back to work but when he sees what he's become, he runs away. So he stays in his room but then he can't even do that because they turn it into storage. One day, he tries to leave and his dad is so disgusted by the sight of him that he throws apples at him. That's the saddest thing in all of literature, the bastard dad throwing apples at his helpless insect son. One of the apples gets lodged in his back, in a tender spot beneath his shell, and wounds him.' He turns to the side and points to a spot between his ribs. 'Eventually, the insect realises that nobody loves him, not even his closest family, and he lies down and dies.' He slouches against the wall. The room is dark but his face nevertheless displays his unabashed self-pity. 'I'm not talking about my illness,' he says. He wants to continue, to explain, I think, that he has felt like Gregor Samsa for as long as he can remember, but he stops because the room fills up with the headlights of my mum's car. She has pulled up outside the house. The engine stops and the car door slams. Her footsteps draw nearer and she knocks four times on the door.

Andy was reclining in his armchair beneath a blanket in the dark and a voice was coming through the speakers under the TV. 'What's this?' I asked, passing him the coffee I had brought from Caffè Nero.

'Audiobook,' he replied. '*A Child Called It.*'

'You like this one?'

'Yeah, poor little bastard.'

'What do you like about it?'

'I don't know. It helps me get in touch with my feelings.'

I opened the curtains and he groaned as sunlight filled the room.

'How are you feeling this morning?'

'Tired. I was up until five playing poker.'

I sat in my usual spot, on the couch opposite his chair, and tried to lure him out of his reticence, but he ignored my questions, wouldn't hold my gaze, and sometimes seemed in physical discomfort, as though he had toothache and could hardly draw his attention away from his nerves.

'I want to hear more about Kelly,' I said. 'I want to hear about your trip to New York. At some point we need to talk about your illness.'

'Where do we start?'

'Let's pick up where we left off.'

'I don't mean that.' He raised a hand to say that I shouldn't get excited, that he remained in control. 'I mean, how do I even begin?'

'You've already begun.'

He shook his head and finally looked me in the eyes. 'Sometimes it feels like it's all happening at once,' he said. 'It feels like a lie to say this happened and then that happened. With me, it's all happening all the time.'

'This is good,' I said. I had begun to wonder if the

discontinuity in Andy's life – its regular changes in setting, the disharmony of its parts – would be better served by a form that was likewise discontinuous. But I had been nervous to raise the question, fearing it would put him off or scare him into silence. Now I thought I had my chance. 'I wonder if I can put this in the book somehow.'

'What do you mean?'

'So much of you is the impression you make. The way you live with these memories in the present. I wonder if we could find a way to get that into the book.'

'I already said we should start now and then go back to the past like I'm sitting by a fire. I wrote to you about it.'

'I remember. I don't mean that. I mean, could we jump between these parts where your memories flow and you tell a story and these other moments, the ones where you can't remember, where you go in circles and re-examine the same memories over and over, or where everything seems to collapse.'

'I don't want that.' He shook his head. 'The whole reason I'm paying you is to make it flow.' His voice grew louder. 'My head is chaotic.' He leaned forward in his chair and extended a stubby index finger in my direction. 'It's a mess. I don't want my book to be chaotic too. Your job is to clean up the mess.'

'I hear you.'

'I don't like that idea at all, Luca.'

'I'm sorry I suggested it. I've heard you. I'll make it orderly, I promise.'

'Orderly, that's it.'

I made some notes to emphasise to Andy that I had listened to him and then asked if we should carry on, but he ignored me and gazed out the window towards the park. 'Shall we pick up where we left off?' I said.

'Where were we?' He didn't look at me. His mind appeared to be elsewhere and I suspected that he was still turning over my suggestion unhappily.

'You had just got back from meeting your dad.'

His face remained still but I heard his breathing grow heavier. With each breath, it rose further, grew louder; through his T-shirt, I saw his chest rise and fall. Then he shook his head and said, 'No.'

'No?'

'No.' He shook his head again and made a cutting gesture with his hand. 'Not today. I can't do it today. I'm not in the mood.' Sensing that he would not budge, I suggested that I leave and we resume tomorrow. 'You can stay for a bit if you want,' he said. When I did not respond to this ambiguous suggestion, he added, 'Do you want a game of *FIFA*?'

It took me a moment to understand what he was proposing. I looked outside, where the sunshine fell on the long grass in the park. It was almost June. Spring was turning into summer. I wanted to breathe the fresh air outside and feel the sun on my face, but I felt guilty when I thought of leaving Andy alone with his unhappiness.

'Why not?' I said. 'We can have one game.'

He cackled and his mood seemed to shift in an instant. 'Are you good?' he said. 'I'll probably batter you.' He leaned forward, took the PlayStation remote from the table and immersed himself in setting up the game, thumbing the buttons roughly. 'Your controller's over there.'

'How do you shoot?' I said.

'Circle.' He was now focused on the screen, where his players were passing the ball around at tempo while my players jogged after them. After just a few minutes, he had scored. Placing his controller on one of his thighs, he raised his arms in triumph.

'I'm getting used to the controls.'

Play resumed. Andy continued to manipulate his controller, muttering to himself as his team of sky-blue avatars zipped the ball to one another. He scored a second time. 'It's too easy,' he said, slapping his thighs and releasing a squeal of delight. Because we seemed to be sharing something like camaraderie, I thought the time might be right to ask directly the question that had been hovering at the peripheries of my consciousness since the day I met him: had he known my dad? If I supplied him with some details, if I pushed him, could he pull one more box from the archives of his memory? Even just an impression might help me understand who he had been or become, what I had inherited from him, and what lay ahead of me. I was desperate to know. I had waited long enough to ask and there would be no better time than now. As I began to phrase the question in my mind, my heart pounded and my palms became sweaty. Andy, meanwhile, had brought his goalkeeper out with the ball at his feet and he carried it all the way to the corner flag, where he put a cross into the box for a striker to head in at the near post. As his players ran to the corner flag to celebrate before the fans, he turned and looked into my eyes with a cruel smile. It was a look I had seen in flashes, but which he had never directed towards me, and which killed off any chance of my asking him about my dad. Anyway, I knew what had happened. He got sick and began to drink again until he no longer wanted to live. There was nothing left to discover, only my desire to revive his fading memory and delay its sinking into the past, the way a sad drunk always wants a can for the walk home, as though he could keep the party going a while longer.

'Do you want a rematch?' Andy said when the game finished.

'Maybe some other time.' I seemed to have given him what he wanted and I didn't feel like spending any more time with him. While I stood up and gathered my things, Andy set up a new game for himself against the computer or some other player somewhere else in the world. 'See you tomorrow,' I said. 'We'll get back to it.'

'See you.' He was already absorbed in his new game as I let myself out.

There were several hours to go until my appointment at the Job Centre and no point in going home. I thought about walking across the park to the Whitworth Art Gallery to look at some paintings, but there was something off-putting about this idea. When I thought of all the times that I had stood in front of paintings and felt consoled by them, believing that their mere existence meant there was hope of a better world, I felt duped. I had spent too much of my life in thrall to representations, had too often chosen art over life. A sizeable cast of morning drinkers sat on the plastic chairs outside the Ford Madox Ford, smoking and exchanging intermittent commentary, and I was tempted by the thought of a cold, midday pint in the proximity of some other lonely men, but I hadn't had a drink for almost six weeks and it was better that way: no consolations, no illusions.

I turned off Moss Lane by the carwash, where a group of men were buffing up a Nissan Almera, onto Heald Place. It was a narrow street parked up with cars, old cobbles visible where the tarmac had worn away. Houses from different eras were built of different shades of red brick. The new builds were darker, almost brown; the post-war council houses were the colour of black tea with a splash of milk; the older houses were brilliant cochineal. Strips and patches of garden broke up the concrete here and there, a square metre of grass between a wall and a fence; the odd sycamore. Then you got into the estate and it was just houses: two-up two-downs, opening directly onto the street. Bars lined some of the windows; net curtains hung in all of them. I walked up to 28 Lindum Street, where my mum and I had lived in the early 90s, when she had got her first job at the council and I was at the nursery on Claremont Road. The curtains were drawn and I didn't feel much looking at the house. It seemed to have nothing to do with me. And yet, in America, I had believed this house, this street, these places lived inside of me and shaped the course of my life. A man came out of the opposite row and looked at me with suspicion. I nodded and set off again, walked down to Fleeson Street, where my dad had lived for the last few years of his life, when he could hardly walk. I went into the kebab shop on the Curry Mile, where I had been for lunch a few times after tough sessions with Andy, and ordered a falafel and a can of Coke.

'You alright, pal?' the man said.

'Yeah, good thanks, pal.'

'You working around here, yeah?'

'Yeah, just on my lunch.' I sat down facing the street and hid my face in my hands. Then I ate my falafel and watched the traffic and the pigeons until it was time to go to the Job Centre.

As I entered the waiting area and the other job seekers looked up at me, I realised I had dripped tahini sauce all down the front of my T-shirt and jeans.

'How's it been going, Luca?' Phil said, closing the door to his office.

'Oh, you know. Up and down.' He raised his eyebrows. 'I still haven't had my first payment.'

'It'll come. Shall we have a look at your work diary?' He clicked around with his ergonomic mouse. 'I see you've been busy.' He consulted the list of jobs I had pretended to apply for. 'Not had any interviews yet?'

'None.'

'That's disappointing, isn't it?' He kept clicking and looking.

'I don't know what I'm doing wrong.'

'What about the civil service? Did you find anything there? I'll print some out for you, shall I? And why don't you bring in a completed application next week so we can look at it together?'

When I returned the next day, Andy was playing *Call of Duty* in his boxer shorts and a T-shirt, so I went to the bathroom to give him the chance to dress. Val pulled me aside to whisper that he was having a bad day and there was nothing to do but wait for it to pass. When I returned, he had neither put on his trousers nor turned off the console. I sat for several minutes, watching his avatar crawl around the desert with a sniper rifle before I finally interjected to ask whether he would consider pausing the game so that we could start. He sighed as he turned off the console and proceeded to answer my opening questions with monosyllabic answers. I tried to direct his focus towards the areas of his story that we hadn't covered, but Andy kept returning to the subject of his dad. Why had he not wanted to build a relationship? he asked me and I said I didn't know. Why had he agreed to meet for lunch when he didn't want to be his dad? I said that people could be difficult to read. He might have been intrigued. He might have felt a sense of responsibility that only extended so far.

'I could see myself in his face,' Andy said. 'It was my dad.' I said that it must have been as strange an experience as any he'd had. 'They should have got married,' he said. 'My mum and dad should have got married and raised me in a house with brothers and sisters. Put that in the book.'

I wrote it down. 'How long were you with Kelly?'

He shrugged defensively. 'I don't know, nine months?'

'Nine months?' I said with audible surprise.

'A year? I don't know, Luca. I don't remember everything.'

'I thought it was longer for some reason.'

'It was long to me. She was the love of my life.'

It took me a moment to understand that I'd offended Andy but before I had the chance to rectify my mistake, there was a knock at the front door, followed by the sound of Val's footsteps thundering along the corridor. 'Who's that?'

'My social worker.'

I heard the door open and Val greeting another woman.

'Do you have an appointment now?'

Andy was about to answer when the woman walked into the room. 'Hiya,' she said. 'I'm Helen, Andy's social worker. Are you his writer?'

I said that I was.

'Brill.' She took a seat beside me. 'How are you, Andy?'

'I'm alright.'

I stood up and packed my things away.

'I hope I'm not disturbing,' the social worker said, but it was clear that it didn't matter if she was.

'You are.' Andy laughed.

'You're not,' I said, though she was. I let myself out.

It was quiet in the Waterstones on Deansgate. A few customers, mostly women who I suspected had recently retired, browsed the well-stocked shelves and a few members of staff stood behind the counter or rearranged table displays. Several of these were dedicated to books about Manchester: books of local lore, facts, and trivia that seemed to have boomed in recent years, all decorated with the bee of the city's insignia. Another display advertised a new novel by a Mancunian writer named Jonny Fletcher: *Cotton City*. It seemed to be about a DJ who gets drawn into Manchester's criminal underworld when he begins to research his grandfather, a militant trade unionist who disappeared after murdering a mill owner in the 1960s. The author, who looked about the same age as me, was pictured wearing a plaid shirt, braces, and flat cap, standing in front of a red-brick wall with his thumbs tucked into the beltline of his jeans. The *Guardian* had called the novel 'a gripping, poignant portrait of a family and a city'. Other broadsheet newspapers had published similar reviews, one describing Fletcher as 'a fearless new voice'.

I took the escalator to the first floor, went to the wall of biographies and autobiographies, and selected a few titles, read their first lines. Andy had cancelled our session, so I had spent the morning writing. Worried that I was making his book too novelistic, I decided to ease or aggravate my worries by doing some research into his competitors. An entire table was dedicated to copies of Michelle Obama's *Becoming* and I picked up a copy and read the opening paragraph. 'When I was a kid, my aspirations were simple. I wanted a dog. I wanted a house that had stairs in it – two floors for one family. I wanted, for some reason, a four-door station wagon instead of the two-door Buick that was my father's pride and joy.' That was not so different from what I had done. I browsed the shelves and picked out a copy of the book Andy had mentioned during my first visit: Ricky Hatton, *War and Peace: My Story*. It began with a prologue: 'It was not supposed to end this way. I was in the Manchester Arena and the fans were singing my name. That part was right, at least.' I scanned on. The paragraphs were short. 'They always say comebacks are ill-advised but I never did listen to them much. It was my life, my career, my decision.' That was a whole paragraph. I skipped forward to the first chapter: 'In the Beginning'. I read the first paragraph and then put the book back on the shelf, took out a few more and looked at their contents and first pages. A different face looked at you from the cover of each book, a different name printed in bold capitals below it, but all of them spoke in the same voice and followed the same structure so it was hard to give credence to the idea that each of them told the unique story of an individual's life.

I stepped into the adjacent room, which once contained books on philosophy and religion. More than any other, that room fascinated me as a child because of its studious, serious atmosphere. When I was ten or eleven years old, I had taken a book by Hume from the shelf and opened it on the carpeted floor. I still remembered the wonder I felt on seeing that strange language and the unfamiliar cyphers and characters that surrounded the words. I sensed my dad behind me, above me, looking down over my shoulder. 'Might be a bit hard for you, that one,' he said. Now, this room contained books on travel, music, self-help, and 'Smart Thinking', while philosophy had been moved to a smaller section on the second floor. I went up there. In Costa Coffee, an elderly woman sat alone, a cappuccino on the table before her. Behind the counter, a man with long, black hair was fiddling with the nozzle on the milk steamer. I looked at politics, history, and philosophy, but the more I looked around the shop, the more I had the feeling that the life had drained away from the books, that the awesome power they had held when I was younger had not only diminished for me, but had objectively diminished, that a book had never meant less than it did now.

I thought I could hear Andy shouting when I arrived the next morning but when he opened the door, I discovered that he was alone. He was wearing a sky-blue T-shirt with an Oasis logo on the chest. 'Is that one of yours?' I said.

He looked at it. 'No. This is good quality.' I sat down while Andy heaved himself out of his wheelchair and into his armchair. I looked away because I had come to hate his movements, his uncanny combination of strength and infirmity. He shifted his weight a few times, adopted the posture he used to talk business, and said, 'When are we going to start writing?'

I had been fearing this question. By now, I had around

fifty pages of passable manuscript, but the more I wrote without showing the work to Andy, the more I worried that he would reject what I had written. Though I had departed increasingly from the parameters that he had set, I hoped the manuscript would win him around to a more ambitious project. It was important, however, that he not see the text before it was guaranteed to make a good impression; the window for possible scepticism had to be kept as narrow as possible. Ideally, it would enchant him on page one. We were not quite there yet, so I tried to talk him down from the idea. 'I want to hear the whole story first,' I said. 'There's so much you still haven't told me: Kelly, Brendan, your trip to America.'

'You know me now. I've talked to you for hours. I've told you things I've never told anyone else. I need to know that you can make it come alive. I've given you my money.' His eyes were full of wild feeling and I sensed that I would not escape a fierce argument without giving up some ground so I said that I could bring a sample of writing the following day, which seemed to satisfy him. 'Have you got enough material for the Haçienda section?'

'I've done what I could with what you've told me.'

'They were the best days of my life.'

'I'll write that.'

'You need to show it.'

'I'm trying.'

'You need to make it come alive. I want it to be like you're there.' He jabbed a finger towards me as he went on. 'I want opening the book to be like stepping through the doors of the Haçienda on a Saturday night.'

'Please.' I raised a palm because I felt under attack, a gesture that seemed to cause him offence.

'What? I'm just telling you how it needs to be. Do you think five grand comes easily to me? Do I look like a millionaire? I have a right to tell you what I want, don't I?'

'Yes,' I made my posture feeble to calm his nerves. 'You do, I'm sorry. And if I take a bit of creative licence here and there? For the sake of atmosphere. Would that be okay? If I make up a few details to fill in the gaps?'

'There's no need to make anything up when it comes to my story, Luca. I've had a life you couldn't make up.' He exhaled slowly and nodded, as though in agreement with himself. For a moment, I thought we had settled our minor dispute and that Andy's temper had abated but now he covered his face with his palm and his breathing became heavy. Unsure of the gesture's meaning, I decided to remain still and wait for his lead. I was not calm. The atmosphere between us had never felt so fraught.

'Shall we pick up where we left off last time?' I said, eventually, once I was desperate to break the silence. 'You had met your dad. You were in love with Kelly. Maybe you could tell me about your diagnosis. Do you feel up to talking about it?'

Andy took his hand away from his face and looked at me. His eyes were red but not teary. 'What?'

'Your diagnosis.'

'We were talking about the day I met my dad.'

'True,' I said, not wanting to contradict him, 'but then we moved on. Your dad passed away. You were beginning to have tremors and so on.'

'I don't think you've understood. My dad didn't want anything to do with me. It was one of the worst moments of my life. I tracked him down after twenty-one years and

197

he didn't want to know me. I thought your mum and dad were supposed to love you. Why didn't mine?' I shook my head as though the question were rhetorical and I agreed with its implication – that life had been cruel to him and that living with this knowledge could not be easy – but he asked the question again, changing its inflexion so that it now seemed to demand an answer. 'Why didn't mine?'

My palms were sweating, my mouth was dry, and I could think of no good answer to his question. 'I don't know.'

'Did yours?' he said. 'Did your parents love you?'

'Not perfectly,' I said, 'but yes, they did.'

'Mine didn't.'

He turned away so that he no longer faced me but looked into the corner of the room. For quite some time, we sat in this way, with me looking at Andy while he looked away. A minute passed, perhaps two, and still I did not know what I could say. I wondered if he needed me to share in his frustration or just to witness him. When the silence became unbearable, hardly giving it a thought, I said, 'Why do you think they didn't love you?' But no sooner had I spoken than I could hear how insensitive a question it had been.

Andy turned to look at me with eyes full of indignation. 'I don't know, do I?' He began to sob with all of his being. Convulsive, snotty, unrestrained sobbing. 'I don't know,' he said between the tears. 'I'll never know.' It was not easy to see him so defenceless, wailing and blubbering and still not finding adequate expression for his suffering. As I watched Andy sob, I realised there was something cruel and selfish at the heart of my interest in him. I had seized on him as a substitute for an authenticity I could not access. I had used his suffering as a way to access my own feelings.

And now that I had him at his rawest and most openly hurt, I wanted nothing to do with that suffering. I was sick of him and I wanted to go home but, for the sake of politeness, I waited until he had the composure to say goodbye.

I sat down to review my manuscript after arriving home from Andy's and saw that it was bad. After the uncomfortable direction our meeting had taken, I was afraid of how he might react to a manuscript he didn't like, so I worked all through the afternoon and deep into the night, only managing a few hours of sleep before it was time to wake up and submit my work to his judgement. Before I left, I printed out the neatly formatted sheets, slipped them into a transparent folder, and placed it under the cover of a *Guinness Book of World Records* I borrowed from the shelf of my absent hosts. This was to protect it. I wanted the immaculate manuscript, with its bold title and justified paragraphs, to suggest the book it would one day become, hoping that would make Andy view it more favourably.

Knocking on the front door, I was more nervous than I had ever been, but when Val greeted me cheerily with the offer of a coffee, I sensed the atmosphere was placid. I heard the sound of canned laughter and found Andy lying on the sofa where I usually sat while an episode of *Friends* played on the television. 'What's wrong?' he said as he paused the TV, leaving a still frozen on the screen: Monica and Ross against the purple-painted walls of the former's apartment. I had assumed we would begin by addressing what had happened the previous day but that thought did not seem to have crossed Andy's mind. The look on his face suggested that he was puzzled by my hesitancy.

'Nothing.' I pointed to Andy's armchair and he nodded. I sat down. 'I've got some writing for you here. As requested.'

'Of mine?' he said with surprise in his voice, drawing himself into a semi-recumbent position.

'Yes, I thought we could read it together.'

'I'll read it when you're gone. Otherwise it's too much pressure.'

'Are you sure? I could read it to you now and we could discuss it together.'

'No, Luca. I want to read it in my own time.'

Sensing that he wouldn't let me win, I decided to drop the issue until later. 'Shall we pick up from where we left off then?'

'Can we slow down?'

What did he mean? I asked.

'It's moving so fast. I feel like we're racing through my life.'

'I know, but you have to keep momentum. Trust me on this. You really need to keep your momentum if you want to get anything done.'

'I don't want to rush it.'

'I don't either. I just think we should keep moving if we can. We can fill in the details later.'

'This is my legacy. I want it to be perfect. I've got all the time in the world to get it right.' I didn't know what to say to this. I could hardly force him to recount his life under duress but I did not want this to drag on any longer than it needed to. He looked at me obstinately, as though he were testing me. 'Let's have a game of *FIFA*,' he said.

'Andy, please.'

'Come on, I'm paying you. I'm not ready to start yet. Let's play a game of *FIFA*.'

'You're paying me to write a book for you. For that only.'

'This is part of it. I'm not ready to start yet. I need to get in the zone.'

I could see that he wouldn't budge. There was a manic look in his eyes and I had little hope that I could get him talking on the subject of his diagnosis when he was in this mood. 'Let's make a deal,' I said. 'One game of *FIFA* and then we carry on with your story.'

'Deal.' He was already leaning across to the remote on the table and turning on the console. Ross and Monica disappeared into blackness. 'I'll be someone else so you have a chance of beating me. I'll be Burnley.'

Val came in and placed our coffees on the table. 'Aren't you two supposed to be working?' she said and I shot her a look that was supposed to capture the complexity of the situation, though it might not have. When the game finished, 5–1 to Andy, I said, 'Alright. Shall we carry on with the book?'

'One more game.'

'No, Andy. If you don't feel up to it today, that's fine, but I'm not going to sit here and play *FIFA* with you.'

'One game.'

'No. Please, Andy. Don't make me do this.'

'Do what? I'm not making you do anything.'

'I'm here to help you write this book. I want to make it happen. Don't you feel up to carrying on with your story? I want to know what happens.'

'You know what happens.'

'Not yet. Come on, you haven't even told me about your trip to New York.'

'Everything goes to shit,' he said. He was lying in a position that could not have been comfortable, supported by a few pillows beneath his head and craning his neck to look at me. 'One day I'm going up in the world, the next day I'm going down.'

'I understand what you're feeling,' I said.

'You don't.'

'To an extent I do. And I know that it sometimes feels pointless. But don't forget how much you want to do this. People want to read your book.'

'What people?'

'I do.'

'You want to write it because you need the money. I saw you coming out of the Job Centre the other day.' I was caught off guard by this and couldn't find any words with which to reply. 'I thought you were a proper writer.'

'I am. Why don't I read you what I've written so far?'

'No. I need to read it on my own. Give it to me.'

'Please let me read it to you. I want to feel your reaction.'

'I don't want to.'

'Okay. But promise me you won't be too harsh on it. It's a draft. It's like a lift shaft with no building around it or a skeleton with no flesh. Do you understand?'

'I'm not an idiot. I'll tell you honestly what I think of it.'

'Just remember that it's not the finished thing. It's a start.'

'I just want to see what your writing is like.'

I didn't want to give him the pages I had written. I wanted to work on it some more, make it stronger. I was afraid that he would hate it and everything would fall apart. 'Please, promise me that you won't panic if you don't like it.' I took the transparency from the *Guinness Book of World Records* and read the first sentence: 'It is with considerable difficulty that I remember the original era of my being; all the events appear confused and indistinct.' I had pinched that from another novel, as I had many of the better lines. Reading it, I felt sure that I had made his text too novelistic but there was nothing I could do about that now. I removed the documents and placed them on the table.

'Read the bit about the T-shirt business. That's the best bit.'

'I'll decide which is the best bit.' He picked up the document and cast his eyes up and down the first page before placing it back on the table. 'I'll let you know what I think when I've read it.'

'Do you want to carry on with some narration today?'

'No, I'm not in the mood.'

'How about a game of *FIFA*?'

'No,' Andy said. 'I want to be alone.'

The front room was dark when I arrived for our next session. I knocked on the door but nobody answered so I knocked harder and waited, relieved by every second that the door remained closed and the hallway quiet. Once I got back to the house in Chorlton, though, I didn't know what to do with the day. The anniversary of my dad's death was approaching – it would soon be sixteen years since he had died – and the time of year always unsettled me, the bright light and the manic lifefullness of early summer. I took the bin out, dragged it over the cobbles and stood it in the mouth of the alleyway with the others.

I went to Beech Road to get a flat white in a takeaway cup and drank it as I walked towards the street where my mum had lived before she moved away. I remembered the last time I saw her there. It was four or five years earlier, when I was still an undergraduate. I didn't visit home often because I was happy in my new life and didn't want to be reminded of the past, and because my mum had moved out of the house where we used to live and was renting a one-bed flat. Tom and I were going to play football and then stay at his house-share in Whalley Range before I took the train back down south the next morning. He stopped by to pick me up and came in for a cup of tea. When we left, my mum came out to the front step to wave. 'Goodbye, boys,' she said. 'See you soon, honey.' It was a sunny day in July and she was wearing a yellow dress that made her look young. Tom and I were wearing our football gear and as we waved goodbye and climbed into the car, I felt protected by the air of normalcy around us, the sense that we were two young men going off to have fun and she was my loving mother at home, even as I knew that she was struggling with money and planning to leave, that it might be the last time I saw her at home. I had since been to visit her in Torrevieja but it was clearer there, as we walked along the quiet seafront, that she was a person like any other with complex needs and disappoint-ments, tired of working and looking with fear towards old age. As I passed her old flat and looked in through the ground-floor window, some part of me still hoped I might see that previous version of her, the one whose radiant presence meant that I was still wrapped up in the world of my childhood. The flat was empty, its decor changed. I took my phone out of my pocket and called my mum but she didn't answer and soon I turned around and walked home.

The next morning, I texted Andy to say I wouldn't head over until he texted me to say that he was home. I didn't expect a reply, but I waited for one anyway and when it didn't arrive I became angry. What did he expect me to do? What else could I do with his selfish, merciless demands but fail to satisfy them?

I must have looked quite mad standing on the step of Mia's condo with my hiker's rucksack on my back, hair dishevelled from seven hours on the Greyhound. She opened the door and laughed, though in her eyes I detected a faint alarm. 'What did you do?'

'I quit.' I stepped inside and let my rucksack fall to the floor by the shoe rack. 'Is there anywhere we can go for a drink? It's a beautiful evening. It gets dark so fast this time of year.'

'My hair is wet,' she said, 'and you can't just walk out and have a drink around here. It's not that kind of place. Don't you want some dinner?'

'I'm not hungry.' The door opened directly into a living room, smaller than I'd imagined. 'What a nice place you've got.'

A small piano stood against one wall next to a few shelves of books and what appeared to be various Polynesian statuettes. A framed print or original of an abstract expressionist artwork hung on the wall above them – some thick black lines on a white background. 'Whose house is this again?'

'An emeritus professor in the English department. He lives on a Scottish island.'

'That must be nice for him.' A selection of framed photographs stood on a sideboard: some were of children; some were of adults. It wasn't clear whether the adults were the same children fully grown or their parents.

'Come.' Mia led me to the kitchen at the back of the house. Here, she poured some crisps into a bowl and set it down on the granite island. Then she opened the giant fridge, took out two bottles of lager, and opened them using an instrument she fished out of a drawer. She handed one to me and held my gaze as she took a crisp from the bowl and placed it in her mouth. I tried to feign being laidback but no stance, no placement of the hands could be natural. Mia's phone had been off all day so we hadn't texted since I set off from home that morning. The mood between us remained unestablished.

'Do you want to have a shower?'

'I'm okay.' She kept her eyes trained on me as she took a sip of her lager. 'Actually, yes. I'll have a shower.'

She led me up the narrow staircase and showed me to the bathroom. I locked the door behind her and pushed open the window so that I could peek at the little fenced-off yard and the backs of the adjacent houses, all painted the same sky blue. I already felt that my turning up here in a moment of crisis broke the terms of our relationship, assumed a degree of interdependence that exceeded the reality of our situation. For a moment, I wondered if I could fit through the window and escape, but it was too small and there was nothing to cushion my fall. Standing beneath a tepid shower felt good; it was the first warm day of the year and I had spent most of it on a stuffy coach. Waiting at the station, I got an email from the English department's administrator informing me of what I already knew: I had failed my exams. I was invited to meet with my supervisory panel and the department head the following week. I scanned it and swiped away the open tab. The seat beside me remained free for the first hour but then a large and nervous man got on at Portsmouth, New Hampshire and sat next to me until Waterville, Maine glancing down the aisle as though waiting for an accident to happen. Sit still, I wanted to say to him. Stop fucking jittering around.

I turned the temperature right down until the water was ice cold and gritted my teeth as it hit my scalp and upper back. I wanted to emerge as a different person. I had always feared being an unwelcome guest and yet, routinely, I seemed to make myself unwelcome. I could walk downstairs now and tell her that I was sorry for coming, I thought as I dried myself off. I had made a mistake. I could say that I would stay the night – downstairs if that were easier – and take the bus back to Boston the next day. But when I went downstairs and stepped out into the small backyard, where Mia was sitting at a garden table, that no longer seemed necessary.

'So, what happened?' she said. 'Give me the gossip.' She listened as I told her and when I'd finished, she said, 'You didn't go back in?'

'I feel embarrassed about it now, but no. I left them to wait for me out of spite and pettiness.'

'So, what now? I assume you can't carry on there.'

'No.'

'Well.' She laughed. 'You always said you had your doubts about it.'

'I did, didn't I?'

'What will you do?'

'I don't know.' I smiled at her, but she didn't smile back. I didn't want to talk about plans, restrictions, realities. I wanted to slip into our fantasy world, but that world was diminishing now.

When I came back from the kitchen with two more beers, her head was tilted to a contemplative angle. 'It probably wasn't wise to burn your bridges that way,' she said, 'but I don't think you're wrong to quit. You only had bad things to say about the place and the work didn't seem to make you happy.'

'No.' I liked hearing this. I wanted more.

'And you still had another – what? Three years?'

'Four at least.'

'You can't force yourself to do work you don't want to do.' I didn't think this was exactly true but I didn't argue. 'And you were probably trying to protect yourself.' This additional suggestion I did not like because it raised questions that I was afraid to ask and alluded to an aspect of my character that I feared she understood better than I did. I nodded as though to convey that we saw it the same way and then I asked her what she had been up to. She told me the university had asked her to run a poetry workshop for undergraduates. She'd also had to present her research to her colleagues in the English department. They all seemed impressed, she said. Now she just had to finish the article she'd been working on all year. 'And then I'm done here.' The wind seemed to pick up and rustle the trees and I was glad because I didn't know what I could say by way of a reply. Thankfully, Mia now placed a hand on my thigh and we began to kiss. We were careful at first, explorative, and the longer we kissed, the clearer it became that beneath the discomfort and all that remained unsaid, we still desired one another. We left our half-drunk beers on the garden table and she led me through the kitchen, up the stairs and beyond the closed door of the bedroom, where she lay down on her back and pulled off her tights. A glass of water toppled from the bedside table as I climbed on top of her and I made as though to clean up the mess, but she dismissed this gesture and pulled me back towards her. There was nothing I found more gratifying than when she wanted me, when that want broke through her perfect composure. Sometimes I wondered if the truest part of my near obsessive attraction to her lay in the petty cruelty of how gratifying I found my ability to break her composure and bring her down to my level. But when she closed her eyes and told me not to stop, I felt that it was she who was in control. After we came, she rolled away, leaving a wide expanse of creased, damp bedsheet between us.

We woke up late the next morning. I had slept deeply beside Mia's naked body with the cold, spring air blowing through the insect-netted window. My arms were wrapped around her back and her face was close to my chest. The previous day's unease seemed to have left us in the night.

I made us coffee and we stayed in bed for a while. She took out her phone and opened Twitter, showed me some memes and screenshots from *The Simpsons*. Then she opened Instagram. All her friends were poets, novelists, academics, translators, artists. She went through their stories and interpreted them for my benefit: one was on a residency in Italy and had posted a picture of an Aperol spritz and a pack of cigarettes on a marble tabletop, another of the sparkling Adriatic. Another had received the proofs of her new collection of poems and posted a picture of the partially opened box. I took all this in with an ambivalent combination of envy and pride. If it was mine, I loved it. If it could never be mine, I hated it. And as she went through the images and explained who these people were – though I had heard of most of them and knew their names and faces – I was silent, because I knew that if I spoke I would give away that it was more the latter, that this was her world and not mine and I was jealous of it. Two friends were in Copenhagen and had posted a picture of themselves drinking wine on a veranda and another of a plate of oysters.

'I love oysters,' Mia said. 'I miss my friends.'

The next image was of her closest friend, a Belgian novelist whose debut I had read. She was sitting on a rug and scratching the belly of a big dog. 'Oh.' Mia made a pained noise. 'I miss her. Who is she with? I'm jealous now.' She opened up the comment box. 'What should I write? Whose dog is that? No.' Her body tightened as genius possessed her, 'No question mark.' She wrote: 'whose dog is that' and took a moment to admire her work before she pressed send. I turned to look at her directly and smiled as though to say I loved her and I wanted her world and her imagination to be mine. She looked directly at me and for a moment, held my gaze with a cool, steady expression. Then she got up to take a shower.

'You really can't walk here,' she said as we set out walking along the road that led downhill towards the town, through an area where large commercial units were separated from the road by car parks: there was a supermarket, a dispensary, and a diner called Governor's, where we ordered a five-stack of blueberry pancakes, of which Mia ate one and I the other four.

'It must be lonely. Where's the campus?'

'A mile or so up the road. It's small. I rarely go.'

'It's just you in that house? In this town?' She nodded

as though to say that I ought to have understood her situation sooner.

'What do you feel like eating?' I said as we entered the car park of Hannaford.

She shook her head. 'You decide. Don't even involve me. I vowed when I left my marriage never again to stand outside a supermarket with a man, discussing what to have for dinner.'

'I can make a fish pie,' I said.

'Don't talk to me about fish pie,' she said.

I filled a basket with smoked salmon, artichokes, blueberries, two local cheeses, a pack of overpriced crackers and a bottle of Chablis.

'Your regular shopping list?' Mia asked.

'We're on holiday.'

'I like your accent,' said the girl at the checkout and Mia smiled at me as though she was proud.

Back at the flat we had dirty sex and fell asleep for an hour. When we woke up we did it again and then got drunk and fell asleep on the couch. I woke up at three in the morning with a splitting headache and Mia's head on my chest and when I woke her up and coaxed her upstairs to bed, I wondered if I was leading the best days of my life.

The next evening, I was cooking dinner while she sat at the table and wrote notes on a manuscript. I was thinking about the future, about what we would do during the coming summer and whether we would stay together beyond that time. The mood had been so good between us that I was beginning to believe this conversation – when we had it – would lead to the kind of outcome I had been dreaming about.

Come back with me to London, I wanted her to say

when we sat down. We can make a life together. 'I like the way you dress salads,' she said.

'Thank you,' I said, and the look she returned seemed to express such tenderness that it almost resembled fear. I could have said, 'I love you.' I would have liked to say those words to her but I didn't. We ate in silence. I didn't know what she was thinking about. I was thinking that it would be easier to propose a trip than a whole future and I was reassured by the memory of the last time we had seen each other, when we had lain in my bed and discussed going to Chicago. I wanted to see the city where I was born and to which I had never returned, to discover it with her. She wanted to see the Lee Bontecou prints that were exhibiting at the Art Institute. 'So how about you and me take the Lake Shore Limited to Chicago, Illinois?' I now said. But it didn't sound natural the way I'd hoped it would.

'I would really like to,' she replied quickly, as though she had been waiting for this suggestion. 'But I don't know if I can.'

'That's okay.'

'I have to finish this article by next week and then I have to start packing up. I need to be in London by June.'

'Do you? What for?'

'I'm judging the Sainsbury Prize.'

'That's great. It sounds as though you're busy. I should take care of a few things myself. Maybe I'll head back tomorrow.'

But I was reluctant to leave. I felt that if I left now, our relationship would be over for ever and she must have felt the same way because she said, 'You could stay a while longer.'

'Would you like that?'

She looked me in the eyes and nodded. 'Stay a few days longer.'

'Alright.' I filled our glasses with Chablis.

We slept late again the following morning and stayed in bed for an hour or two after waking. Downstairs, while the coffee was brewing, I checked my phone and found a second email from the English department, urging me to reply to the first.

'What's wrong?' Mia said when I returned to the bedroom.

'Nothing. I just hate getting emails.'

While I prepared lunch, Mia sat at the table and wrote feedback for the undergraduates who had taken her workshop. Though she was not looking at me, my body became unwieldy the way it did when I felt unsure of my place. Reaching for a wooden spoon, I knocked a jar of pickled beetroot over on the kitchen island. 'Fuck,' I said, and she looked up to see me throwing down a tea towel before it spilled onto the floor.

'It's okay. Don't worry.'

After lunch, we walked along Broadway in the opposite direction, to an ice cream stall named Gifford's that stood in a shack surrounded by parking space at the side of the road. We sat on a picnic table and ate our ice creams in silence, watching the traffic pass on the main road and the American flag ripple in the car park of Dunkin' on the other side.

'I need to start working again,' she said when we got up.

'Of course.' I wasn't sure exactly what this meant. 'Shall I head back in the morning?'

'No need to head back right away. I'll just need to do a bit of work.'

'I should start applying for jobs anyway.'

'What will you apply for?'

I told her that I didn't know. In fact, I wanted to ask her advice but I didn't because I was afraid that doing so would accentuate the difference between us and leave me feeling young and naïve.

Back at the house, she went upstairs to work. After tapping around on my laptop for a while, I opened a beer, smoked a cigarette in the backyard, and then watched football via an illegal stream on my laptop while I made a pasta sauce. When Mia came downstairs a few hours later, she looked preoccupied, harried in a way that I had only seen in flashes. I turned around with my mouth halfway towards some words and saw that she was sitting down at the piano. She lifted the fallboard, played a few loose notes, and then began to play the opening arpeggios of Debussy's *Arabesque No. 1*, which sounded more beautiful for their roughness. She knew that I could hear her, standing no more than a few metres away, but she did not appear self-conscious and may not have known that I had turned down the gas beneath the pasta, placed my beer on the countertop, and was standing, watching her slim back and her bony shoulders moving left and right as she now began to play the descending pentatonic scale. She played them quickly, at first so quickly that I wanted to ask her to slow down, but as I listened, I thought that it was better she not linger over the notes sentimentally. She descended a second time and I could see the long fingers of her left hand stroking the keys at a half tempo while the right hand, which worked harder, was obscured. Fleetingly, I believed the moment was perfect. The music had been so unexpected it had caught me off guard, like perfume or tobacco smoke on a breeze. The climate was so pleasant, the golden evening sunlight falling through the french windows onto the kitchen table was so warm and radiant, and I was more alive, further away from home than I had ever been. Then I thought that perhaps it was a terrible moment, that the music gave me a glimpse into a paradise that I would never be allowed to enter and the situation in which I found myself was unsafe, unstable, impossible to sustain. She made a mistake, tripping over herself with the right hand, and stopped suddenly. Then she turned her head and saw me looking at her.

'What?' she said. 'Stop looking at me like that.'

I smiled as though she had said it teasingly. 'You're good.'

'I'm hungry.'

'It's ready.' I turned to the stove and carried the pasta to the sink, trying to imbue my actions with some of her grace as though it would make us equals. I had made a Ragu with porcini mushrooms and carried it to the garden along with a bowl of salad.

'Where are you going to go?' Mia asked.

'How do you mean?'

'Are you going to stay in Boston?'

'Oh, no. I don't know. Maybe to Manchester.'

'I thought you might say that.'

'We wouldn't be so far away,' I said and she returned an ambiguous look.

The next day, she was upstairs writing when I received another email, stressing the importance of my responding. I deleted it. With regret, I thought of Jacob, my under-graduate mentor, who had done so much to help me. He would be disappointed; he would not understand what I had done. He had never understood the nihilism that ran through me like a bruise in an apple. Mia's typing, her long fingers striking the keyboard, was audible from upstairs. I had nothing to do. I took a can of beer from the fridge and cracked it open.

'What's wrong?' Mia said when she came downstairs for a cracker and a piece of cheese to find me lying on the couch, tipsy at 3 p.m.

'Nothing's wrong,' I said and she retreated to the office.

It rained that evening. Mia shut herself away for a long Skype meeting with the editors of an Australian publisher who wanted to reissue her two collections of poetry in a single volume. I didn't feel like reading and it was already past midnight in England, so all my friends there were asleep. I scrolled through my WhatsApp conversations, trying to find someone in Cambridge whom I wanted to text. Kareena had messaged to ask if I was okay but I didn't know how to respond so I put my phone away, played some music on YouTube, and got drunk. It was midnight by the time Mia finished and she didn't feel like talking.

I awoke to the sound of her crying the next morning. She was facing the window, where the insect screen dulled the morning light. 'What's wrong?' I asked her and she didn't respond. I placed a hand on her back, but she flinched to make it clear she didn't want to be touched. I lay still for a while. Then I rolled towards her and said again, 'What's wrong?'

'I had a bad dream.'

'What happened?'

'I don't want to talk about it.'

'Was it about us?'

'It was about Henry.'

'Did he die?'

'I don't want to talk about it.'

I sat up, leaned over, and kissed her unmoving face. It was only as my lips touched her cheek that I realised my anxious affection had given way to a creeping resentment. A moment passed and Mia got up, went to the bathroom, and then went straight to her office and closed the door. When I realised that she wasn't planning to come out again, I left the house and walked the long street into the centre of town.

'Where are you?' Tom said when he answered the phone.

'Orono, Maine.'

'What are you doing there?' He was driving. I could hear the car in the background.

'I came to see Mia.'

'Is it going well?'

'It's going alright.'

'Yeah?'

'Yeah.'

'Alright. I'm driving.'

'I can tell.'

'Right,' he said. 'Call me another time.'

'Okay. Bye.'

I thought about calling my mum, but we hadn't spoken for a while and I didn't want to tell her about my situation. She would have heard the self-pity in my voice and responded with pity of her own, which would have been intolerable, so I walked along without thinking much about anything. Orono was not unpleasant. It was a small town in spirit but on foot it was large. I passed colonial houses with long lawns and rows of squat, shack-like clapboard houses with beat-up facades and doors that opened onto the narrow sidewalks. Downtown, the buildings were three or four storeys high and built of the North American variety of red brick. A police car drifted by and the officer looked me up and down as he passed. I went into a bar on Main Street and ordered a strong IPA. There was nobody around except for me and the barman.

'What brings you to Orono?' he asked.

'A woman.'

'Figures.' He set my beer down on a napkin in front of me. 'We don't get a lot of tourists here.'

'Where do the tourists go?'

'They mostly head down to the coast. Mount Desert Island, Stonehaven, Portland.'

'Is it nice down there?'

'Oh, it's beautiful. You gotta check it out if you've never been.'

'Can you get there without a car?'

'Not that I'm aware of.' He was drying wine glasses, running a towel around the inside and then holding them up to the light.

'So, what do people do in Orono?'

'How so, bud?' If they were clean, he hung them upside down on a rack.

'For work and so on.'

'Used to be a lumber town.'

'Not anymore?'

He shook his head. 'Not so much.'

'Can I ask you a question?'

'Of course.'

'Is there anywhere nearby where I could see a moose?'

'A moose?'

'Yeah,' I said. 'In the wild.'

'Not in Orono. Only time most folks see a moose is when it comes out of nowhere and ends up on the windshield. You gotta go up north to see one in the wild. They're pretty shy.'

'No problem.'

'You asking for a particular reason?'

'I'd just like to see one while I'm here.'

'Yeah, they're cool animals alright.' The barman hung another glass and disappeared into a back room.

I looked at my phone. 'Hey,' Mia had texted me.

'Hey,' I wrote back.

She appeared online. 'Where have you ended up?'

'I'm in the town.'

'Having a nice time?'

'Yes.'

'Good. Coming home soon?'

'Sure.'

'Good. Can you get toilet paper?'

'x,' I wrote.

When he came back and noticed that I'd already drained the glass of beer, the barman said, 'Thirsty? Want another?'

'I'd better not.' I gave him a ten-dollar bill and told him to keep the change.

'Enjoy your stay,' he said. 'I hope you see that moose.'

I thought that Mia's text had signalled an apology of sorts and a willingness to move past the morning's bad atmosphere. She'd expressed a desire to see me and even referred to her place as 'home'. So I had a small bounce in my step when I nipped into Hannaford to buy toilet paper, olive oil, condoms, a six-pack of bottled lager, and a packet of Marlboro Lights, stuffing them merrily into a paper bag and walking back to the condo.

Mia was on the phone when she opened the door and I must have been making an idiotic, romantic sort of face because she looked at me with disgust and turned her attention back to her phone call. 'I can't believe they would even publish it,' I heard her saying as she made her way up the stairs. In the kitchen, I set the paper bag down on the counter. Mia had tidied while I'd been out. A bottle of antibacterial spray and a crumpled J Cloth stood next to the sink. Perhaps she was trying to purge the place of my presence. This was a bad state of affairs. It reminded me of visits to my dad's house, during the period when I saw him frequently. He was often bad-tempered and I didn't know why. He seemed almost to hum with frustration as he walked from his desk to the kitchen to brew a cup of tea. Then he might fall into a daydream as he waited for the kettle to boil. It was possible to mistake his stillness for tranquillity and, if I disturbed him, his impatience would be doubly upsetting because I had expected him to greet me with a warm smile.

I remembered a time when I was staying at his house in Stretford. My mum had gone away for the weekend and left me in his care. All week I looked forward to the visit but when I finished school on Friday afternoon and saw him at the school gates, standing apart from the other parents, wearing a black leather trench coat and running his fingers through his hair, I could see right away that he was not in the mood for my company. We walked in silence to the bus stop on Wilbraham Road and only when we took our seats did my dad say that he had some things to deal with and I would have to entertain myself until he was finished. When we got to his house, he left me in the living room with a can of Diet Coke and told me he was going up to the study for a while. There was no TV and I didn't have my Gameboy so I played some of my dad's CDs and read an issue of *Kerrang!* that I had left at the house on my previous visit. I'd already read most of the features, so I soon tired of the magazine and instead sat in the armchair by the window, gazing out at the quiet cul-de-sac and the derelict house opposite. On hearing my dad's footsteps on the stairs, I brightened, believing that he was coming to spend time with me, but he walked straight by the door and to the kitchen. After a few minutes, I followed quietly and found him standing by the open back door. He was looking out over the small yard, wearing a blue and grey plaid shirt tucked into his blue jeans, holding a cup of tea and smoking a cigarette. He was shaking his head as though in disappointment or disbelief. At first I thought that he was talking to the neighbour over the wall but when he continued, I realised he must have been alone. He shook his head a few times, stopped, and shook it again. It seemed strange to me that he was not aware of my presence and so for a moment I wondered if he was shaking his head with disapproval at my having snuck in behind him. He exhaled with a kind of snort that I thought was a laugh and then I smiled in anticipation of him turning around, but it wasn't a laugh and he didn't turn around. He only shook his head again and leaned against the doorframe with a frustrated sigh. Quietly, I retraced my steps to the living room and closed the door.

I had misunderstood everything. It was essential that I escape and regain my autonomy. I had to pack my bag and leave right away, but my bag was in the bedroom and Mia was still up there. It would be much too dramatic to walk in and disturb her conversation. From upstairs, I heard the sound of her laughing. She was still on the phone and there was nothing I could do but wait.

I had drunk three beers and smoked three cigarettes by the time she stepped through the kitchen doorframe wearing gym shorts and a T-shirt and holding a can of beer. I had intended to be annoyed at her but I wasn't. She moved her hips in a subtle, playful motion that reminded me I couldn't have been much fun and then walked towards me like nothing at all was the matter and sat down on my lap. This was strange behaviour, not in keeping with her usual repertoire. It was not unwelcome from my perspective but it was unexpected and I stiffened my thigh as she took her seat. She regarded me the way I might regard a dog with whom I had struggled to build a rapport. It would not have been a surprise had she tickled me under the chin. 'Are you moody?' she said.

'Yes.'

'Are you?' She seemed excited by the idea.

'I really am.'

'Have I not been very nice?'

'No.'

'I've not, have I?'

'Not at all. Who was on the phone?'

'It was Marijke,' she said. 'The *New Statesman* have published a bad review of her new novel. By Lottie Schneider – do you know her?' I shook my head. 'She's a poet, a shit poet. She's written this review that hardly engages with the novel and just accuses it of being "self-indulgent" and "opaque". Who is she? She's not even done anything!' She stopped speaking and widened her eyes as though she might have offended me. 'Sorry,' she said, placing one hand on my shoulder. 'I didn't mean that. I'm in a strange mood. I had an upsetting dream last night.'

'Would you care to tell me what happened?'

She shook her head.

'Please, I'm interested in dreams.'

She shook her head again. 'I'd rather not tell you.'

Perhaps she and Henry had gone to a dog shelter: a long, dank corridor, a cacophony of barking. They had approached a cage at the furthest end, where a mangy Alsatian lay on its side. It took her a moment to realise that its organs were spilling onto the concrete floor. Or perhaps she and Henry were kayaking on a placid lake. She began to drift away from him and felt that she was losing control but when she called for help, he couldn't hear her. Or it could have been the other way around: the dream was that he was calling out to her and she could do nothing to help.

'I'm not the same as you, Luca,' she said. 'I don't believe a person's memories and impressions are the most interesting thing about them. I keep my feelings to myself.'

'I don't?'

She smiled as though this were a silly question.

'Are we so dissimilar?'

'In this respect, I think so. I'm like a crab whereas you're like an egg. A soft-boiled egg in a cup. You want nobody and nothing to disturb you until someone comes and cracks you over the head and all your insides run all over the place.' Her face lit up as she delighted in her invention. I was about to protest when a sound carried over the fence from a neighbouring garden. A door opened. Footsteps walked across the flagstones and we fell silent as though we were hiding. Our eyes met and I became more aware of her weight and warmth in my lap. An erotic tension grew in the silence. An object was picked up or placed by the fence. Mia shifted on my thigh. Then the footsteps went back to the door and the door closed.

'I'm going to go home soon.'

'I tend to withdraw when I'm working,' she replied as though she had expected me to say that. 'I need my privacy.'

'I understand,' I said, though I didn't. That had been one of my problems. I didn't have the discipline to withdraw and focus. I would always have put my work aside in favour of Mia, not out of any virtue, but only neediness.

'Why don't you stay for the weekend and leave on Monday?'

'Will it be nicer?'

'Yes, I need to take a break from work to clear my head.'

I thought it was better to leave now, but that if I left in these circumstances, our relationship was over, so I agreed, hoping the weekend would allow us to rediscover what we had lost or were now losing.

'I told my parents I would call them. I'm going to go for a walk while I do that. Then I'm finished for the evening.'

'I don't mind if you do it here.'

'I'd rather not. They weren't happy about me and Henry separating. I don't want them to know you're here and I don't want to pretend you're not.' She got up, went inside, and a few minutes later, slipped on her boots and jacket and stepped outside. I watched her through the small window in the door, walking slowly towards the end of the parking space in front of the houses, where the low sun was setting behind the bare trees. Once she had disappeared around the corner, I went upstairs to get my laptop from the bedroom and, on the way, pushed open the door to the office. It was a small room with a window overlooking the backyard and its tranquillity suggested it had once been a child's bedroom. By the window stood a desk and on it lay Mia's Mac, a few books and pens, a pot of Nicorette gum, and a printed manuscript, annotated in black pen, titled: 'An Open Book Confronts Me: Elizabeth Bishop and Lyric Futurity'. I moved closer to inspect it and saw that another document lay beneath it, partly concealed and poking out, a poem printed on A4. Most of the lines had been crossed out but a few were legible and I began to read them:

> Yolk wet and molten sediment in flesh,
> History compressed into the body like
>   bitumen,

A key scraped in the lock downstairs and I retreated from the office, closed the door, and retrieved my laptop from the bedroom so that I could walk down the stairs holding it as Mia kicked off her boots.

'What were you doing?'

'Just fetching my laptop. That was quick.' I passed her at the bottom of the stairs as she hung up her coat.

'They didn't answer.' She gave me a look that I couldn't read. 'Do you want to draw a tarot card?'

'We could do that.'

She looked at me and seemed to take pleasure in my discomfort. 'The cards are in the bedroom.'

'I'll let you get them.'

I sensed that she enjoyed my standing up to her and wished I were able to do it more often. She went upstairs, returned with the cards, and sat down on the end of the couch. 'Shuffle them a bit.' She passed me the cards and I shuffled them while she watched over me. 'That's enough.' I took a card and laid it on the coffee table. 'Eight of Swords, upright.'

'Is that good or bad?' I asked.

'It's not as simple as that. You have to interpret the cards and think about what they might signify in the context of your life. I'll look it up.'

I leaned over and looked at the card. It depicted a blindfolded man with his hands tied together, surrounded by swords. 'It doesn't look great.'

On her phone, Mia consulted a website or app from which she began to read. 'The Eight of Swords can represent feeling trapped, confined, restricted or backed into a corner. It signifies fear, anxiety and psychological issues.' She looked at me and said, 'Remember not to take it too literally.' Then she continued: 'Hopelessness, helplessness, powerlessness, persecution.' A smile broke out at the corners of her mouth.

'What?'

'Nothing. These descriptions are often overblown. You may be in crisis or facing a dilemma. However, the overall theme of this card is that you are the one keeping yourself in this situation through negative thinking and allowing yourself to be paralysed by fear. The swords depicted in the card are surrounding you but you can take the blindfold off and walk away at any time. This card also represents consequences and judgement which may take the form of trial by jury, imprisonment and punishment.'

I reclined into the sofa and sighed, but Mia slapped my leg. 'Don't be glum,' she said.

'It's not sounding great for me. Helplessness, persecution, trial by jury.'

'Interpret freely. You might be trapped by an idea. You might be imprisoned by an outdated self-conception.'

'Is that what you think?'

'They're examples. Who are the jurors?'

'I don't know. Let's do you now.'

'Stick with it for a minute. You can't just go around abandoning everything as soon as you get uncomfortable.'

'Please.'

'Okay,' she said, 'we'll come back to it.' While Mia shuffled the cards, I got up, went to the fridge and removed two bottles of beer from the six-pack I'd bought. She popped hers open, took a sip, laid a card on the table. 'The Hermit, upright.' She found the card on her app and handed her phone to me. 'You read.'

'The Hermit card in an upright position indicates that you are entering a period of soul searching, self-reflection and spiritual enlightenment. You may find that you need time alone to gain a deeper understanding of yourself, to remove yourself from daily chores and discover your true spiritual self, contemplate your existence, your direction in life or your values. The Hermit can also indicate isolating yourself or withdrawing into oneself in order to recover from a difficult situation. You may be going through an anti-social phase where you just don't want to interact with people as much as you normally would. This is a time to focus on yourself and meeting your own needs.' I placed her phone on the table while she looked across the room, her brow furrowed in contemplation. 'There's not much to interpret, is there? It sounds quite unambiguous.'

'There are always nuances to interpret.'

'You want to be alone.'

'There are different ways of being alone, of withdrawing.'

'I can only think of one.'

'For example, all year I've been working on Bishop, reading everything she ever wrote, her prose and letters as well as her poems. I haven't been so involved in another person's language and ideas since I did my PhD. Now I'm finished and I realise this attachment has served a second purpose: it has allowed me to direct my attention away from myself and so avoid a reckoning with the aftermath of my failed marriage. When I look at this card and think about how it resonates with my circumstances, I realise that the end of this year must represent a return to myself. This is what I mean. It's not so literal. I've spent more time alone this year than at any other time in my life, but when I go back to London and pick up my old life, even though I'll be teaching and seeing friends, I'll be with myself again.'

'Okay,' I said. 'I take the point.'

I rested my head on the sofa close to hers, as though it were natural for us to move on from this topic and relax into each other's presence but she remained watchful and ignored this gesture.

'How are you trapped?' she said.

I looked at the books and statuettes lining the shelves, the photographs, the framed prints on the walls. 'I suppose I'm trapped in an old idea of what my life ought to be like or holding on to some redundant idea of who I am. I don't know. I see how this is a useful heuristic for interpreting your life but I don't think I believe in tarot cards. I'm sorry.'

'I hate the word heuristic.'

'So do I. I don't know why I said it.'

'It's one of those awful words used by academics with no ear for language.'

'I agree. I regret saying it. Shall we smoke?'

'I'm okay. Do you think you're sentimental?'

'No.'

'No?'

'I can be nostalgic.'

'Is that different?'

'Very different. Why, what are you?'

'I'm neither.'

'Alright, fuck this.'

'What?' Now she laughed and smacked my foot playfully. 'Don't be moody.'

'Tell me a secret.'

'Why would I?'

'Please. To make it fair. And fun.' I went to the fridge to get two more bottles of beer.

'People don't tell you what they don't want you to know.'

'Unconsciously they do.'

'Not everyone. Do you think you're an alcoholic?'

'Do you?' I had now returned from the fridge and was standing before her with a beer in each hand.

'You drink a lot.'

'So do you.'

'Only when I'm with you.'

'Well, I only drink a lot when I'm with you,' I said, though that wasn't true.

'What are you going to do?'

'What do you mean?' I said.

'What are you going to do? You can't just stay here getting drunk and sleeping in late.'

'I know,' I said defensively. 'I wasn't planning to. I'll go back to Boston and speak with my advisor. Then I'll take things from there.'

Sensing, I supposed, how that statement had embarrassed me, she placed a flat, neutral hand on my thigh and gave me an apologetic look.

'Would you like some dinner?' I said. 'There's leftover sauce from yesterday.'

I went to the kitchen and Mia followed, taking a seat at the dining table and then asking, 'Can I read you a poem?'

'Yes, that would be nice.'

She got up promptly and went up the stairs while I boiled some water and tipped the leftover pasta sauce into a pan. I thought it would be the poem I saw on her desk, the part that was concealed from view or a newer version, and though I knew she would not have written a love poem, the two lines I had read did not preclude the possibility that the poem had something to do with us, but she re-appeared a few minutes later with a book in her hand. 'It's by Peter Gizzi,' she took a seat by the table. 'A Winding Sheet for Summer':

'I wanted out of the past so I ate the air,
   it took me further into the air.
It cut me, an iridescent chord
   of geometric light.
I breathed deep, it lit me up, it was good.
All these years, lightning, rain, the sky,
   its little daisies.
Memento mori and lux.'

She turned the page, pinned the new one with her fore-finger and read on:

'And you can't blame me.
This daisy feeling.

I was a poet with a death-style of my own
    waking.
I occupy the rest of it.
A blue-green leaving feeling.
To no longer belong to a body sometimes
    open to air.
In rain, in early morning rain.'

She read clearly, the same way she had read her own work at the Barker Center, when I had watched her from rows back and desired to be alone with her, her voice rising from her stomach, her teeth and tongue machinating the consonants precisely. I stood by the cooker, watching her eyes cross the page, her posture shifting subtly with the moods of the poem. The sun had set now and darkness was pressing up against the windows.

'It will say this long agony is great being awake. It is being lovely now,' she said. Then she turned the page again, crisply, quickly, so that she incorporated the sound into the rhythm of the poem. 'I built my life out of what was left of me. Sky and its procedures.' She never looked up or acknowledged my presence, but it was not as though I were not there, rather that she seemed to take pleasure in my being the audience for this communion with herself. I began to feel jealousy the way I did as a teenager, when a girl I fancied was flirting with another boy. 'When the words came back their fictions remain. Thunderheads and rain.' She turned the page again and carried on. The water was boiling violently, so I turned down the heat and stirred the fusilli. 'For a long time, the names of things and things unnamed. For a long time, hawks and their chicks, fox and their cubs, mice and their mice.' She kept reading but the performance, which had captivated me at first, was beginning to repel me. I felt that to stand and listen represented a small humiliation, an assertion of her eloquence over mine, a lesson. I had hoped the poem might contain a message, communicate what she couldn't say in ordinary speech, but as she read – 'A soft electro-fuzz enters the head. A soft fuzzy opiate lightness' – I understood that language, for her, did not have that expressive function that I still wished it did – naïvely, romantically. She played it like an instrument and the point was for me to behold her mastery. I turned away and dislodged the tomato sauce where it stuck to the edges of the Teflon pan. 'I came from a different world,' she was saying behind me. 'I will die in it. Someone saw it, I love them for seeing it.' I stirred the sauce and thought, finally all the illusory possibilities are cooking off so that only my fate remains: not to belong here, not to speak this language, to go back where I understand people and am understood. She flipped the page; I turned the dial on the cooker all the way to the left. 'I am that thing in morning, whatever motors in the skull.' I took a cigarette from the packet on the kitchen island and walked past her, pushed open the door to the garden and sat on the step, half inside and half out. The night air was cool. 'And what have you been given, the blue nothing asks, who are you under clanging brass? Are you listening?'

'I'm listening. Carry on.'

I looked up into the dark, cloudy sky and let her speech become an indistinct murmur as I took a few long, deep drags that made the cigarette butt hot between my fingers. Then I flicked it into the dark of the yard and went inside. Mia was still reading and I had more or less stopped listening. I turned off the heat under the sauce and tipped the pasta into the colander. Then I stood, watching the steam rise from the sink and listening again to the words that, although they had stung me, although I had taken their opacity personally, after all, were beautiful. 'The sun remains a yellow sail tacked to the sky,' she said. 'I am climbing air here. I am here in the open. The kestrel swerves. Its silent kerning. A stunning calibration of nothing. I'm left to see.' She finished, closed the book, and looked at me in that penetrating way that seared me with its frankness and left me feeling exposed.

'Dinner's ready,' I said.

She seemed pissed off as she ate, looking down as though her dish of fusilli demanded her full attention. She forked one, blew on it once, and then chewed it carefully, looking out the windows into the darkness of the garden, tilting her head to the angle that meant she was thinking a thing over, turning it this way and that. Several minutes passed without either of us speaking: too long. A mood had come between us, too layered with small annoyances, fears and misunderstandings to come apart with just a few words, one that would need a real conversation, confessions, perhaps even an apology. The longer we didn't speak, the heavier the silence became, until I almost could have laughed but didn't. 'Do you want to watch a film?' she finally said.

'Sure,' I said, but I didn't really. I wanted to talk. I felt that something needed to be articulated, though I couldn't think of anything to say.

'I'll do them,' she said when I got up to wash the dishes. 'Is there anything you want to watch?' She went nonchalantly to the sink while I remained standing, unsure of where to put myself. 'Have you seen *Black Narcissus*?'

'No.'

'It's Powell and Pressburger. Do you like them?'

'I don't know.'

She found the film on the internet and connected her Mac to the TV. Then she sat on the sofa with her legs folded beneath her and directed her full attention to the film while I sat next to her, a few inches away and wished that I'd sat at the other end of the sofa. If I'd sat further away, it was possible that our not touching would seem to be a sign of our ease in each other's company, whereas this position made it impossible to think about anything apart from our not touching. As the film began, I kept wondering why she had chosen this one; why this film about a convent of nuns in the Himalayas? Was it something to do with their isolation, which resembled ours? Surely not because of its sexual tension? When David Farrar's character appeared on the screen, bare chested and ruggedly hand-some, smoking while a monkey played on his shoulder, I wondered if she were trying to send me a message: that she had believed I was more like him – cool and self-possessed – and that she was disappointed with who she had discovered me to be. Several times, when he appeared, I looked across at her and hoped she would look back at me to confirm or refute this idea, but she didn't. Throughout the whole film, Mia never diverted her attention from the screen, nor reacted in any overt way, while I could hardly take in what was happening because I was thinking about us, about what had happened in the past few days and why the mood had been changing so rapidly, why I had come here at all. By the time an hour had passed, I had lost track of the plot altogether and could hardly take in the images, so pitiful did I feel. While Mia, even when Kathleen Byron was falling to her death in the canyon, remained still and focused, her steady, pensive gaze unmoving.

'Did you like it?' she finally said when the credits began.

'Yeah.'

'Don't lie! You were bored.'

'I wasn't bored.'

'I could tell,' she said, standing and heading upstairs.

When I followed a few minutes later, I found her lying in bed on her side, facing the window. I brushed my teeth for longer than I usually would, washed my face, and sat down on the toilet seat for a moment. Then I got in bed beside her, lay on my back and looked at the ceiling. 'Mia,' I said, 'are you going to sleep?'

'Yes,' she said.

'Okay.' But don't you want to talk? I wanted to say. Don't you want to find some way back to where we were a few days ago, when it felt as though we were falling in love? I formulated several remarks to this effect but couldn't begin because the tension in Mia's unmoving body made the answers clear. I turned and looked at the back of her head and the part of her neck that was exposed where her blonde hair fell towards the pillow. I didn't know if she was tired or if she just didn't want to speak to me and I began to feel indignant about my powerlessness. I searched, panic-stricken, for any course of action I could take that might change our fate: could I apologise, scold her, laugh, cry, get up and leave without a word? My feelings towards her impassive body flitted between tenderness, anger, hatred, forgiveness, and desire; several conflicting soliloquies ran parallel in my head until I had worked myself into such a state of distress that I finally said, 'Mia, are you asleep?' She didn't respond nor even move a muscle and I sensed that she really had fallen asleep.

So I got up quietly, pulled on my jeans and T-shirt, and grabbed my rucksack from the chair by the window. Then I crept downstairs, put on the living-room light and gathered my laptop, charger, and my books, packed them into the bag, took my cigarettes from the table by the back door, put on my coat and shoes, and left, closing the door quietly behind me and walking towards the main road leading into town. It was cold and dark outside and I felt tired, the way I did when I had to wake up at 3 a.m. for an early flight. At the same time, the feeling of freedom was exhilarating, even more so when I imagined Mia waking up to discover that I had left. I wanted to be there to see her reaction, or to comfort her and tell her that I wasn't really gone, but it was too late now. I had finally done something decisive and I couldn't change my mind. I knew there would be no buses until the morning but I had seen a hotel downtown whose bar I thought might be open and I decided to go there and have a drink while I figured out what I was going to do next.

'Dear luca,' Andy texted me after several days without a word, 'been staying wiv a mate in Rochdale was good to get away. You may come over tomorrow cheers Andy. We can talk about your writing.'

As the front door swung open, I found him lowering himself back into his wheelchair. I hoped that Val would be there because his moods seemed to be better when she was around, but as I followed him into the front room he said, 'Just me today,' as though he had read my mind. My manuscript lay on the table among an unusual amount of clutter. There were two Coke cans and some weed-smoking paraphernalia: a grinder, a packet of long papers, a packet of tobacco. There were the two PlayStation controllers, an open bag of peanut M&Ms, a notepad and a letter from the NHS. 'I had a mate over last night. Darren Walker. You don't want a cup of tea or anything, do you?' There were markings on the manuscript in two different hands, red and blue. Andy stood up, wobbled on his feet, and then lowered himself into his armchair. He took the manuscript in his hands and said, 'I don't like what you've written.' I nodded, as though agreeing would protect me from feeling hurt. 'I don't like it. I hate it.'

'What is it you don't like?' I asked him with as much neutrality as I could manage.

'It's all wrong.' He shook his head and now used his

fingers to count the key points: 'It's whiny. You make it sound like I blame everyone but myself for everything that's wrong with me. It's boring. There are too many long words that I would never use. It makes me seem like a moany bastard. Darren thought so as well. He said, "You're a happy-go-lucky guy, Andy. This makes you seem like a miserable bastard."'

'But it's meant to show how hard your life has been. That's the only way we can show how brave you are for living through it.'

'It's meant to be uplifting. This is just miserable. And it's full of errors.'

'We can fix them. That's the easiest thing in the world to do.'

'Why didn't you fix them before you gave me the book then?'

'It's a process, Andy. Back and forth. I write a bit. You give me feedback. I make it better.'

'I don't see how this can be made better. Listen. This is what me and Darren came up with last night. How it should be.' He swiped on his phone and held it close to his face. 'Manchester, the greatest city in the world. The year is 1970 but the swinging sixties are still in the air. A dapper young gentleman, Mr Frank Barton, is coming to the end of his shift on the production line at Kellogg's, working to feed a hungry nation. The bell rings at the end of the working day and the men pile out into the streets in high spirits. With his chums from the factory, Frank heads into the city in search of a hearty meal, a good drink, and who knows what else?' He looked at me to make sure that I was listening. 'He steps into a little place called the Twisted Wheel. The music is grooving and Frank can't help but click his fingers and shake his hips. Everyone is dancing and having the time of their lives. The girls look gorgeous. A beautiful petite blonde catches his eye. "May I have a dance, madam?" he says. "Certainly," she responds and gives him her delicate hand. Sparks fly and these two young things dance the night away. I don't need to say what happens next but these are my parents and nine months later, I am born.' He shot me a look of reproach. 'That was just me talking and Darren writing down what I said. It's better than what you've done in six weeks.'

'It's a different style. The whole point of me sharing some writing was so that you could tell me what you like and what you don't.'

'I don't like any of it.'

'Well then, I'll change it. I'll do it how you want it.'

'We need to do it like this. The way me and Darren did it. I tell you what to write and you write it. If you go off and do it on your own, you'll just do it in your own way again. You need to do it here.'

'Andy, I don't think there's a writer in the world who would agree to sit with you and write on demand.'

'That's how it needs to be done. You've not listened to what I told you. You made it sound like it was the most miserable time in the world. I was happy!'

'I'm sorry. I tried to capture the story as you told it.'

'You've made a load of stuff up.'

'I was trying to add colour.'

'The wrong colour. If I said the sky was blue, you would write that it was black. What's this? "It was nearly six o'clock, but only grey imperfect misty dawn, when we left the Haçienda." What's that?'

'A descriptive flourish. I'm sorry. We can change everything.'

'We're not changing anything. We're starting again.'

'Fine. I'll start over. I can do it quickly now that I have the material.'

'I'll need to tell you the whole story from the beginning again and you make sure you listen this time.'

'No. Andy, we don't need to do that. I've got recordings.'

'We need to get it right. We've tried doing this on your terms. Now we're going to do it on mine. You need to come here and work. You can write while I dictate to you like I did with Darren.'

The idea of being interminably bound to Andy filled me with dread and yet, upon hearing these orders, my first instinct was to accept their inevitability and concede. I felt so much pity for him that I could hardly imagine saying no, but there remained in me a kernel of resistance and a will to live that, if I didn't seize it now, I might lose it for good, and so I said, 'No.'

'What do you mean, no?'

'I can't do that. It's a terrible idea. I hate it.'

'It's the only way to get it right.'

'If that's the only option for you, you'll have to find a different writer. I can't do it.'

He shook his head as though he were disappointed. 'I knew this would happen. You're going to abandon me.'

'Come on, Andy. Don't say that. You're making it impossible for me to help you.'

'You're going to abandon me like everyone else.' His first utterance seemed to have stoked his anger and this second was louder and full of indignant righteousness.

'Andy, please,' I said, trying to calm him down. 'We can

still find a way to make it work if you'll meet me in the middle and be reasonable.'

'I knew your dad, you know.' Andy raised his voice and leaned towards me. 'I realised when I saw you coming out of the Job Centre. It's the way you walk – just like him.' He was watching me closely to see how I would react. 'He used to drink in the Albert. He was a pisshead who thought he was better than everyone. He looked down his nose at me and everyone else but then he'd get hammered on gin and fall asleep at the bar.'

'Please, Andy.' I tried to stay calm but I was filled with rage, beneath which I detected a long, implacable sadness.

'I remember he had a son who he hardly saw because he was always too pissed. That was you!'

He laughed and looked giddy with the power his words had to upset me.

'Stop,' I said. 'Stop saying this stuff.'

'Don't tell me what to do. You're not in charge of me. I'm in charge of you!'

I got up and began packing away my things.

'What are you doing?' he said. 'You can't leave. You've got my money.' I zipped my bag and walked out the door without looking him in the eye. 'Come back,' he called as I left. 'Luca, you little dickhead, come back!'

It took me a long time to recover from that session. My nerves were shot and I had to lie down for several hours before I could begin to think clearly again. Andy had so taken over my life these past few weeks that I seemed to have lost track of myself. But it was still in there, rattling around: irritable, needful, hungry. I lay down on the living-room carpet and listened to the silence. How still it was in this house, how quiet, and how incessant was the noise inside one's head. How tedious were the voices that spoke behind our ears, always repeating the same stories, speaking of the same mistakes, insults, injuries: their moaning, braying, their unceasing attack that pulled my head this way and that until I could only shake it and say no, please no more, and even then it wouldn't stop. I opened the desk drawer where I had hidden the bills Andy had given to me on our first meeting. £1,760 remained. Did I have to give them back? Would he demand them? If I insisted the money was owed to me for my labours, what would he do? Would he send his mates to beat me up? Would his image haunt me? I sat on the office floor and allowed my mind to fill with images of big men threatening and punching me. Then I ran downstairs again, sure that he would now have texted me, demanding his money back, but I didn't have any notifications. I turned my phone off. How terribly quiet this house was. How menacing time was when it loomed without shape or variation.

Several days passed before I woke up to find the following message from Andy, sent at 03:36 am:

Dear Luca,

Following the termination of our professional relationship, I hereby request a refund of the money paid to you for services not rendered. The outstanding sum is £2,000. This is to be delivered to my residence in cash ASAP. Failure to comply will result in action being taken.

Mr Andy Barton

Letting my phone rest face down on my chest, I sighed with resignation. I didn't want to give Andy his money back. I had dedicated hours of my time to listening to him and writing up his story. It was he, anyway, who had insisted there was no need for a contract when we agreed to work together. I had nothing to feel guilty about, I told myself. If I paid Andy back, I would be left with nothing. That wasn't okay. I had been working for him and he had to pay me. I began to type out a message, explaining this, but I stopped myself. I was too angry to think straight. I groaned, deleted everything I had written and saw that the word 'online' appeared beneath Andy's name. Afraid that he had seen I was typing, I closed the app and placed my phone on the table. 'Leave me alone,' I said aloud to the empty room. 'Please, leave me alone.'

I awoke the next night to a sound like wood splitting. Without turning on the bedside lamp, I stood up and moved to the window. A rustling sound was coming from the alleyway behind the house. It stopped after a while, but I tossed and turned for the rest of the night and allowed myself to imagine the multiple ways Andy might choose to punish me if I didn't, or even if I did, give back his money. Several times, I decided that the money was not worth the hassle and resolved to return it, but when I thought of how little money I would have left and of all the hours I had spent listening to him and painstakingly transcribing his words, I became angry and resolved again to keep it and face the consequences. I cycled through various iterations of these same thoughts until the crack of sky between the curtains turned pale. When I turned on my phone, I had nine messages:

I thought you was sound luca
I trusted you
You had everything I never had
Family
Love
Good uni
If you don't want to help me it's your decision
     but don't steal my money
You are stealing from a sick man
You are stealing my soul

I began to pack my things into my suitcase and clean the house. I put my bedsheets and towels in the wash, took the plates and mugs down from the office, wiped the desk, cleaned the windows. I gathered the cigarette butts from the backyard, emptied the fridge, wiped the shelves, did the dishes. By midday, the house looked as though I had never been there. Jem and Brenda weren't returning for another two weeks, but I didn't want to spend any more time alone. I double-checked the wardrobes and drawers, made sure all the windows were closed, took the bin out, and locked the front door behind me. Then I dragged my suitcase to Chorlton Metrolink and waited for the tram into the city.

Andy was writing:

You leave me no choice but to get my money
     back by force
Val told me where you live when she gave you
     a lift home
In chorlton near mcdonalds
Don't push me luca

He was still typing and I waited a while for the next message to come through but he kept typing and typing. The tram arrived and I found a seat. Andy was still typing and I turned off my phone and put it in my pocket. It wasn't even one o'clock when I got off at Piccadilly Gardens, where I sat down on one of the benches by the concrete wall. The streets were busy with shoppers and people loitering. It was one of those warm cloudy days that nobody knows what to do with. A few police officers were questioning some young men on the bridge over the fountain area. Water shot up from the holes in the ground and a mother leaned over her son's shoulder and pointed. Pigeons were gathering around a discarded paper bag. My plan had been to sit in a café and read while I waited for Tom to get home, but I didn't feel like reading. I never wanted to read a book again. They were nothing but trouble.

Instead, I took a walk around the city, dragging my heavy suitcase behind me across St Peter's Square, which had been remodelled, cleared and flattened so completely that I could hardly remember how it had looked before, and then down Whitworth Street West, where the old site of the Haçienda had been knocked down and a block of new apartments had been built in its place. Finally, I found a new café in an old railway arch, ordered a flat white and an overpriced cookie, and sat on a metal chair at a small table in the corner, where I used my phone to apply for teaching jobs in the oil-rich states of the Persian Gulf.

When I arrived at Tom's shortly after six, he looked me up and down before I entered, carrying out a thorough examination of my face, clothing, and bearing before asking in an accusatory tone if I was okay. I said that I was, but that the past few weeks had been challenging. 'Hard, is it?' He led me into the living room. 'Hard sitting and listening to a man speak and writing down what he says?'

'It is actually.'

'Just kidding. He's a nutter.' Tom opened the balcony door and a couple of pigeons took flight from the balustrade. 'How's all of that going anyway?'

'It started well.' We stepped outside and took in the view of the ring road.

'It always does.'

'Then it became more difficult.'

'Say more.'

'He had unrealistic expectations.'

'He thought it was going to be a bestseller?'

'He wanted a theodicy, an explanation of God's ways and a justification for the presence of evil in the world.'

'His words?'

'It's what I inferred. He thought it was going to save the past from oblivion and make him happy, make him feel heard.'

'Couldn't you have done it anyway? Leave it up to him to face the disappointment?'

'I don't think he even wanted to finish it. I think he wanted the process to last for ever, so that the hope would never die.'

'Could have been a full-time job.'

I laughed and said I couldn't imagine anything worse.

Tom shrugged as though to say that he could. 'Are you sure he didn't just want a different sort of book?'

'That's also possible.'

We stepped back and I noticed that a hardback cover of

Cotton City by Jonny Fletcher was lying on the table. 'You're not reading that, are you?'

'My uncle gave it to me as a present. What would be the problem if I was? Are you jealous? Because he's a successful local writer?'

'I'm not jealous of him.'

'You are.'

'I'm not. I'm jealous of a lot of people but not him. A local writer is a type of local, not a type of writer.'

'That's a good one.'

'Are you going to read it?'

'Nah,' he said. 'Looks shite. I'll drop it off at Oxfam. How is your writing anyway? What about this novel?'

'What I was doing was no better than Andy.'

'Fiddling with yourself? Makes you go blind. So, what will you do now?'

'I don't know. I've got some irons in the fire. How are you? Did you have a nice time in Anglesey?'

'Very nice, but we had to come back early. We put an offer on a house and it's been accepted.'

'Have you?'

'In Levenshulme.'

'That's nice, pal. You're moving up in the world.'

'By increments, yes.'

'I'm moving down.'

'At the moment, but it's not too late to change direction.'

'Do you think I should stick around here? Maybe I could buy a house as well. Get a cat or a dog. Live a simple life.'

Tom laughed. 'Not you. You'd be bored. You have to keep struggling through life.'

'Thank you,' I said. 'That's nice.'

'Anyway, you need money to buy a house. You don't have any money.'

'I've got a bit.' I opened my suitcase and showed him the stacks of £20 notes.

'What the fuck is that?'

'It's from Andy.'

'Doesn't he want it back if you're not writing the book?'

'Don't I deserve some payment,' I said. 'At least some recognition for all the work I've done?'

'No,' Tom said. 'You have to give it back.'

'Why?'

'Because you do. You can't steal from a poor lonely bloke. He's sick. He's not well.'

'I'm poor and lonely, too.'

'It's different. You only have yourself to blame. Come on.' He stood up. 'We'll go over now and you can give it to him.'

'I worked for it.'

'Come on.' He was already putting on his shoes in the hall. I gathered the notes together in a plastic bag and followed him out the door. 'Nasty bastard,' he said in the lift. 'You were going to take the money, weren't you?' I met Tom's eyes in the graffiti-covered mirror and shrugged. 'Stinks of fucking piss in this lift.'

After stopping at the cash machine so that I could withdraw £300 to replace what I had spent of Andy's money, we pulled up outside his house. I had texted to say that I was on my way with his money and he had replied – 'Good man' – but I wasn't without trepidation as I knocked. A commotion could be heard from within and the door opened to reveal Andy lowering himself into his wheelchair.

'Hello, Luca,' he said. 'Hi, Tom.' He reached out and shook Tom's hand.

We followed him into the living room, where a man was sitting with a notebook in his lap. He was around forty, with a head of modish brown hair, and he sat hunched over his notebook at the table, wearing a zipped-up raincoat despite the warm weather. 'Hi, lads,' he said. 'Don't mind me.'

'Matt is going to be my new writer,' Andy said.

I gave Andy the plastic bag. 'It's the full amount.'

'Thank you, Luca. You've done the right thing. Here.' He reached into the plastic bag and withdrew a £20 note. 'Treat yourselves to some dinner on me. For your troubles. I think it will work out better with Matt. He's a proper Manc, born and bred. He understands what I'm trying to do. There are things about me I don't think you could ever understand. You weren't the right man for the job but you tried your best. And I didn't mean what I said about your dad. He was a nice bloke really. I had a chat with him quite a few times.'

'You did?'

'Yeah, I remembered the other day: the bloke who worked at the university who'd been to America. You look like him. I remember him saying he had to stop drinking so he could see his son again. He talked about you a lot. He was proud of you. I didn't know he died. I'm sorry for your loss.'

'Thank you, Andy,' I said. 'That's nice. Would you like me to send you my notes and recordings?'

'No, it's alright. I want to tell Matt the story from the beginning so that he understands who I am.'

I looked at Matt, who was busy scribbling in the notebook in his lap. He looked up and smiled. 'I'll be fine, thanks, mate.'

'If you wouldn't mind excusing us, Luca. We're in the flow.'

'Of course. Sorry. Bye, Andy. Good luck.'

'Come round for a brew sometime or drop into the centre. I'll make sure you get a copy of the book when it's finished. Matt reckons it'll be out by Christmas.'

The new writer looked at me and nodded with a sheepish look in his eye. I felt a pang of concern for Andy when I considered that he might be getting ripped off but I decided not to give it another thought.

Outside, the late spring air was warm and balmy.

'Doesn't that feel better?' Tom said.

'Not really.'

We got in the car. 'It does. You don't want that on your conscience for the rest of your life.' He started the engine and set off driving along Moss Lane. 'Am I dropping you in Chorlton or are you coming back to mine?'

'Do you mind if we head back to yours? I don't want to go back to that house.'

'Come on then.'

We drove along Moss Lane, past a new apartment building and then an older one with boarded-up windows, its front yard overgrown with tall weeds. 'Elizabeth Gaskell's *Mary Barton* opens around here,' I said. 'It's an evening in May, a holiday, and the workers are out in the fields and meadows for some respite from the city. It's a pastoral scene.' We rounded the corner and the fermentation silos of the Heineken brewery came into view.

'Do you think you'd have been happier then?' Tom asked. 'Working twelve-hour days in a cotton mill? Getting your fingers crushed by a spinning mule?'

'Of course not. That's not what I'm saying.'

'What are you saying then?'

'Things change.'

'They do. It's important to remember that. You have to look towards the future. Otherwise you're going to end up like Andy.' We were approaching the Mancunian Way. 'Your whole future is in front of you.'

'And my whole past is behind me.'

'So what? Forget it. It's happened now. Move on. Why can't you move on?'

'I don't know.' I looked out the window at the new student flats in Hulme and my stomach filled with that familiar sense of dread. 'What do you do on the anniversary of your dad's death? When you go to the cemetery?'

'How so?'

'What do you do in there?'

'I lay flowers at his grave. Then I light a candle and weep.'

'You weep?'

'Like an old Italian woman at the funeral of her first-born son.'

'Really?'

'Seriously, I do. It's important.'

'Even though he's dead?'

'Because he's dead.'

'Alright. I think I'm going to give that a go. I need to bury something before I leave. Otherwise, I'll end up back here again.'

'The anniversary is coming up, isn't it?'

'Tomorrow.'

'You should do it. It'll be good for you. I'll give you a lift.'

'Thanks, mate,' I said. 'That would be nice.'

I slept on Tom's couch with the balcony door wide open and woke to the sound of pigeons cooing overhead. We set off early, drove to Chorlton, and stopped at a florist near Southern Cemetery where Tom told me to go inside and buy some flowers and a candle.

'What sort of flowers?'

'Whatever you like. What do you think your dad would have liked?'

I didn't know. I went inside and looked at the colourful flowers arranged in buckets around the room. 'Y'alright, love?' said the woman behind the counter. I had no taste in flowers and hadn't a clue what to buy. Not roses, obviously, but perhaps lilies? I pressed my nose into the bud of a white lily and pictured my dad as best as I could, wearing his leather trench coat, smoking a roll-up while we waited for the 86 bus. I didn't know him well enough to guess what sort of flowers he might have liked. Then I saw a fat bouquet of lilacs, which made me think of the opening lines of *The Waste Land*, a book my dad had given to me not long before he died, in the 1999 Faber edition with a black and white photograph of St Paul's Cathedral on the cover. I hadn't understood the poem at all then but I supposed that he knew I wouldn't and had given me the book ahead of time, knowing that he wouldn't be around to give it to me later. I took the lilacs, picked up a memorial candle and paid the woman behind the counter.

'Lilacs,' Tom said when I got in the car. 'Nice choice.'

'What are we going to do exactly?'

'I'm going to wait in the car. You'll go in and mourn.'

'I don't know if I can do it. It seems affected.'

'It's one of the fundamental rituals of human civilisation. You'll work it out.' He pulled over beside the cemetery gates.

'You know he was cremated, don't you? There's no grave.'

'Doesn't matter. Find a nice spot. Find a tree.'

'Can I use your dad's grave?'

'No,' Tom said. 'I don't think that would be appropriate.'

I got out of the car and entered the cemetery, carrying the lilacs in one hand and the candle in the other. I walked a while in the shade of the sycamores, reading the stones and looking for a quiet spot away from the road. A few times, I almost stopped but either another mourner was too nearby or the spot I had chosen was too close to another grave. Eventually, I came across a poplar tree standing in a patch of grass. Nobody was around and the only sound was the hush of light wind in the canopies. I went to the tree, kneeled down on the earth, and laid the lilacs on the roots protruding through the soil. Then I lit the candle, placed it beside the flowers, and tried to concentrate my thoughts on the memory of my dad. It wasn't easy. My head was so full of trivialities and petty concerns that I didn't think I would find room, but after a while, I managed to fix upon an image of him, not a particular memory, only a ghostly outline. Then, for a moment, it was very clear that he was gone from the world and had been for a long time, that his death had not been inevitable but was, finally, immutable, and I cried for the person he had not lived to be, for the father I had lost, and all the years I had been tormented by his memory. When my knees were sore from bending and the tears were running dry, I stood up, wiped my eyes, and made my way back to the gates, where Tom was waiting in the car.

'Well done, buddy,' he said. I closed the car door and we joined the traffic on Barlow Moor Road. 'How was that?'

'It was good. I feel lighter.'

'Good. It's important.'

'Do you think it will help me to live better?'

'Might do, might not.'

'Yeah.'

'I wouldn't get your hopes up.'

'No.'

'But good to do it anyway.' We drove past the KFC where where Blockbuster used to be. 'So, what are these plans you've got? I don't know if ghostwriting is the one for you.'

'I've got an interview with a teaching agency on Friday. There's a position at a school in Abu Dhabi.'

'You're joking.'

'I'm not.'

'What the fuck are you going to do in Abu Dhabi?'

'I'll work, live in some kind of complex, save money.'

'I can't see it. How will you excite yourself?'

'No more excitement for me. It's time for a shrewd course of action. Five years over there and I could save enough money to buy a house.'

'Where?'

'I don't know. Somewhere.'

'You won't do it.' He opened the window and the smell of hot tarmac rushed into the car. 'What about your intellectual ambitions?'

'Folly. I was just putting off getting a job.'

'If the fool would persist in his folly, he'd become wise.'

'Not me. I'm packing it in. So, do you think you'll come visit me out there, wherever I end up? It could be Abu Dhabi, Oman, Bahrain. All these jobs come with a flight allowance for visitors.'

'Nah.' He leaned back into the headrest and placed his

arm on the window frame. 'I don't see myself visiting you over there.' Then he put the radio on and switched through the stations until he got to Mint Radio, at which point he affected a look of concentration to make clear that he had some professional interest in knowing what they were playing. Two men were bantering in Mancunian accents. Then they started playing New Order's 'Blue Monday'.

'Don't you get sick of it?' I said. 'All the same shit from the past over and over again?'

'Yeah,' he said, turning the radio off. 'Some days I can't stand it. And listening to those boring bastards go on about the eighties is even worse.'

Because it was a fine evening, Mel suggested the three of us take a walk before dinner so we went out around six and walked beside the heavy traffic on Chester Road until the point where you could turn off and cut through a new development, walk under the tram tracks and cross the canal via a footbridge. Then you could squeeze through a gap in the fence and get onto Pomona Dock, the mile-long strip of disused land between the Bridgewater Canal and the River Irwell. It had once been part of the Manchester Docks, which were decommissioned a decade before we were born, but unlike the Salford Docks across the river, which had been turned into apartment buildings, a shopping mall, and an arts centre, this one had been left empty. On either side of the disused road that ran lengthways along the island, grass, thistles, and brambles had grown wild and wherever a slab of concrete stopped the grass from growing, moss and lichen had covered it in a layer of green and umber. Along one part of the water's edge, there was even a row of gorse with bright yellow flowers. It was not exactly beautiful; the road was strewn with broken glass and nestled amid the vegetation were car tyres, rubbish bags, and a fridge freezer; across the canal, you could see the tall pile of a scrapyard and across the river, cranes, diggers, and apartment buildings. But it was spiriting, in a place so determined to hide its decay beneath regeneration projects or banish it to the margins, that a site like this could remain an undeveloped ruin and a testament to the old city that had been buried before it was even fully dead. I was trying to articulate this as we walked along the disused road in the direction of Salford Quays.

'They'll get to it soon,' Tom said. 'They get everything.'

'They might not,' Mel said. 'There's a campaign to make it a park.'

'They'll get to it,' Tom said. 'Give it a couple of years and this will all be flats. Scrapyard View: Boutique Waterside Dwellings.'

'Was it okay this morning?' Mel asked me.

I felt embarrassed when I remembered kneeling on the ground by the tree and crying, but at the same time, I felt a kind of lightness. 'It was, thank you,' I said.

'Have you had a good stay overall?'

'It's been good, yeah.'

'And I hear you're off to the UAE now?'

'Let's see about that. It's one idea among several.'

'What are the others?'

'I could go and stay with my mum in Torrevieja. I guess those are the two options for now.'

'You wouldn't think about staying here?'

We reached the end of the dock and looked for a moment

across the basin, where the mucky film on the water's surface shone in the evening sunshine. Then we turned around and walked in the direction of the flat with the sun at our backs.

'What would I do?'

'Live here,' Mel said. I waited for Tom to speak but he kept his eyes on the gravelly road with a serious look on his face, as though the two of them had consorted to have this conversation. 'You can stay with us for as long as you need to. It's no bother. We can stay at mine sometimes so you have a bit of space.'

'You're here now,' Tom interjected and though it was tempting to mock the self-evidence of this statement, it had a persuasive logic that appealed to me. 'Do you remember Jamie Clayton from school? I saw him on the tram the other day and told him you were here. He said you could work for him if you wanted to. Home clearances. It's basically going in a van and stripping the houses of dead hoarders. They recycle all the crap and anything of any value they sell at auction.'

'That doesn't sound too bad,' I said.

'It's hard work, but that might be good for you. And the money's decent.'

They were both quiet then, as though they were surprised that I had been so amenable to their suggestions and were afraid of saying anything that might scare me away, but they had no need to be. I was pleased with the offer and considered it happily as we walked along Pomona Dock. In the past, I would have worried about the fate of my inner life, about what space I could make for it in such a situation, but I had turned myself inside out like a trouser pocket and discovered that its contents were no more deserving of scrutiny than a sweet wrapper and a ball of fluff. So I liked the idea of being on my feet all day, lugging junk out of old houses and dropping it off at the tip with hardly a moment to think.

'Do you think he'd take me on?'

'He said he would. I'll give you his number and you can text him.'

'Alright, nice one. That sounds like a good plan.'

We stopped at the chippy on the way back to the flat and I bought dinner for the three of us using the £20 note from Andy. I was happy as we walked home along the narrow pavement beside Chester Road, even though it was noisy and ugly and the air was thick with fumes. I was happy about the weight of the plastic bag in my hand, about the parcels of fish and chips wrapped in white paper with dark patches where the fat was seeping through and the smell of hot batter and vinegar. I was hungry and I thought that might mean I had regained the appetite to carry on. It was summer. I was going to work hard, earn money, and improve my situation by small degrees. If I could keep in check that old, objectless desire for something transcendent, I could plausibly tell myself that I was ready to integrate into society and live.

ACKNOWLEDGEMENTS

I'm extremely grateful to Peter Gizzi for allowing me to quote from his poem 'A Winding Sheet for Summer' on pages 231–4. One of the dissertation topics on page 10 is Mathilde Montpetit's and is cited with her generous permission. A few quotations appear without citation in the text. On page 19, the rain falling on the windshield of a car recalls the lyrics to 'Small Fires' by Karate. 'Little puffs of industry' on page 54 echoes Billy Collins's poem, 'The Best Cigarette'. 'Twas not the will but the way . . .' on page 59 and 'Hard-hearted parents . . .' on page 60 are from Robert Burton's *Anatomy of Melancholy*. 'Only those who know the supremacy . . .' on page 64 is from *Middlemarch*. The phrase 'a specialist in failure' on page 71 is José Mourinho's. '. . . directly interwoven with the material activity . . .' on page 77 is from Marx and Engels's *The German Ideology*. 'They preferred the name . . .' on page 95 is from Tony Hoagland's poem 'Among the Intellectuals'. '. . . alternate between work and want . . .' on page 114 echoes Elizabeth Gaskell's preface to *Mary Barton*. 'It is with considerable difficulty . . .' on page 203 is from Mary Shelley's *Frankenstein*. 'I keep my feelings to myself' on page 224 is from Elizabeth Bishop's poem 'Strayed Crab'. 'If the fool . . .' on page 255 is from William Blake's 'Proverbs of Hell'. The title is from *Hamlet*.

Thank you to my agent, Matthew Marland, for his

encouragement, guidance, and advocacy, and to my editors at Sceptre, Ansa Khan Khattak and Nico Parfitt, for the intelligence, care, and hard work they put into making this novel better. Thank you to all my teachers, especially Claire Messud and Thomas Karshan. Thank you to Dana Flynn, my first reader, for everything she has taught me about reading and writing. Thank you to Mike Allen, James Barnes, Al Bell, Leah Foster, Vijay Khurana, David Lynch, Rob Madole, Emily Waddell, Madeleine Watts, Alex Wells, and Elvia Wilk, for reading drafts of this novel – sometimes several times over – and providing invaluable feedback. Thank you to Patrick Cornwell and Dan Hampson, for their love and support. Thank you, Camilla, for her patience and belief and for sharing her life with me, which made writing this novel possible.